You saw something you shouldn't have

Brandon Faircloth

Published by Brandon Faircloth.

Copyright 2018 Brandon Faircloth

All rights reserved. This book may not be reproduced in whole or in part, in any form or by any means, electronic or mechanical, including photocopying, recording, or by any information storage and retrieval system now known or hereafter invented, without written permission from the author.

This book is licensed for your personal enjoyment only. This book may not be re-sold or given away to other people. If you would like to share this book with another person, please purchase an additional copy for each person you share it with. If you're reading this book and did not purchase it, or it was not purchased for you, then please purchase a copy. Thank you for respecting the hard work of the author.

Please visit Verastahl.com for up-to-date news, links, and contact information for Brandon Faircloth.

This book is dedicated to the love of my life, Leslie. Thank you for always reading my stories, sweet girl.

Other Works by Brandon Faircloth:
Mystery
Darkness
On the Hill and Other Tales of Horror
Whimsical Leprosy
The Outsiders: Book One
One Bite at a Time (Coming Soon)

Table of Contents

We made up a ghost. And now it's killing us.

Part One

I just got off the phone. One of the Stonebrook Six, one of my best friends in the world, was killed last night. His husband Anthony called me, voice raw with fatigue and emotion. He said that the police didn't know the details of what had happened yet, but last night Ellis' remains were found in the parking garage of the building where he works. Where he worked.

They told Anthony that they would have thought it was an explosion, but there were no signs of any fire or damage to anything other than Ellis himself. They would have said it was an obvious murder, but they don't know how someone could crush and dismember a human being that thoroughly without heavy machinery, much less spread him across the twelve foot ceiling of Floor 3B in that monolithic parking structure like a thick layer of chunky peanut butter.

Anthony was crying again by that point, so I assumed I had just heard him wrong. Then he repeated it, his voice coming in hitching gasps. A co-worker had come out just a few minutes after Ellis to find my friend dripping and plopping back onto the relatively clean concrete below where he had been pressed into the ceiling.

Anthony said that the only way they even knew it was him initially was due to the security footage of him going out toward his car. The video cut out as he approached the area, and when it returned the time stamp showed thirty seconds had passed without footage. The girl who found him was out less than five minutes later, and no one else had entered or left the garage in that time so far as they could tell. Crushed personal effects and initial blood work confirmed it was him.

I could feel myself teetering between arguing with Anthony that he must be wrong and breaking into tears myself. I had just seen Ellis two days ago when we were all together mourning the first of our circle of friends to die. Those of us that were flying back out of Chicago had ridden together to the airport, and after Mills had caught her flight back to Austin, me and Ellis had just hung out at an airport restaurant until my flight came up. Our mood had been sad because of Cassidy's funeral and everything that followed, but we were trying to make the most of the time we had left. Ellis was telling me about his wedding and showing me pictures. I still felt guilty for not making it in person, but I had just started my new job at the time. Ellis, like always, understood and worked to make me feel better about it.

I told him some about the girl I've been dating—the relationship was still improving after six months, which was a record for me. Ellis said that very thing, but then quirked an eyebrow at me. He asked if I had realized how I was looking at Mills the past couple of days, and I tried to play it off like he was joking, but I knew he wasn't. In that subtle way he had, he was trying to nudge me to consider if I was still in love with Millicent like I had been when we were growing up. But my head was too full already from everything else, so I pushed the question away, gave him a hug, and headed to my flight.

That was the last time I talked to Ellis before something tore him apart.

I hung up with Anthony after an hour, my throat raw and a feeling of exhaustion weighing down my every step as I went to the bedroom and collapsed onto the bed. I wanted to cry but couldn't, as though the engine of my heart was too busy burning through gallons of fear and guilt to allow even a drop of sadness into its chambers. I tried to sleep, but after awhile I gave up on that as well and began to write this account. I need to get it all out and away from me.

I realize that I've jumped in at the middle of all this rather than the start—I'm tired and not thinking straight. Let me provide a bit of background and then I'll talk about Cassidy's funeral and everything that happened after it.

****

I had four best friends growing up—Ellis Mackery, Millicent Davis, Thomas Wall, and Cassidy Friel. I think we were unique among many groups of childhood friends in that we had all come together at the same time (Mrs. Webber's third grade classroom) and were all equally close to each other. Aside from occasional childish arguments, we never fought with each other, and as we got older, we somehow managed to safely navigate the choppy hormonal seas of two pairs of hetero guys and girls and a third guy that was gravitating towards bi-curiosity.

This is important because as I start to question my memories about so many things, I keep returning to my idea of my friendships with the people closest to me. Ellis, who was always the kindest of us. Mills, who was the smartest and kept the rest of us out of trouble on several occasions. Thomas, who was always so moody around others but so light and happy when it was just the five of us. And Cassidy, who was shy and sweet and I now think died terrified.

I don't have any close family left—my father died when I was fifteen and my mother doesn't like talking to me anymore. My old friends fall into two categories: College friends that I rarely keep in touch with beyond social media, and my best friends from my days at Stonebrook. It sounds strange because we didn't meet at Stonebrook, which was our middle and high school before it was closed. We had spent three years together at Jackson Elementary across town, and were just as close then as we were later, but it was almost like our group identity wasn't fully cemented until we got to Stonebrook.

Fifth grade rumor was that the place had been a small college fifty years earlier, and I do think that was true. It was certainly an old building, and the shape and layout of the rooms retained faint traces of its earlier life. The building was shaped roughly like a hash mark, with two long, wide corridors intersected perpendicularly by two other long, wide corridors. The center square of those crisscrossed lines was filled by a small gymnasium that actually had a pool underneath its motorized floor, though the floor was kept locked and the pool had supposedly long been drained dry.

But the age and uniqueness of the school, its quiet sense of history and mild creepiness, it had an effect on us. We stuck together even more than usual, making few outside friends. We worked to get into the same classes, and the few times when one of us was by ourselves, the wait until the bell rang was interminable.

It was during one of these isolated classes when I first thought about the school being haunted, and even now, having talked about everything this past weekend with the others, that's still one of my few clear memories of our time at Stonebrook. Some small idea, an idle daydream, a simple what-if. What if the school was haunted by a ghost?

****

I got the news about Cassidy's death last Wednesday. It was Thomas that called me, just as he had called the others. After I had moved away at fifteen, after Stonebrook was closed, the group had drifted apart. Thomas and Cassidy had stayed the closest, and sophomore year of college they had gotten married. In the ten years since, they had generally seemed happy the few times we talked or got together, but I knew they had ups and downs. Thomas told me on the phone that they had been legally separated for the past three months but were trying to work things out for themselves and their little girl. And then Cassidy had gone missing one morning and was found five hours later in the groundskeeper's shed of the park across the street from their apartment.

The police were investigating it as a potential homicide due to the strangeness of the death, but there were no leads. Thomas had been on duty at the hospital where he worked as a physician's assistant, so his alibi was solid. Worse was that she seemed to have been drowned, despite being in a dry room with no clues as to how she got there.

I couldn't get into Chicago until the morning of the funeral, but afterward we all went back to Thomas' house. They had been living together during the separation, and as the four of us sat around his living room, I found myself looking out the window at the park across the street, wondering where the shed was where my friend had been found.

We had been talking about Cassidy for the last three hours, telling funny stories and listening to Thomas go on emotional monologues about how much he loved her and how he had failed her, which was always followed by us reassuring him that she had loved him too and that none of this was his fault. He would always glance at me at this point, and I would try to give him a comforting smile while hoping it was enough, because I didn't know what else to say.

But as the evening wore on, you could feel the conversational momentum grinding to a halt. It was just past eight, but our tiredness and sadness were palpable. Still, I looked at Thomas, and I knew that his daughter was staying at his parents' house overnight, and I hated the thought of him being alone. So at the next lull, I suggested some or all of us spend the night with him. He looked like he was going to argue, but then he nodded with a weary look in his eyes.

"Yeah, I think I'd like that. For any of you that want to, though I know some of you have rooms already paid for."

Millicent grinned. "My hotel looked like shit anyway." Ellis murmured agreement, and I felt a slight buoyancy that I had found a small way to help. That's when I ruined everything.

"The Stonebrook Six are back together again!"

As soon as I said the words, I regretted them. I had meant it as a joking, overly dramatic and silly proclamation to get a cheap laugh out of the others. But as soon as I said it I realized that Cassidy was barely in the ground and I was talking about us all being together. Thomas glared at me while Mills started shaking her head, her eyes wide.

"Why would you say that?" Ellis' tone was more hurt than accusatory. "Why the fuck would you say that, Alex?"

I felt like I could hardly breathe, my eyes roving between the three of them. "Fuck…I'm so sorry. That was so stupid. I'm just not used to Cassidy being gone, and…"

Thomas stood up, his expression hard. "This isn't about Cassidy. Why would you call us the Stonebrook Six again? Is that some kind of fucking joke to you?"

Mills was on her feet now, putting herself between me and him. "Tom, chill out. He doesn't remember. You know that."

Thomas glanced down at her, his face reddening. "Then how the fuck does he remember the Stonebrook Six?"

I was growing more confused and alarmed by the second. "What…that's what we called ourselves. I remember we called ourselves that. The Stonebrook Six. It was a joke."

Ellis had stood up now too, moving closer to me. "Okay, Alex. That's right, sorta. But do you remember why it was a joke?"

I could feel tears stinging my eyes now. I didn't understand why everyone was so mad at me, especially if they weren't mad about me saying it with Cassidy gone. "It…well…It was because there were only five of us. We were talking about nicknames one day and about how our group should have one, as a joke. We talked about calling ourselves the Stonebrook Five for some reason, but ended up all agreeing that the Stonebrook Six sounded cooler. Like an old outlaw gang. So we called ourselves the Stonebrook Six even though there were only five of us."

Thomas took a step closer. "Bullshit! Such bullshit. You know, I've never fully believed your convenient 'I don't remember' shit, but how the fuck are you pulling out shit like that and not remembering what it really was?" Mills gave him a shove that didn't move him but got his attention.

"Fucking back off him. He's not lying. He lost more than we did, so try to remember that." Mills' glare melted away as she turned back to look at me. "Alex, it's not exactly like you think. A lot happened, and…well, you blocked out most of the bad I think. We don't understand how or why you don't remember, but you need to know that we believe you and love you."

Thomas snorted. "Typical. Alex makes Cassidy's funeral day about him."

Ellis shot him a dark look. "Button it. We all loved Cassidy. You don't have the market cornered on missing her." Looking back down, he gave me a sad smile. "Alex, what you were saying, about how we started calling ourselves the Stonebrook Six… that never happened. We started calling ourselves the Stonebrook Six because of the Professor."

I felt a rush of fear running through my body at the name. My mouth went dry and I shot up like the room was on fire. "No…what…no."

Mills looked at Ellis. "You shouldn't have said anything. You should have left it alone."

Ellis shrugged. "I didn't bring it up, but he has a right to know. Alex, do you remember the Professor?"

I shook my head violently and started trying to move past them out of the room. "No, I don't want to talk about this."

Thomas caught me in a strong grip and pulled me into a bear hug that was equal parts angry and loving. "We're going to talk about it, bro. I think it's time." Mills was yelling at him but he went on. "The Professor was the sixth in the Stonebrook Six. It was the…" I shoved him hard enough that he lost his grip and went staggering back into a low coffee table, his arms pinwheeling as he tried to regain his balance before sitting down hard enough on the small table that one of the legs gave way and sent him sprawling on the floor. For my part, I imagined I looked like a trapped animal. But that was okay, because that's exactly what I felt like.

Mills had her hands raised as she stepped forward and touched my cheeks. "Sweetie, it's okay. We should probably go ahead and talk a little about it now, just so you're not confused any more. Is that okay?"

I still wanted to run, but her cool, smooth hands on my face were like a soothing balm. I nodded reluctantly, looking down at Thomas. "Are you okay, man?"

He stood up slowly and gave me a slight smile. "Yeah. I'm sorry, I was being an asshole. Are we cool?"

I nodded. "Sure man. I'll replace the table. I'm just…really freaked out at the moment."

Mills stepped back and nodded. "I know. So let's try talking it out, and if you reach a point you get too scared, we'll stop, okay?"

“Okay.” I paused and then pushed on, my eyes going between Millicent and Ellis. “So who was the Professor?”

Ellis is the one who answered. “It was the ghost. The one we made up. The one that hurt all those people.”

Part Two

What follows is my best recollection of what Ellis told me that night. I want to be clear before I start that I truly didn’t remember anything more or different than what I told them or what I’ve written previously. And it wasn’t like I just had a giant blank spot from age 10 to 15 or 20. I have memories, plenty of memories, of both my time at Stonebrook and what came after. It’s just now I believe that I’m missing a great many things, and that at least a few of the things I do remember never actually happened.

That’s the best and only explanation I have for my relative ignorance of our collective past. It scares me, at least in part because I now know that I’ve had one or more conversations with the rest of the Six…with my friends…about me not remembering things at all or correctly. This was before they realized how deep-seated my block was and gave up trying out of some combination of frustration and fear that forcing me to remember would do me harm. So not only don’t I remember the events themselves, I don’t remember them trying to remind me of them. It makes me feel that my memory lapses go beyond shock or trauma. More like someone or something intentionally fucked with my head.

Even now, going over what I’m about to relay in this writing, I don’t really remember it—at least not well. It’s like I saw a movie of a portion of my life and now I have trouble distinguishing what I actually remember from my life and what I’m just remembering from the movie. When I finish writing this I’m going to call Mills and see if she’s okay.

Again, below is my best recollection of one of the last times I got to talk to one of my best friends.

****

Alex, I know you say you don't know what we're talking about, and I—we—believe you. We do. But stuff like you mentioning the Stonebrook Six, your reaction when I mentioned the Professor…I think you still have those memories in there somewhere and have just blocked them somehow. Or maybe they're being kept from you. Either way, I think it would be good for you, for all of us, if we explained a bit and see if it'll stick with you this time. See if you're ready.

Now as you know, we all transferred from Jackson Elementary to Stonebrook Middle at the start of fifth grade. The building was weird and kind of spooky, and we all mainly hung out with each other. Between classes we started out meeting up at the big oak tree that stood at the edge of the bus drop-off parking lot. But by seventh grade we were changing classes as much as the high school and started running into older kids that were pissed that we were crowding their secret smoking spot behind the tree. We looked for another good hangout spot for a couple of weeks, but then Thomas and Cassidy found us a way into the lower rooms.

You look a bit lost, so let me explain. The hallways of the school crisscrossed, with the vertical four halls being used for fifth through eighth grade, as well as special classrooms for things like music and clubs. The horizontal halls were used for ninth through twelfth grade, and had the administrative offices and the teacher's lounge. But as we figured out over time, each of those halls had another floor below it that wasn't connected to each other like the floors above. It gave each floor its own private basement, and while the rooms had been used for classes at some point in the building's past, by the time we got there they were mainly for storage…or a secret hangout if you could find a door unlocked.

The door to the basement of six grade's hall didn't lock securely, and by the time October of our seventh grade year had rolled around, we were already hanging out down there regularly. It wasn't as bad as it sounds. There was electricity, and the space was surprisingly clean, though there was a certain air of decay and disuse that always hung in the stale air. It was a spooky place, and the few times I was the first one to arrive, I had to fight the urge to go back upstairs until one of you got there. I think maybe that's what got us talking about ghosts.

****

“No,” I interjected. “I remember daydreaming in class about there being a ghost at the school. I was by myself and bored. I think I brought it up to the rest of you.”

Ellis frowned, glancing at Mills and Thomas. “Well, that could be right. Either way, it doesn’t matter who brought it up first. We were all talking about it, and we were all a part of what came next.”

****

At first it was us just swapping rumors and speculation we had heard about the school as a way to pass time during breaks or lunch. Truth be told, most of it was fairly tame. It seemed the place had been a college at one point, but nothing bad had ever happened there that we could tell. No grisly murders or dark rituals, no crazy people or monsters.

Of course, mundane fact didn’t satisfy us for long. We would talk about the school being creepy. About maybe having seen something or heard something one time. There would be passionate debates about how a place that old and creepy must be haunted by at least one ghost, despite the lack of any evidence to support it.

Then we turned to talking about what such a ghost would be like. Cassidy is the one that came up with the idea that it was probably the dead soul of a former college professor. The Professor, she suggested, had probably fallen in love with one of his students, and when his advances were rejected, he had killed himself at the school, possibly in the very room we sat huddled in between fourth and fifth period.

It was just a story, of course, and we all knew it. But stories have power. So does belief. I’ve been thinking a lot about that the last few days, and I think stories are living things. Whether you’re telling the tale or hearing it, you feed it with emotion and thought, with imagination and belief, and it evolves and grows. In time, a story can take on a life of its own.

Over the next few weeks, we added a great deal to the Professor. It became a kind of informal story contest, where we would all take turns creating stories that either plumbed some chamber of the ghost or school's past or reported on some more recent indication of the Professor's continued presence at the school.

Thomas was the first.

****

Thomas' Tale

Thomas told us more details about how the Professor was seen lurking around the halls of the college in the months following his death. The girl he had been in love with had dropped out after his suicide, but returned the following quarter. She was one of the few women at the school at the time, and this combined with her prior absence caused her to redouble her efforts to catch up and surpass her peers.

One night when she went to leave the school library, she found that she was locked in and all alone. Well, except for the Professor. The next morning they found her bruised and bloody in a gibbering heap. She never returned to school and people say she died just a few weeks later of some unknown malady.

****

Millicent's Tale

Mills added in how the building was actually built on the tribal grounds of the Arikara, a Native American tribe that once lived in the area. Or to be more accurate, she had added with dramatic flair, a banished offshoot of the Arikara that had been shunned by the tribe for their extreme cruelty and dark magic practices. They had used the location as a site for their black rituals, and when they were driven from the land, European immigrants found themselves drawn to the place as well.

A village had grown up in the spot in the early 1800s, being a prosperous trade hub for local farmers and distant merchants for nearly fifty years. Then, during the height of the Civil War, a small band of travelers had come to town to find every man, woman and child slaughtered. The initial reactions were to blame a rogue detachment of Confederate or Union soldiers, but closer examination showed that the townsfolk appeared to have all turned on one another until the last one died of wounds she inflicted on herself.

It was another thirty years before anyone dared to build in the area again, but people have a short memory where there's money to be made, and by 1900 the current town had started growing in that direction and soon the school was being built. Some say the same dark forces that plagued earlier generations caused the Professor to commit suicide and may still stalk these halls today…

****

Ellis' Tale

When they bought the closed down college and started renovating it into the middle and high school, they found all these weird lower floor hallways. Apparently they had been used for classes at one time—all except the one we were meeting in. That one had been a lab the college had set aside for faculty to use, though only a couple ever did. One of those was named Arthur Chester, a chemist that was known for his obsessive devotion to his research and isolated lifestyle.

When the school closed, everything was very chaotic, but they did try to make sure that everyone was out before they sealed everything up. They went into every underground chamber, calling out for people and checking for signs that someone was being left behind.

But Arthur had taken to testing his compounds on himself and lay passed out in a dim corner of a back room. He never stirred and they sealed him in with no idea at all. When he awoke, it was another two days before he even knew he couldn't leave, and the theory was that he suffocated himself with gasses from a concoction intended to blow the door off its hinges. All that's known for certain is that his face and hands were torn and broken from where he had frantically flung himself against the heavy metal door until his lungs or his heart finally gave out.

****

Cassidy's Tale

A few years back, before we were at Stonebrook, one of the freshmen saw something moving in the woods near the school. They thought it was a deer at first, and they pointed it out to a friend, but the friend didn't see anything. Intrigued and wanting to prove their friend wrong, they tried to get their companion to go with them to the woods' edge, but they refused.

Determined now, they set off by themselves while their friend went off to class yelling a stern admonition that the teacher was going to skin them alive for missing class. When the freshman didn't come home that night, everyone began to search for her. It wasn't long before they zeroed in on her friend and what she might have seen.

This led them to the woods, and while they had brought ten people and a pair of dogs to search for her, it was unnecessary. She was hanging thirty feet up in the branches of a large tree not far in and along the main trail through the woods. Her skin had been flayed away and spread like ragged wings behind her, and her lipless mouth was held open by what they first took to be one of her own notebooks. However on closer inspection, they saw that it was actually an old essay blue book. Written on the inside cover was the name of the girl the Professor had loved.

****

These stories were told and retold over the course of several weeks, and every time that it would come to your turn, Alex, you would pass, saying you were still working on yours. We didn't push you, but we were starting to get tired of just rehashing the same old material and for whatever reason we didn't feel like we could move on to new stories or something else entirely until you were finished.

So we started telling the stories to others. I think we were all doing it on our own at first. I remember the first time I talked about it to any of you, about how I had told a couple of buddies in gym class about the Professor, I was surprised to find you had all been doing the same thing.

Stuff like that isn't uncommon, of course. Every school or town or group of more than five people have rumors and superstitions. Most of the time they have their time in the limelight and then fade away. Some stick around long enough to become urban legends or folktales. But when we started telling people about the Professor, it spread quicker and more powerfully than any of us expected.

Part of it is that we were all telling it like it was true. We had taken to telling each other's stories among ourselves, you included, so we were all practiced at telling details of the tales without stumbling or lacking confidence. Another thing was that even though we were all known to be friends, we were all telling different people who then spread it to others. Within a month, our versions of Professor stories had been told probably fifty times. That's not even counting the mutated versions, the spin-offs, the rip-offs, and straight-up new stories other people were creating out of some kind of strange drive, whether it was just an urge to be part of the current trend or something darker pushing them to do it.

By Christmas, people were telling each other to "watch out for the Professor!" and "don't go in the woods alone" during the holiday. We thought it was hilarious, and were more than a little proud that we had inadvertently created a school spirit, at least for a little while. We had kind of figured it would die back down when we came back in January, but that was before Jenna Hastings went missing.

Part Three

Jenna Hastings was a sophomore at Stonebrook, and she went missing the day before Christmas Eve. The last time anyone had seen her, she was leaving the mall, bags of last-minute Christmas gifts in her hands, and walking across the parking lot towards the fast food place on the corner. We were already out for the holiday break at the time, so it wasn't until a few days after Christmas that it became a big enough deal that the news trickled down to us.

I remember us all sitting in my attic, playing Sorry! because we were tired of being outside in the cold. Cassidy had just gotten there and was telling us about Jenna, and at first it was mildly troubling and interesting, but that was all. Jenna was three years older than us, which at twelve might as well have been thirty years, and while we all had some vague idea of who she was, we didn't have a clear idea of her as a person. Instead she was more of a point of interest or a cautionary tale.

But then Thomas decided to make a joke out of it. Cassidy had finished her short recounting of what she had overheard from her mother's phone conversation, and we were about to get back to the game when Thomas piped up with, "Maybe the Professor got her."

We all froze and looked at him. His proud grin started to fall away and Mills punching him in the arm finished the job. "Idiot," she said with a scowl. "That's not funny. And it's dumb. The Professor is made up." We were all nodding our agreement, and even at the time I knew that something felt wrong. We were all either 12 or 13 and none of us were known for being overly sensitive or afraid of dark humor. But we all shared a kind of desperate intensity in that moment—a need to not only rebuke what Thomas had said, but deny it.

I've thought about us sitting in that attic, scolding him while he grew sad and sullen. He didn't like being yelled at, but he didn't fight back like he usually would. It was as if he knew as much as the rest of us that he had made a mistake beyond bad taste. I think that's one of the first times I knew we had somehow started to believe in the Professor too.

****

The following week we were back in school, and we had carefully avoided any further mention of the Professor among ourselves during the break, maybe in some unconscious attempt to kill the idea before it took deeper root. But our hopes that the rest of the school would have forgotten about our stories over the holidays were dashed as soon as we got off the bus that first morning back.

Two of the school janitors had just set up a pressure washer to blast paint off of the concrete walkway just a few feet from the bus lot. They had already started spraying, but we could still see the neon green words emblazoned across the ground like a brand.

We found out later that the vandalism had just been discovered half an hour before the buses started arriving, and they had it removed by that afternoon, but the damage had already been done. The school was on fire with fear and speculation now, and the larger world had started to take notice too. During a class change, we saw two policemen out at the walkway taking photographs of the now partially obliterated message. Then after lunch, we realized that they were still there, questioning several staff about it as well.

The reason was obvious to everyone. They thought it could be connected to Jenna's disappearance, or at the very least, they wanted to cover every base just to be safe. Either way, this investigation just further validated the Professor's existence to most of the students. Within the week we were all hearing new stories about the school and the Professor pop up, sometimes told to us by the same people we had initially told the original stories.

For the first few days back we tried to laugh it off or ignore it, and we didn't talk much about it among ourselves, but there was a tightening cord of tension running through all of us. It was quickly becoming something we didn't just not discuss, but something we actively avoided discussing. Then a couple of things happened that changed everything.

The first was that the third week of January, Jenna Hastings was found. She had run off with a boy from the next town over that she had been secretly dating for over a year. He was an older boy who had made promises of taking her away from the drudgery of high school life and bossy parents--and who wound up leaving her two states away at a burger joint not dissimilar from the local one he had picked her up from the day before Christmas Eve.

The town breathed a collective sigh of relief, and no one was more happy that she had been found than us. We began joking about how stupid people were to believe in the Professor, how silly it all was. We would sit in our underground hideaway, sounding superior and proud of how everyone had come to believe in something we had made up. But the jokes and the laughter weren't quite the same as they had been before. Now they felt like we were whistling as we walked through a graveyard, our forced humor and bravado meant to keep dark things at bay.

In the next couple of months, talk of the Professor did die down from its fever pitch after the graffiti, but it never really went away, and by the last week of school that year we had just come to accept that for good or ill, we had created a new legend for the school and the town. I say for the town because there was actually a newspaper article about the Professor about two weeks after Jenna Hastings was found. It was a puff piece in the local paper, and it was trying to trade on the drama of the missing girl who had been found while not explicitly saying her name. But it was undeniably about "the teacher ghost" that locals had started talking about in recent months and gave poor summaries of a couple of the stories. A few of our parents asked us if we had heard anything about this ghost crap at school, and we all denied it earnestly. We were ready to put it behind us.

Then Ellie Marks, or as she was frequently called by her cruel fellow freshman, "Ellie Skidmarks", made the mistake of picking on Cassidy at school.

****

Ellie was a heavy-set, unfortunately proportioned girl, and that combined with a dim intellect and a terrible temper led her to frequently shift between pitiable victim and merciless bully depending on her surroundings. Likely from the outside it was like watching some kind of social causality experiment play out. She would get picked on, she would become hurt and angry, and she would take it out on younger, smaller students.

Our group rarely had much problem with bullying, in part because we stuck together and kept to ourselves, and in part because Thomas and Mills would happily beat ass if someone tried to test things. Ellie had tried to test things a couple of times in the past when Cassidy was alone—Cassidy who was small and beautiful and delicate, who had boys already noticing her despite her best efforts to fade into the background. I think we all knew that Ellie had been dealt a harsher hand in life than Cassidy had, and that's part of why she had never gotten worse than a strong warning from Mills when she had tried saying mean things to Cassidy in the past. But the last week of school, the P.E. classes were all devoted to some combination of field relays and dodgeball, and Ellie just couldn't resist.

Myself, Mills, and Cassidy were all in the same dodgeball game that day, and we were on the second round. Dodgeball always runs the risk of turning into a brutal free-for-all, but the teacher, Ms. Perkins, did a good job of keeping her P.E. classes in line. No one had gotten hurt and everyone was having a pretty good time so far.

When Ellie got the ball in that second round, she headed straight for Cassidy. Based on the rules, she wasn't supposed to go over her team's half of the basketball court to make her throw. And the first throw she didn't. The rubber ball thudded into Cassidy's lower back, startling her more than hurting I think, but it was enough to get her off balance and send her to the floor.

It was like seeing a falling gazelle for Ellie. She scooped up another ball as she charged towards Cassidy, waiting until she was standing over her before throwing it hard at her upturned face. Cassidy let out a yell and Ms. Perkins began running over, blowing her whistle and hollering for Ellie to get back. The older girl started mumbling some half-hearted excuse that it was an accident, but the smirk on her face said that she knew she was caught and didn't care.

Me and Mills rushed over to Cassidy, who was sitting up but had a large red welt starting to rise on the left side of her face and her eye kept pouring water. When she saw the two of us, she started crying. I bent down and hugged her. Behind me I could hear Mills talking to Ellie.

"You just fucked up, Skidmark. We're going to get you for this."

Normally Ms. Perkins would have jumped Mills for language and a threat like that, but I think she half wanted to hit Ellie herself. So she just told Ellie to go to the principal's office immediately and that she would be coming along in just a minute. She then turned back to Cassidy, who I had helped to her feet. Perkins was asking if she was okay, if she needed to go to the nurse, when we started to hear Ellie scream.

It took a moment for anyone to find Ellie because the sound of her screams seemed to echo down the twelfth-grade hall and into the gymnasium. Perkins and an assistant principal (who left the school at the end of that year) finally realized she was screaming from behind the locked metal door that led down into the lower rooms beneath the twelfth-grade hall. They fumbled around until they found the key, and when they opened the door they saw Ellie laying at the bottom of the stairs in a screeching heap. Her right leg had been broken, which could be accounted for by a bad fall down the concrete steps, but what was stranger were the bones of her hands, which had been crushed. They were damaged to such an extent that she could never use the left one well again, and the right one—the one she had thrown the dodgeball with—ultimately had to be amputated after several failed surgeries trying to restore bloodflow.

It wasn't lost on anyone that this had all happened right after she hurt Cassidy, and it didn't take long for everyone to also realize that you and Thomas were in class when it happened, and the three of us were standing in front of a couple of dozen witnesses at the time. Plus, there was the fact that Ellie had somehow gotten past a locked door before she fell.

But all of that was secondary to the biggest thing that made everyone at the school certain of what had caused Ellie's injuries. It was Ellie herself. While she never returned to school at Stonebrook, and we never heard of anyone talking to her about it later, close to a hundred people had heard her screaming down in the dark that day. They heard what she said before her cries of pain and terror had compressed into a wavering animal wail.

AHHHHH! OH GOD. OH NO. FUCK, ITS GOT ME.
NOOOOOOO! GET IT OFF OF ME! MY HANDS...NOOOO!
PROFESSOR, NOOOOOOOOO!

Part Four

Stories and beliefs have power. So do names. When Ellie screamed out the Professor's name in pain and terror, she cemented the idea of its existence in the minds of everyone that heard it. Even those that didn't want to believe, that called the stories of ghosts and dark rituals childish fairy tales, had a black sliver of doubt slid into their heart that day. And for those that already believed or wanted to, it was confirmation of something both wonderous and terrible.

I remember us all talking about it one time a couple of years after Ellie was attacked, before the worst of it started happening. We were still comfortable and confident at that point—feeling special. And we talked about it all more freely in those days, about what the Professor might actually be and how it all worked. About how other people must look at it and why they were all at least a little afraid of us. That's when Mills had spoken up.

She said that if you took a town full of people, most any town, you'd have some people that believed in God, some that didn't, and some that fell in between. But if one day that town saw a miracle, something that seemed to clearly point to the existence of God and beyond that, seemed to indicate that God liked some people better than the rest, it would be interpreted differently by different people. Some would ignore or try to explain away the miracle, even if there was no reasonable alternative available. Some would embrace it and find comfort in the proof it provided. But some would just be scared. Because what's more terrifying than the idea that God does exist, but He really doesn't like you very much?

Now I believe in God, and I think whatever God is, it's a lot kinder and fairer than the Professor. But after Ellie's fall, we weren't worried about the Professor being kind and fair. We were focused on it being on our side. I'd like to think that we were somehow manipulated by it in the weeks and months and years that followed. Pushed to turn a blind eye to the true nature of the thing we had let into our group.

But I think that's a lie. Having proof to match what our hearts already knew was a relief in many ways, and knowing that the Professor would protect us went a long way towards easing our fears about what we might have played a hand in creating or at least waking up. We felt chosen and special, and if it accorded us extra respect and deference from the other students, what was the harm?

It reminds me of a story my grandmother told me growing up.

There was a little boy who lived in the wilds of India with his family for most of his childhood. When he turned 12, he got work as a servant for the prince. One day, the prince went out riding with two of his friends and took the boy along to act as his steward. They had been riding for several hours when they came to a clearing. In the middle of the clearing was a massive tiger sunning itself in the tall grass. The prince and his friends began excitedly boasting to each other about what they could do, how they could fight the beast, even without a weapon. They were somewhat drunk at the time, but they were also feeding off of each others' foolishness and ego, so it wasn't long before one slipped from his horse to address the others.

This first friend said, "I will go into the grass and wrestle the tiger into submission." With that, he stripped off his shirt and ran at the tiger, leaping onto its back. The animal roared in surprise and anger, and within a matter of seconds, it had torn the man apart. The Prince and his other friend were horrified, but they were more determined than ever to dominate the tiger and avenge their friend. The boy tried warning them to stop, but the prince slapped him and told him to be silent.

The second friend vowed, "I will go into the grass with my club and beat the tiger into submission or kill it if it will not submit." With that, he hunkered down and began creeping through the tall grass toward the great cat as though to sneak up on it. When he was ten feet from the tiger, it leaped on him and ripped his throat out.

The prince was now beside himself with fear and anger. He roughly shoved the boy forward, intending on sending him to his death so no one would be alive to contradict the prince's grand tale of how he fought valiantly to save his friends from a giant tiger. The boy did as he was told and went out to the great beast.

The tiger studied the boy carefully as he approached, his large yellow eyes narrowed as he glanced between the small figure and the prince who stood back at the treeline. For his part, the prince already had one foot in the stirrup, ready to make a run for it if the tiger headed his way. He wanted to see the insolent boy killed, but not badly enough to risk himself.

But the boy wasn't killed. Instead, the tiger licked his face with a giant pink tongue and if the prince wasn't mistaken, he heard the beast begin to purr when the boy put his arms around that massive shaggy neck. The boy said something in low tones to the tiger before releasing his neck and returning to the prince.

"How?" The prince demanded, all fear now forgotten in the face of his wounded pride and indignation. "How did you face the tiger and not get killed, boy?" When the boy said nothing, the prince pulled a musket from the sash at his waist, his jaw hard with anger. "No matter. If you can face it, so can I."

The prince let out a grunt as the small knife was shoved into his gut, and when he looked down, the boy twisted the knife and yanked it back out. Incredulous, he went to point the gun at the boy, but the tiger was on him now, removing the gun and the arm that raised it with a single swipe.

As the prince lay dying, the boy and the tiger stood over him covered in his life's blood. The tiger absently licked the back of the little boy's head as he answered the prince. "I grew up near these woods, your majesty. This tiger has been one of my best friends for years. He would never harm me or let me come to harm, nor I him."

The prince, choking on blood, gasped out a response. "But why? Why not warn us before we tried to fight it?"

The boy laughed, bending over to wipe his small knife off on the prince's fine brocade. "Do you need the advice of a servant boy to tell you not to fight a tiger? You thought there was fun to be had, and there was. It's just that it was for my friend the tiger, not for you. And why should I spoil his fun? He's a true and loyal friend, while you? You I hardly know at all."

****

"Damn, your grandmother told you some fucked up stories," Thomas said with a snort, getting a dirty look from Ellis. It was getting late now, and I was reaching my limit for what new and terrible things I could hear for the night. Yet I found myself asking Ellis for more.

"What do you think the point of the story was, Ellis?"

Ellis smiled, his eyes tired. Telling all of this, dredging it up, was taking a toll on him too. "I've never been sure. I used to think it meant be careful who you fuck with because you don't know when you'll run across someone badder than you. Or maybe that people will do or accept just about anything for something or someone important to them, regardless of who might get hurt in the process. But now…now I think the message is that when you're best friends with a tiger, you start looking at other people as nothing more than prey."

****

The summer after Ellie was a fun and exciting time for us. We were scared, but only enough to make it more interesting. We'd come around to the idea that there was a tiger in town, but that it was our friend. We debated trying to communicate with the Professor, but Mills and me were against it from the start. And with nothing new happening around us, at first we weren't even sure that the Professor could leave the school grounds.

But by late June we had heard several stories of people having strange encounters in the town. A man being chased by a shadowy figure while walking through General's Park late at night. A store downtown having all its windows broken out with several employees inside, with no signs of how it was done or why. These things, if they were related to the Professor, had sinister connotations. In truth, Mills and I argued, even though it was arguably payback for her hurting Cassidy, Ellie's "accident" was fairly brutal and extreme. Maybe the Professor was friendly to us and maybe it wasn't, but it was certainly dangerous either way.

Then the car accident happened. Or almost happened. Do you remember that part, Alex? Okay. Fuck. Well, one day you and your mom and…you were going to the grocery store. You know that big intersection up from where you lived? A gas truck missed the light as you were crossing the intersection. It should have hit your car right where you were sitting in the passenger seat. The fucking thing was going better than forty miles an hour and would have killed you. I'm sorry, Mills, but it's the truth. It would have killed him if it had hit.

But it didn't hit. Less than five feet from the outside of your car door the truck hit something else. We went and looked at the truck the next week at the junkyard. It was crushed up to the window of the cab like it had ran into the side of a battleship. Hell, I don't know how it didn't explode, but it didn't. The driver died, but you were all fine, and...well, after that we knew. The Professor really was our friend.

We didn't talk about it with other people, but news of the wreck had spread through the town. There was even a picture in the newspaper. By the time we got back to school, our social standing had changed again. Some people avoided us like the plague, while others actually started trying to befriend us, to get into the circle. But, of course, the circle already had its sixth and final member.

You were the one that called us that first. The Stonebrook Six. We laughed at the time, but it stuck. When it somehow got out into the rest of the school, we weren't worried or embarrassed. We wore the name as a badge of honor, a symbol of how special we were to have a tiger as a friend. But then...

****

Ellis stopped, looking around at the others and back at me. "I'm...I'm beat, man. I'm starting to...I'm going to start messing up on some of the details and I think you've heard more than enough for now. We can talk more later about it, okay?"

I nodded my understanding, feeling a mixture of disappointment and relief. We all hung out quietly for a few more minutes before finding spots to sleep for the night. The next day none of us discussed it, and I haven't talked about it further with anyone yet.

But that needs to change. I'm about to stop writing for now and go call Mills. See if she knows about Ellis and how she's doing. I don't want to talk more about this with her over the phone, so I'm going to see about flying out to visit Mills in the next couple of days, possibly after I've talked with my mother.

Because I know my mom has to know some of this. Or know something about something. There has to be a reason why she abandoned me with Aunt Judy at 15 and will barely talk to me even now. I trust what Ellis told me, what I might learn from the others, but I'm not taking anything for granted and I just don't know. I feel like Ellis was hiding things from me, even if it was with the best of intentions. I don't think my dear mother will be as worried about my feelings.

Part Five

I don't remember much from when I was fifteen, but I remember the ride to my Aunt Judy's house down in Tennessee. It was just me and my mother in the car, the air conditioner the only noise for the several hour drive, though it wasn't the only reason for the chill in the air. I remember knowing that my mother hated me and being terribly sad about the fact, especially because I deserved it. That's the fucked up thing. I remember feeling that I had earned everything I was getting somehow, but I didn't know why.

Until the last few days, I've been sleepwalking through a life built on an obscured past without even questioning what would cause me not to remember something so important. But I've woken up now, at least a little. Every day bits of memory are coming back to me, but only about those things I've been told, as though someone has to point out objects in a shadowed room for me to notice that they're there.

I had decided I would talk to Mills on the phone and get more details of what went on before visiting my mother. The idea was that I would be better armed with knowledge, and to be honest, I wanted to be able to learn enough to talk myself into abandoning the idea of contacting my mother at all. The last time I spoke to her was over the phone on my 18th birthday, and it was not a long or heartwarming conversation. It ended with her saying she hoped she'd never hear from me again, and I have lived up to that hope for over a decade.

But despite repeated calls and texts, I hadn't been able to get Mills yet, though I kept trying on the road to Euclid, Ohio. Hearing Mills' voicemail always makes my heart jump slightly, though increasingly it was from fear rather than excitement or joy. I didn't want to panic, and I'd already booked a flight for Austin from the

Cleveland airport for late that night, but it was still hard to keep my mind on what I was doing while worrying about her.

In some ways it was a blessing, because I arrived at my mother's house before I realized it. I had never seen it before, only knowing where she lived thanks to my Aunt, who kept hoping we would reconcile someday and would periodically slip me unsolicited updates on how my mother was faring and what she was up to. It's not that I didn't care—I cared a lot. It was just that reminders of her were also reminders of a lot of pain and loss.

I had always been closer to my father growing up, and when he died suddenly when I was fifteen, it sent both me and my mother into a tailspin…I froze as I realized something. I didn't remember how my father died. I didn't remember anything other than that he's dead. What the fuck was wrong with me?

The terror and anger of realizing how profound my memory gaps truly were drove me from the car and up to the front door of the house. It was a small but nice house in a pleasant neighborhood, and I tried to knock as demurely as I could both for the neighbors' sake and my mother's. Still, I knew I probably looked wild-eyed when she opened the door.

"Hi…um, Hello, Mom. I'm sorry I didn't call or warn you, but I was afraid you wouldn't see me if you knew I was coming." I smiled weakly, my stomach churning in knots. I was afraid if I stopped talking, she would just slam the door in my face, which might still happen anyway. "I just really need to talk to you for a few minutes. I won't stay long and I won't ever bother you again if you want. Can I please come in and talk to you for a few minutes? It's very important." I could hear my voice shaking, and I hated it, but it couldn't be helped. For her part, my mother's initial look of surprise had slowly slid down into a look of suspicious anger.

"Are you on drugs? Is that what this is?" Her voice was dry and hoarse sounding now, and I wondered if she had started smoking again. She had stopped when I was little when…something happened. Fuck. "I hear on t.v. about junkie kids coming to kill their parents." She raised a thinly penciled eyebrow. "I think you've done enough killin' already."

I clenched my teeth, my anger and frustration burning away my guilt and fear for the moment as I took a step forward and jabbed a finger at her face. "There. That right fucking there. I'm so sick of this. Of all of this. People are either treating me like I'm a piece of glass or they're shitting on me for things I don't remember. No. Fuck that." I realized I had made it five steps into the house now, my mother retreating from my angry tirade. Taking a deep breath, I started over. "Look, I'm sorry. I know you don't want me here. I don't want to be here. But I need answers for things I don't remember. I'm not on drugs, and I'm not going to hurt you. I just need your help."

My mother looked up at me, her lips pressed into a thin line. "I don't have any money to give you."

I rolled my eyes. "I don't need money. I just need help remembering things."

Studying me carefully, she narrowed her gaze again. "What kinds of things?"

I had been mostly looking down at the floor since entering, but now I met her eyes again. "Like why you hate me for one. I really don't remember why or what happened when I was 15."

I saw her eyes begin watering, and at first I thought it was sadness at how far apart we had drifted or regret for sending me away. Then I realized it was raw hurt and anger.

"Get out. I won't hear any more of this bullshit in my own shitting house!" She was screaming like a madwoman now, her eyes wide and her face red as she advanced on me. "That was always your problem, you'd never admit to what you done. Never admit to killing them or letting them get killed, whichever it was."

I stood my ground. "They? Who is they? Who did I kill or let get killed?"

She had reached me now, beating upon my chest with her small, thin hands. "Damn you, Alex. What is wrong with you? Are you telling me you don't remember? Are you still going to play this game after all this time?"

I gently grabbed her wrists and held them still for a minute. "Mom, Cassidy and Ellis are dead. They've been murdered because of something we all were doing as kids. And if I don't figure out what is going on, it may happen to the rest of us too." I sighed. "Fuck, it might even if I do figure it out." I let go of her wrists and stepped back. "I'm not playing games. I really don't remember. I never could. I can't explain it, but it's only since I've been talking to the others the last few days that I've started to remember any of it. So I'm going to ask you one last time to please talk to me for a minute. Explain to me what went on. Then I'll go away forever."

My mother wiped at her eyes and I could see her fingers were yellowed with age and cigarette tar. I realized I had smelt alcohol on her breath when she was close by as well. She was looking at me like a wounded animal, and I hated myself for making it all worse for her by being here. And if she wasn't going to…

"I don't know everything. I don't know much, really. But I'll tell you what I can, and then you have to go."

****

You were always so close with your friends. When you were younger I was happy for you—I know how hard childhood can be, and to have so may close friends can be a blessing. But as you got older and moved to…that damned school…things started changing. You were more quiet and you barely talked to us about what was going on with you anymore.

At first, I chalked it up to adolescence. You were a growing boy, and I knew from my brothers growing up that a teenage boy can be hard to be around. And you weren't mean or getting into trouble. You were just…not there. You were gone a lot of the time, and when you were home, you could tell your mind was off somewhere else.

When strange things started happening around the school and the town, we didn't pay it much mind. Your father liked to joke about the teacher ghost, and we really thought that's all it was, a silly joke or myth. But then we almost had a car accident that one time and…well, you may not remember it, but it was almost really bad. And the way it didn't happen was so strange. I should have known then something wasn't right. Maybe I could have helped you. Got you away from those kids, that school.

Still, people are blind to things so much, right? So time passed, and I heard of things happening, but I guess I ignored it or thought it was just talk. Then one night you came in and said that Alicia was gone. That she had been taken by the thing at the school. I didn't know what you were talking about, but you were all torn up and terrified, so I…

****

"Wh-who's Alicia?" I felt as though my head was being torn apart, and as I spoke, each word echoed across my brain like a monstrous bell being rung. I saw my mother wanting to grow angry again, but she wrestled it back down when she saw how much pain I was in.

"My God. You really don't know. I think you really forgot her." We had still been standing at the edge of her living room while we talked, and she moved now to her mantle to retrieve a picture frame. In it was a photo of me at about age twelve, along with my parents and a young girl that looked to be about eight. My mother held the picture in front of my face, tapping the girl with a long, yellow nail. "That's Alicia. That's your sister." She dropped her arm and staggered back, her face looking impossibly old and tired.

"That's half of why I couldn't be around you anymore. I could never believe that you really forgot her. How do you forget a person? Especially her. She was so sweet and good, and she loved you so much." She was crying freely now, and I wanted to comfort her, but didn't quite dare. "We all loved each other so much. But then you got caught up in whatever was going on at the school."

Her face was harder now, tears sliding down her cheeks like water on granite. "I don't know what you got tangled up in, whether it was some kind of cult or if there really was some ghost or something at that school. All I know is that when you came in all scared and bloody, your father went to bring our baby girl back. I tried to get you to stay with me, but you ran out after he left."

"I called the police, but they were already out there. Seven people died that night. They never found my baby girl, but they found your father's body in the gymnasium. Or parts of it at least." Her eyes were dry and blazing again. "And you…I was so scared for you. Even when I knew you must have had some hand in her being at the school so late in the evening, especially when you were the one that knew where she was. When we found you and your friends out on the football field later that night, all unconscious, I was so relieved. Both because you were safe and because maybe you had answers. Maybe you could help us find your father and Alicia."

Her tone grew more wooden as she talked, and her eyes had wandered to the picture in her hands. She stroked it absently as she went on. "But then they found your father around the time the EMTs were checking you kids out. They said you were scraped up but otherwise fine. Rescue crews were still searching the school, but I took you to the car and asked you what had happened. Where you had seen Alicia last." Her grip tightened on the frame until I heard it crack. "And you know what you said to me?"

"Who's Alicia?" I finished with her, remembering it as it was being told. I still didn't know what had led up to that moment, but I remember my mother that night, so sad and scared, staring at me with her mouth open for several moments. Asking me again and again, shaking my shoulders. And then she slapped me across the face.

I could see she was remembering that too. "I know it seems like I've treated you bad, Alex, and I guess I have. But just like you couldn't help what you remembered, I couldn't help how that made me feel. I tried getting investigators, psychologists, even a preacher, to talk to you. Tried to help you remember or quit lying if you weren't being honest about what you knew. But nothing helped. And every day…every day I felt like you were slowly killing your sister by either being intentionally evil or just stupid and weak enough to block out the most important thing you could ever know."

She wiped her nose as she shook her head. "I'm sorry, but I'm done. I've spent years trying to forget all this, to forget about you. I'm sorry you're in trouble now, especially if it's not your fault. But I can't be around you anymore. I don't hate you, Alex, but I don't love you either. Not anymore."

I left my mother's house and drove to a nearby parking lot where I just cried for a few minutes. I think part of me had always thought we would reconcile, and the loss of that hope coupled with memories of my baby sister flooding back as I tried to cope with losing her too…it was more than I could handle at first. I didn't know how much I was to blame for what had happened to her and my father, but that didn't lessen my grief or my guilt.

After awhile I checked my phone. No word from Mills and two hours until my flight. I decided to try her again, and this time she picked up right away. Except it wasn't her. It was Thomas.

"Hey, Alex. Mills can't come to the phone right now. Mainly because I have her tied up in the other room. Been trying to get the Professor to sit on her chest, which fuck me, you probably don't even know what I'm talking about, but it doesn't matter. We need you buddy. I think it'll work if you're here."

I was momentarily confused, trying to decide if he could potentially be joking or something, but that made no sense. He wouldn't go all the way to Austin for a joke, and his voice sounded strange, like he was caught between laughing and crying. Or just in the middle of going insane. "Look, you're right. I don't know what you're talking about, but I'll come and we'll figure it out. Is she okay? Have you hurt her?"

Thomas gave an uneven laugh. "No, she almost broke my arm, but she's fine. Not trying to hurt either of you. But I need you both to contact the Professor. Ask for its help."

"Help?"

"With Cassidy. With bringing her back to life."

Part Six

"Thomas, you need to stop this. I know you're upset, out of your head with grief even, but this isn't the answer."

I had spent a hellish five hours since my brief surprise phone call with Thomas waiting at the airport, waiting on the plane, waiting for a rental car and then driving as fast as I could to get to Mills' house outside of Austin. I didn't think he would hurt her, but I hadn't thought he would tie her up either. When I knocked on her door, he answered right away, and though I could tell he had been crying, he looked oddly happy to see my face. He actually went to give me a hug before seeming to absently remember he had a small revolver in his right hand. With an embarrassed shrug he gestured with the gun for me to come in.

When I first entered the house, I moved past Thomas and started calling for Mills. She yelled back and I found her laying on the bed in her room, her ankles and wrists tied with thin, yellow rope. I had untied her right away, knowing he was at my back with a gun but not caring. Once I knew she was okay, I hugged her and turned to look at Thomas, who asked us to come sit on the sofa in the living room. It was there that I started trying to talk him back from the edge he was teetering on. But looking at my friend, his eyes weighted down with a hard glaze of insanity, my heart sank as I realized I wasn't going to be able to reason with him.

"No, no, Alex. You're wrong. I've thought it all out. We created this thing, right? And it's powerful. Able to do all kinds of things. It's magic. So what's to stop it from helping us out with Cassidy?"

"How about the fact that it just fucking killed her last week?" Mills snarled at him, the anger and fear in her voice scaring me more than Thomas. I needed to get her out of here. At least she'd be safe and maybe I could calm him down alone. But Thomas didn't seem angry. He was nodding and smiling as though being patient with children who just didn't understand.

"I see your point and why you'd think that. But the last few nights, I've been having dreams. Or really the same dream repeatedly. At first, I thought it was just stress and grief, but when it happened the third time…well, I realized it had to be the Professor. It was sending me a message. Telling me about what it could do."

Mills gave him a warning look. "Thomas, stop it." Looking at me, her eyes worried, she said. "Do you remember a girl named Alicia?"

I had been holding her hand and I gave it a squeeze now. "Yeah, I do now. I came from my mother's. It…didn't go well, but she told me about my little sister. I've spent the last few hours remembering more and more about her since." I felt myself getting choked up again and pushed it down, turning back to Thomas. I loved Mills for being worried for me, but I was tired of being protected. "So what did you see in the dream that makes you think the Professor will help? What doesn't Mills want you to tell me?"

Thomas smiled wide, his eyes glittering in their sunken hollows. He looked ten years older than even after Cassidy's funeral, and I wondered for a moment when he had last gotten any restful sleep. His voice and his movements had a disquieting jerkiness to them, like a corpse dancing to an electric current. I stifled a shiver at the thought as I tried to listen.

"…and then I was floating in the old gym at Stonebrook. Floating past the floor and down into that old pool. You don't remember when we were down in that pool, do you, Alex? Well, that's all right. But I was down there, and I could feel the ol' Professor down there with me too. But I wasn't scared. I was happy. It was like seeing an old friend, except I couldn't really see him too well, of course, and he kept looking like different things. But then I heard something moving around in the shadows of the pool, sloshing around in that smelly water down there in the dark. It was funny—I could see down there, but I couldn't see either. Not everything. It wasn't until it started floating out into the middle of the pool that I saw clearly what it was."

"It was Alicia. All grown up, or at least a lot bigger than when we lost her. And she was alive! I don't know how, but she was alive down there in the dark. I saw her look at me, and…well she kind of smiled I think. Just think, Alex. If it can keep her alive all this time, it can bring back Cassidy. I felt like that's what it was telling me." He stopped talking suddenly, staring at me as though he expected his words to have answered any questions and solved any conflicts.

"That's fucking crazy, Tom. That's impossible." I stood up, and he raised his gun half-heartedly, but I ignored it. "If it was the Professor contacting you and not just a dream, it wasn't trying to help you. It was trying to trick you. It's killed Ellis. Did you know that? It fucking crushed him against the ceiling of a parking garage like a goddamn roach. That's your buddy the Professor. That's the thing you're siding with over your fucking best friends." I was standing over him now, and his lips were quivering as tears began to fill his eyes. I heard Mills start softly crying behind me at the news of Ellis, but I kept my gaze on Thomas for the moment as he struggled to speak.

"I…No…I…we just need to try, okay? Get the Professor to sit on our chest, any of us. Talk to it. Even if I'm wrong or crazy, we need to try and talk to it, right? Find out why it's killing us?"

I reached down and snatched the gun away from him without resistance. "I don't even know what the fuck you're talking about. 'Sit on our chest'? What the fuck does that even mean?" I cast my gaze back to Mills who had a haunted look on her tear-streaked face. "Do you know?"

She nodded slowly. "I do, yeah. But I think it's a bad idea, if it would even work now."

Thomas looked past me at her. "It would. It would with him here. Alex was always its favorite."

I went to rub my face and realized I was still holding the gun. Frowning disgustedly, I emptied it onto the floor and then set the gun down on the coffee table before stepping back to face both of them. "Look, I want to know the rest of what's going on. Mills, I think you should leave or me and Thomas can. He can catch me up on his own."

She was already shaking her head. "No, I'm not leaving you. No offense, Thomas, but I don't trust you for shit at the moment. And you're too upset to tell him everything anyway."

Thomas was crying softly now, his head buried in one of his hands. "I know. You're right. I'm fucked up. But please tell him. Maybe he'll understand if we tell him the rest." He looked up briefly, his eyes red. "I really am sorry. I'd never hurt you guys. I'm just so fucking scared and alone."

I squatted down next to his chair and gave him a brief hug. "We're all scared, man. But you're not alone. Let her tell me the rest and we'll figure something out, okay?" He nodded and I stood up again, moving to sit with Mills again.

She was still almost painfully beautiful—even scared and exhausted and terribly sad, her face shown with this inner light that touched the core of me. Watching her trying to find the right words, working to find the least painful path through making me relive the worst thing that ever happened to us...I knew then that I was still in love with her. Would always be in love with her and only her. It was a strange time to have such a happy revelation, but I held onto the warmth of it as I waited for her to begin.

****

By the end of eighth grade, the Stonebrook Six pretty much ran the middle school. We didn't bully anyone, but the strange combination of fear and mystery surrounding us was a powerful brew. We were popular without trying, at least on a surface level. And that's all that really mattered, because as always, we really only wanted to hang out with each other anyway.

When we got to ninth grade, things were different at first. Despite sharing the same main building and campus, there was a fairly sharp social divide between the two schools at Stonebrook, and we were now going from being the eldest middle schoolers to lowly freshmen. It meant older kids, different teachers, and more time having passed since the last tangible signs of the Professor.

People like to forget things that don't suit them. They use time and the elasticity of memory to sand off the rough edges of the past, and those things that are too hard to be reshaped are stored away in a musty corner of their mind.

The Professor, as compelling as it was in some ways, was an uncomfortable thought. And like any uncomfortable thought, it spent quite some time walking on the knife's edge of the townsfolk's collective and individual consciousness. On the one side, the eventual oblivion of rationalization and explanation. On the other, the same neglect and dusty demise that befell childhood memories and unpleasant pasts. During most of our ninth-grade year, I think the Professor was teetering between those two kinds of death, and its balance on the blade grew weaker with each passing day. If we had only left it alone, it might have faded away for good that year.

But we didn't. We didn't want the Professor to die, and I think we could all sense it needed our help to survive. Without any plan or coordination, we all began talking about the Professor again in our subterranean hideaway. I mean, we had always talked about it a little, even if just in a joke or passing reference. But by the spring of our freshman year we were back to discussing it regularly, the breath of our words fanning the embers back to life.

I was largely to blame. I had taken it upon myself to do research on different myths and legends--specifically magical creatures that seemed similar to our Professor, if I could find any. That was how I wound up reading about tulpas and telling you all about them.

Tulpas, from what I remember, are supposed to be beings created by the mental or spiritual energies of one or more people. Kind of like an imaginary friend you make real by believing hard enough. It was a strange idea, but it seemed to fit the Professor better than anything else based on what we knew about it.

Around the same time, Ellis came up with the idea of trying to see the Professor. We weren't even sure it was still around, and the idea of verifying its continued presence in some way was attractive to all of us. Ellis' idea led to us getting a large baby pool and sneaking it into a back room down in our secret lair. We filled it with a few inches of water and then began calling to the Professor.

The idea was this: The Professor was always invisible, and past attempts we had made to just ask it to show itself had gone unanswered, so either it couldn't become visible to us or it didn't want to. But if it was at least willing to come and visit us, and if it had some kind of physical form, we might be able to get some sense of its size or shape in the water. It was an odd idea, and Ellis admitted it was a longshot, but we figured it was worth trying, with the fun and challenge of sneaking the pool into the school almost worth the price of admission by itself.

The funny thing was that it kind of worked. We set the pool up, asked the Professor to come as we stood around the water holding hands, and this time it came. We could all feel it there, and after a few seconds Cassidy let out an excited gasp as the water began to slosh in the pool. As the liquid settled, you could see voids where the water didn't go. It was hard to say for sure, but it looked as though the Professor was standing on two invisible legs in the pool. Except then it became four voids instead of two. Then one larger one, then eight small ones. On and on we watched as the water would slosh and settle, slosh and settle, every time around a different shape or configuration.

Then it was gone. We all began talking excitedly, and at first, we didn't really understand what we had just seen. Then I realized what it was. It was changing shape repeatedly as it stood in the water. Big, small, many legs or none, it must have shifted between a dozen things in the span of a couple of minutes. We were excited about all of this, of course, but rather than satisfying our curiosity to know more about the Professor, it just made us hungrier for the next step.

Alex, you were the one that came up with a way of communicating with it. One day when we were all skipping a school assembly together, you started telling us about a theory you had. You said that if we really had made the Professor up, made it what it was, why couldn't we make up a way of talking to it too?

The idea caught on with all of us right away. We talked about it for a couple of weeks, figuring out and agreeing on the details, but by the end of the school year, we were ready to try it out. The end result was very simple, in part because making up rituals can be hard and in part because I think we instinctually weeded out the elements that didn't work. I understand that's contrary to the base idea we were working from--in theory, any idea for the ritual should have worked so long as we believed in it enough. But that's just one example of why I don't think we had as much control of things as we thought at the time. At some point, the newest and last member of the Stonebrook Six started guiding us.

The ritual went like this. We sat cross-legged in a circle, knees touching and one of us holding a lit candle. We repeated the phrase, "Professor come and join us. Professor come and talk to us.", and with each repetition, the candle would be passed to the next person in a counterclockwise manner. If the candle flame turned green, it meant the Professor was present and willing to talk to us. The flame change was important, we had decided, because we wanted definitive proof if the Professor came to talk.

We were all excited to try it out, but when we went to do it the first time, we were all laughing a little and making jokes. I remember thinking it was odd that the year before the idea of trying to talk to the Professor directly would have terrified me, but now I was somehow not only okay with it, but very concerned that we weren't taking it seriously enough for it to work.

But I needn't have worried. The Professor wanted to talk to us, and the candle hadn't made a full circle before the flame turned a bright, eerie green. You were holding it at the time, Alex, and suddenly the Professor was on you.

Having the Professor speak through you is an odd sensation. You don't feel like its inside you, but rather that its sitting on top of you somehow. You feel an immense weight on your chest, and while it completely controls your voice and expressions when it's on you, it doesn't really feel like that most of the time. It's more like someone is sitting on your chest and blocking your face from everyone while drowning out what you're saying with their own words and emotions. Which, of course, is where we came up with the name.

Over the next few months we talked to the Professor several times, and it sat on each of our chests' more than once. Most of those seemed like magical experiences at the time, as though we were talking to a miracle…which I guess in some ways we were. But the first and last times were terrifying.

When you were holding the candle and the flame turned green for the first time, we were all shaken. I don't know that any of us really expected it to work, and even if it did, we had no way of knowing how the Professor would try to communicate. We had actually brought down a small chalkboard and a Ouija board just in case it needed a way to talk to us.

Instead it used you.

****

"Hello, children."

The Professor's voice was always so strange. It would vary from moment to moment much like its shape had in the pool. One word it might be high and squeaky, the next it might be a deep baritone or an almost bestial growl. Odder still was that though we heard its voice through your mouth, we also heard it in our heads. There it wasn't a voice at all really, but some kind of song--one that we could understand and that was somehow the same as the words being spoken.

We all looked around at each other as we heard the voice both inside and out. For a moment I wondered if we would all be too scared to speak when Ellis popped out with the first trembling question.

"Are you the Professor?"

What might have been a short laugh echoed through the room, though it sounded more like a mixture of a crow's caw and a woman's scream. "Yes, Ellis, I'm the thing you call the Professor."

Another glance passed between us and then Thomas was asking, "Are you a tulpa?"

A brief pause and then it answered. "Tulpa is just a name really. A label for a larger concept that goes beyond what the word describes. But to answer your question, no. I'm not a tulpa, though they do exist."

"What are you then?" I asked, my concern growing. "Are you a demon?"

Another cawing scream of a laugh, this one long enough that I began to get worried. "No, no, Mills. Not a demon of any sort. What I am…well, there's no easy way to explain what I am, but I will try."

"This place, this world, is one of an infinite number of such worlds. Alternate dimensions you might call it. And by one way of thinking, these infinite worlds sit at the center of a larger expanse of reality." The Professor turned his gaze--your gaze--to Cassidy. "You remember that time you and Alex cut open the baseball?" Cassidy nodded vehemently, her eyes wide.

"Well, it's kind of like that. If these infinite worlds are the core, the next layer out are the Seven Realms. I don't know everything, and I don't know all of the Realms. Hell is one of them, the Nightlands is another. There's the Incarnata, which is where your tulpas come from, Thomas. And there's the Void. That's where I came from."

Ellis leaned forward, his expression thoughtful. "The Void? What is that? Are there others like you there?"

The Professor shook your head. "Oh no. There's only one of me. And the Void is a place where nothing is…something. It's a place of unthought of and undreamt of things. Some might call it a dead place, but that would be wrong, because dead is something, and the Void's only substance is nothingness. Personally, I think of the Void as a place of endless potential."

It drew back your lips in a ghastly facsimile of a smile. "Look at me, for instance! I was floating in the Void, dreaming lost dreams in an endless sleep, when I sensed something new. It was a small and distant light. In that light I could see Alex here, bored in class and thinking about this school being haunted. In some ways, I was watching myself be born."

"Even though it burned and hurt me, I moved toward that light. Soon I sensed something else. I was hearing Thomas telling the story of the lovesick Professor's suicide. I was hearing all your wonderful stories, pulling myself along them like a lifeline until I pushed through the membrane into this world."

The Professor let your lips go slack as his eyes took us all in. "When I said there is only one of me, I meant it. Even in all the infinite versions of you and this school, only this version had the right combination of ingredients to create me. I've seen worlds where you all never meet or are all dead. I finally stopped looking at them because it saddens me so."

It paused for a moment, so I took the opportunity to ask another question. "Why does it make you sad?"

It didn't use your expressions this time, but its strange voice sounded hurt, as though I should know without having to ask. "Because I hate to see any of you suffer. In many ways, the five of you are my parents as much as you are my friends. And I love you all."

I swallowed and was going to ask something else when Cassidy jumped in. "We love you too, Professor!"

Another ghastly smile from you and I decided to wait on asking my next question. But then your eyes were back on mine as the Professor answered my question without it being asked.

"Mills, I just want to enjoy existing and keep doing so. Help my friends and keep growing." Your eyes stretched wide as though held up by invisible hooks. "In some ways, I'm not that different than having a puppy." It swung your eyes toward Ellis. "Or a tiger cub. I need to sleep and eat so I can keep growing. I've been asleep these past few months, and now I need to eat again."

It licked your lips absently. "And I'm very hungry."

Part Seven

"What do you mean you're 'very hungry'?" Ellis asked. His tone was light, but his face was serious and looked concerned. "Are you talking about eating people?"

Another laugh, though this one sounded a bit more like someone sawing through sheet metal. I tried to repress a shiver and fight the urge to scream at it to leave you alone. That was the worst part of it that first time. Seeing you not being you. The unnatural way the Professor controlled you made you look like a life-sized puppet…or a corpse. Either way, it took everything I had to keep talking to it, which is funny considering how often we talked to it after that. Part of it was because it was the first time, of course, and we grew more accustomed to the strangeness the more it happened.

Part of it was because it was you, and I always had the same unease when it decided it was your turn.

"No, no. Nothing like that. I'm not trying to hurt anyone really--unless they bother any of you of course." It paused a moment and then went on. "But I need people to know I exist, to have stronger belief in me from more sources. Signs that the 'ghost' is around, that kind of thing. There's nothing you need to do…I'm strong enough now to take care of it. But I wanted to let you know I was back and I hope you do talk to me again. Your ritual is very clever and works well enough, and I've missed you."

I tried to smile. "We've missed you too, Professor." And it was true. Despite our fear and worry at what we were dealing with, we were already used to the idea of the Professor being our friend and protector. The thing that made us special. So whatever our misgivings at the time, they took a back seat to our happiness and relief that it was back.

Over the summer we talked to the Professor every few days. Never for too long, as it said it took energy for it to sit on one of us and it needed to conserve what it had. But it always seemed happy to come when we did our homemade ritual, and it was glad to answer questions for us when we asked. At first, we had more questions about what it was or what its end goals were, but we always got variations on the same pleasant reassurances. They were palatable enough and hard to refute, even if we had no real way of knowing if it was being honest or not.

Then we started asking more questions about what it knew. Things about the Void and the other Realms, about mysteries in our own world. We learned about a lot of things, even if we didn't understand all of them very well. But there were gaps in its knowledge too, and I think it was being honest about them, because it enjoyed telling us things we didn't know. For instance, it said there was little it could tell us about the Void because of the Realm's nature. It defied easy description or understanding. But it told us several stories about the Incarnata, which it seemed to know, or at least enjoy, the best.

All it could tell us of Hell was that it existed and was vastly different now than it had been at one point due to some large battle that had taken place there. As for the place it called the Nightlands, it was more reluctant, just describing it as "one of the larger realms, full of power and potential. There is a thing there called the Baron that…well, he's very ambitious."

We had little context for any of that other than Hell, of course, which it knew little about. So we focused on things closer to home.

****

"Bigfoot?"

It was sitting on Thomas' chest this time and gave a small grin. It had gotten better at mimicking natural facial expressions, which somehow made it both more and less creepy when it tried.

"No, not in this reality. There are two species of ape and one marsupial that have not been identified yet and are sometimes mistaken for a bigfoot, however. There's also a genetically modified version of an alpaca that has been the basis of Yeti legends for several hundred years."

"Weird. Ghosts?"

"Aside from me? No, only joking. Yes, there are several kinds of spiritual entities that would fall under what you would call 'ghosts'."

"Vampires?"

Thomas' face lit up slightly. "Oh yes. There are a variety of those, though none that actually fit the most common archetype popularized by Bram Stoker." It surveyed us, its eyes twitching slightly as it moved from face to face. "Have any of you read Dracula, children? It really is excellent."

We learned that while it had vast stores of knowledge from some unknown means, the Professor still loved to learn new things and had a method by which it could draw information from books and computers without having to physically read or interact with them. Back when we had first started telling Professor stories around the school, it had fed on the school library and the textbooks in hundreds of lockers throughout the building. Toward the end we found out it had started exploring the internet, which raised its own concerns.

But during that last summer, we were just having fun. And despite the vast wealth of knowledge we had at our fingertips, we oddly only had a few sessions towards the beginning where we asked the Professor a lot of probing questions about things only it could know. Pretty soon we were just talking--telling it about what we had going on in our lives (even though there was an unspoken understanding it already knew most of what we were doing) while it asked us questions and told us stories. It really was great at telling stories.

I think it's like if you become friends with someone from another part of the world. At first you might be quizzing each other about your respective lands, but if you are truly friends, that phase passes as you move from differences between you to things you have in common. Shared experiences replace novelty, strangeness and excitement give way to familiarity and love.

And we did love the Professor. I think in its way, it loved us too. The problem is, we started treating it like it was a person instead of whatever it really was. Like Ellis might have said, the problem with being best friends with a tiger isn't just that you start thinking like a tiger. It's that you assume the tiger is starting to think like you. But a tiger has tiger-thoughts and loves as a tiger loves. Soon enough, we started finding out what that meant.

****

Over the summer months we had heard tales of weird happenings around the town. The Brigham Well, you know, that stupid thing in the middle of the town square? It froze over in the middle of July. Five different households woke up to find the furniture in their homes all swapped to different rooms--including the beds they were in. The bases at the rec department's softball field all burst into flame simultaneously while over a dozen people were there to witness it after a practice session.

And people did talk about it, and some of them did attribute it to the Professor, but a lot of them just chalked it up to freak weather, an eccentric burglar, and trapped underground gases. Even if none of that made any real sense or had any proof behind it, it was easier for people to handle mundane excuses than extraordinary truth.

I think that frustrated the Professor, and I like to think it really did try to collect more belief without hurting anyone else. But it was learning its own lessons from each experiment, and it saw time and people's aptitude for self-deception inoculating the town against belief in the Professor. But it is very smart. It knew there was no real inoculation against fear or pain. Or death.

****

I had been getting bugged by Timothy Egan to go out with him since the first day of sophomore year. He was a jock, but a smart one, and he had decided that he wanted to date one of the strange girls of the Stonebrook Six. He actually started out hitting on both me and Cassidy, but between the blank, uninterested stare she gave him and Thomas' threatening glower, he had quickly settled all his efforts on me.

Two weeks in, I finally gave in. He was cute, and though I wasn't really interested in him, I had never been on a date before so I thought it might be fun. And it actually was. He was polite, took me to a nice place, and was never aggressive or weird like I had been afraid he might be. I knew that you didn't like it, which is part of why I went out with him at all if I'm telling the whole truth. I decided one or two more dates with him might be enough to get you to talk to me about things if you felt the same way I did. But I'm getting sidetracked, and we have other fish to fry.

The first fish actually came up while I was still going out with Tim. You and Ellis were in Mr. Jameson's English class together, and the guy decided early on that he hated you for some reason. He'd say sarcastic things in class, mark you down on tests more harshly when he could get away with it. Ellis wasn't harassed like that, and no one else in your class or my class with him was either. Whatever his problem, it came to a head in early October when he accused you of plagiarism.

It was the first big grade of the class, and all of his classes had the same project. An essay on one of William Blake's poems.

You probably don't remember this, but me and you actually worked on ours together, with us both reading over each other's work several times to make sure it was good enough, particularly with Jameson looking for any reason he could find to give you a low grade.

When you got it back with an F and a note that it had clearly been plagiarized, you were understandably furious. You told us that you asked him about it after class, and he said he could tell from the writing style that it had been copied from somewhere, though he couldn't offer any proof of course, because it was bullshit. He was smirking and telling you that, as the teacher, the grade was entirely his prerogative. That's when you both heard the noise from outside. I think just about the entire school did.

Jameson's prize possession was a white 1971 MG. He would come wheeling up to his teacher's parking space that was just outside his room, occasionally honking its peppy little horn at the high school girls he liked the looks of, seemingly oblivious to the rolled eyes and snickers he always received. More than once during class I had seen him glance out the window at the car, as though guarding it from some plot to vandalize it or maybe just admiring it and daydreaming he was back behind the wheel instead of stuck teaching English to a bunch of tenth graders at Stonebrook High.

I wish I had looked up and seen his face when the two of you went to the window to see what all the commotion was. From what you told me, I think you both made it in time for him to see the last of it, but I got to witness the entire thing.

I had gotten done with gym class early, which had been sprints around the football field followed by unimaginative calisthenics--Ms. Perkins was out with knee surgery, and Coach Anderson didn't care about anything but football, so his main plan was to tire us out and send us away early. I was cutting through the teacher parking lot on my way back to the main building when I heard a screech of metal.

It was Jameson's MG being slowly balled up and crushed like a piece of paper in some invisible giant's hand. Glass shattered and trim popped, but nothing flew off. Everything was self-contained in an ever-constricting sphere of force--a dying star collapsing into itself. Even with everything we had seen and knew, I would have said it was impossible if I hadn't watched it happen. The small car was crushed into a ball less than three feet in diameter and then unceremoniously dropped back to the asphalt with a ringing thud.

I knew it was Jameson's car, of course, but I didn't know about your essay yet. No one did. But as I looked around at the handful of other people in the lot and saw the terrified faces pressed against every nearby window, I knew that they understood what it meant just as well as I did. When Jameson started wailing, saying that it was somehow your fault, as irrational as that was...well, it wasn't just his car that left the school for good that day.

I remember us all getting together after school and talking about it, and none of us, even those of us that saw it, were really scared of what the Professor had done. What it was capable of now. We were just happy that it had stood up for you and gotten what it needed. Because the Professor was all anyone was talking about now, especially when Ellis slyly let it slip to a couple of people that it had happened while you were talking to Jameson about him trying to fuck you on your essay. We knew that our friend should be well-satisfied.

It took less than a week for us to realize our mistake. We had underestimated how hungry the Professor was and it had given up on trying to be gentle or doing things for a small audience. So at that Friday's pep rally, with the bleachers packed and everyone watching, the Professor murdered Timothy Egan.

Part Eight

After the destruction of Jameson's prized car, we should have been scared of what the Professor was capable of. Shit, we should have been scared long before that. But we weren't. Thomas and Cassidy were more than a little freaked out when they saw the balled-up wreckage of the vehicle being loaded into the back of a dump truck, but even they thought it was pretty great that the Professor was looking out for us yet again. As for everyone else at the school, while the Professor was being talked about more than ever, the five of us actually had fewer people talk to us about it. Now they would usually just get quiet when we approached.

In some ways it was isolating, but none of us really cared. I had told Timothy Egan I didn't want to go out with him again that past Sunday, and at the time I had thought it had gone pretty well. I could tell that he was starting to really like me, and I didn't feel right about hurting him to make you jealous. Unfortunately, on that Monday, around the same time that Jameson's car was getting wadded up by the Professor, Timothy was leaving the same gym class I had just left. But instead of going on to the main building, he had hung back with several of his friends.

I don't know the details, but the rumors and snippets I heard later were that someone had asked him about how far he'd gotten with me. Feeling peer pressure or maybe because he had hurt feelings, he decided to lie. Talked about how big a slut I was and how he was done with me now that he had gotten what he wanted. The words were barely out of his mouth when they heard the yelling from the teacher parking lot and went to see what remained of Jameson's MG.

I didn't know about any of that until after everything was over. We went through the rest of the week, still riding the buzz of excitement but unaware anything else was coming. Then came the Friday afternoon pep rally.

Despite being better known for basketball, Tim was a back-up receiver on the football team as well, and that Friday our school was going to be going against the Brockton Mud Dogs, who rarely won against anybody. The pep rally was relaxed and fairly fun, and they had incorporated a competition of sorts into the rally where all the football players would take turns running up to a small trampoline that had been set up and try to dunk a basketball. It was silly fun, and most of the football players made a big show of hamming it up as they either dunked it or missed terribly. Then Tim's turn came.

Smiling as he took the ball from a cheerleader, he started running toward the end of the court. I noticed that he seemed focused and serious by the time he leapt for the trampoline, but maybe he just didn't want to mess up. When he landed on it, instead of propelling him up, it somehow sent him shooting forward as well. His face caught the bottom edge of the backboard with a sickening crunch, but it did little to slow him. Instead, the blow just caused him to flip head over heels as he continued going toward the cinderblock wall fifteen feet beyond the edge of the court.

When he hit the wall, he was nearly twenty feet up and struck first with the back of his head. We all heard the meaty cracks as his skull and several other bones gave way before he tumbled to the tile floor like a broken doll. It had all happened so quickly that the cheers were still fading when the screaming started.

Even without knowing the reason why, we all knew the Professor was behind it. Tim's path and speed were unnatural and far beyond what would have been possible from him just jumping on a small trampoline. We weren't the only ones that thought that, of course, but what could anyone do? It was easier to just pretend that it was a terrible accident. School was canceled for the day and for the following week, with grief counselors being called in to talk to students and faculty that wanted to come to the campus on Monday through Wednesday. A candlelight vigil was also going to be held that Monday night in the gymnasium.

Timothy's death affected us a lot more than any of the rest of the Professor's actions had. Even if we had known about his shitty lies at the time, none of us would have thought he deserved to die for it. As it was, we met on Sunday and talked about what to do. We knew there was a chance the Professor was listening in on us, but we knew of no way to stop it and there did seem to be times when it was unaware of what we were doing. At first, we just sat around talking about how horrible Tim's death had been to watch and even lamely throwing out suggestions for it being something other than the Professor's fault. Ultimately, it was you that came up with an idea.

"If we made him, we should be able to unmake him, right? We made up a ritual to talk to him, so let's make up one to banish him back to the Void."

Ellis had looked at you worriedly. "It's a good idea, but we have no idea if it'll work. The Professor might could have talked to us anytime it felt like it and just liked us coming up with a ritual. Maybe it feeds it somehow or it just thinks it's funny. Either way, if we do that, it'll know what we're trying to do." He swallowed and looked around at the rest of us. "It'll be angry about it. It'll turn on us."

This led to a long silence. We all had been thinking about that, of course, but Ellis putting words to it made it more real somehow. Finally, Ellis looked back up at you. "But we don't have a choice. We have to try and stop it. It can't keep hurting people like this. And we can't keep acting like it's okay."

****

Our plan was to go down into our normal lower level hangout beneath sixth grade hall and do the ritual while the candlelight vigil was going on. The hope was that the Professor might be distracted by all those people there, and before it realized what was going on, it would be sent back where it belonged.

Our new ritual was a candlelight vigil of sorts, too, though instead of the one candle we used for talking to the Professor, we all had lit candles in the circle. We were going to take turns saying "Professor, we don't believe in you. Return to the Void." and blowing out our candle. It sounded lame to us at the time, but we needed to keep it as short and simple as possible, and we had no way of knowing that anything more elaborate would work better.

So there we all were, staring into each other's candlelit faces in the dark of an abandoned classroom. Cassidy started us off, saying her words with a slight tremble to her voice and tears rolling down her cheeks. It was hard on her; on all of us. Not just because we were scared, but because even after everything that had happened, it still felt like we were betraying a friend.

She puffed out her candle and we heard a distant alarm start blaring. For a moment I thought it was some sign the ritual had worked, but then I realized that made no sense. I also recognized the sound. It was the building's fire alarm.

We went back upstairs into pandemonium. There had been nearly two thousand people in the gymnasium when the floor started splitting open like a scene out of an earthquake movie. Three of the people on the floor, including the principal and Timothy's mother, had fallen into the darkness before anyone realized that it was motorized floor springing to life after decades, opening up its mouth to reveal the old pool below. Another two people got trampled as everyone started trying to get out, running down whatever was the closest hallway and pushing through the doors, triggering the fire alarms as they went.

We were moving against the current, the five of us heading towards the gym together without having to say anything or make a plan. We knew what was going on, and we were determined to try and stop it. By the time we pushed our way into the gymnasium, the floor had stopped moving, leaving a rectangular void in the middle of the floor twenty feet wide and fifty feet long. I remember hearing the dying screams of a little boy that had been stomped to death on one of the lower bleachers, and I was turning to go help him when I heard you yell your sister's name.

I didn't understand at first. We knew some of our parents were going to the vigil, but neither yours or mine were among them. And as far as any of them knew, none of the five of us were going either. So how would your little sister have wound up there? I went to ask you what you were talking about when I heard it. Alicia's voice calling for you from the dark beneath the gym.

I would have said it was a trick, but I went to the edge where you were bent down peering into the shadows. I saw her looking up at us just like you did. She was terrified and soaked, but otherwise seemed unhurt. I started looking around for some way of getting down to her or pulling her up, but that's when the floor began to close.

You tried to go in after her then. Me and Ellis are what stopped you. Maybe that was selfish, but I didn't care then and I would still do it now. I think you would have died down there, and I wasn't willing to lose you, even if it meant we lost your sister. We wrestled and held on to you long enough that the floor closed back up, and when you were free, you just stared at us for a long moment before running off. We tried to catch you, but there were too many people outside. I remember us looking for you for some time around the school, but then…nothing. I was waking up with all of you on the football field, and later I heard about your father dying in the gym that night too.

I'm so sorry we didn't try telling you this again sooner, but you were strange after it happened. You had memory gaps that I was actually a bit jealous of, and I was afraid if you remembered more, it would either hurt you or cause you to hate me. So I talked everyone into letting it go, and life went on. Your mom took you away to live with your Aunt, but we kept in touch and stayed close all these years. I wanted more with you…still do, but I didn't feel right trying to start something with you with all these secrets between us. Just…please don't hate me. Any of us. We really did try to do the right thing—especially you and Ellis.

****

I looked at her for a moment before leaning forward to hug her. I waved Thomas over and he joined in too. It was nearly seven in the morning and we were all exhausted, but the last thing on my mind was being angry at the few friends I had left in the world. Mills looked relieved when we pulled apart. I was about to suggest that we get some rest and then try contacting the Professor when I heard a voice coming from Mills that I hadn't heard for a long time.

"This is all very sweet. I'm glad I could be a part of bringing you all closer together again. But I think we're past reliving old memories for now. Time to make some new ones." The Professor was holding Mills' lips in a nasty smile, her eyes rolling and terrified as it spoke.

"Let her go. Talk through me, damnit."

That old screeching laugh. "In due time. Don't worry. I'm not hurting her. I don't want to hurt you either. I just need you to come visit me. The time's come for a class reunion."

I thought I knew the answer, but I wanted to be sure. "Okay. Where do you want us to visit you? At the school?"

Mills' expression stretched into a grimace that was painful to watch, her eyes watering from the skin of her eyelids being pulled so taut. "Yes, the fucking school." Its voice was rough and angry, and it waited a moment before going on in a softer, quieter tone. "The place that you left me. Left baby sis. Left so much. In the underneath. In the cold and the dark."

Out of the corner of my eye, I saw Thomas lunge forward and snatch up the gun from the coffee table. For a moment I forgot it was unloaded, and I let out a scream as he put it to his temple and pulled the trigger repeatedly, each metallic click bringing a shuddering gasp of breath from him. By the fourth click I saw that he had wet himself, and as I stood to help him he lowered the gun. I saw the Professor in Thomas' face a moment before I heard its voice coming from him, wavering between tinkling bells and grating stones.

"Don't make me wait."

Part Nine

To start out, I should introduce myself as the author of this final part. I'm Millicent Davis, or as my friends call me, Mills. For reasons that will become obvious through my account of what happened to the three of us when we returned to Stonebrook, Alex isn't in a position to write this. Alex finished writing out his last part--what I will call "Part Eight"--as we sat in the back of Thomas' minivan headed back toward our old hometown. Thomas told us they had gotten the minivan when Cassidy first learned she was pregnant, the idea being it would wind up being filled with kids. But so often things don't turn out the way you expect.

It's time I told you that I've been the one posting Alex's writings, which first had to be transcribed from the old notebook he had written it all down in as things happened to him. To all of us. It was hard reading his words, reliving so many painful memories yet again and all with his voice in my head. But it was wonderful too. It let me see into his thoughts, into his heart, confirming to me that the Alex that wrote those words was the same person that I fell in love with back in third grade. Even after all that has happened, despite what I am doing, that knowledge of Alex's heart gives me comfort and…I'm ashamed to say it…joy.

It took us six hours to get to Stonebrook from Austin, and all of us were going on minimal sleep. We had decided to drive in shifts so we could each rest some on the way, but it was hard to do more than doze fitfully as the minivan trundled toward what could be our deaths or worse. It's funny, but the phrase "death or worse" never made since to me before. I've always been terrified of death. My own, of course, but even more so the deaths of those I love. The idea that there was something worse than death always seemed absurd to me.

I was wrong.

****

Stonebrook had been surrounded by chain-link fence and signs that declared the property condemned after the night of the candlelight vigil. Alex moved away, of course, but the rest of us got shuttled to another high school on the other side of the county for the next three years, with a new high school and middle school finally being completed and opened the fall after our graduation. I think most people in town tried to forget about Stonebrook, and no one would dare buy it or try to turn it into something else, but it still sat there like a tumor, malignant and with roots sunk deep into the heart of the place.

I had half expected someone would have just bulldozed it after all this time, but aside from thick overgrowth in the yard and sickly vines covering several of the walls, it looked largely intact. The metal fence was rusted and hung limply in spots, and it didn't take much for us to find a spot we could lift up enough to scoot under. We were all scared, but we didn't let it stop us. I would like to call it bravery, and maybe it was, but it felt more like bleak determination at best. Or at worst, we were caught in the gravitational pull of something much older, smarter, and stronger than us.

We got into the school easy. The first door we tried was unlocked, and after a couple of tugs, it swung open with a squealing protest. We had flashlights, and despite it being early afternoon, we needed them as soon as we entered what I recognized as sixth grade hall. The three of us moved together, our lights and eyes constantly moving in every direction on the lookout for any threat. I think we knew it was pointless, that there was little we could do even if we saw something, but we had to try--or at least pretend to try. The illusion of safety and some level of control was the only thing saving our sanity as we journeyed further into the stale murk of the school.

When we drew near the metal door leading down into our old hangout, music started playing from somewhere in those lower rooms. I recognized the song.

You're nobody til somebody loves you…

You're nobody til somebody cares…

I pulled up short, wondering if we were meant to go down there instead of on to the gym, but Alex silently shook his head and nodded for us to keep going. I relented and followed them into the building's heart.

The center of the floor was pulled back again, revealing the yawning black that led down into that subterranean pool. I looked around with my light, searching for a good way to climb down, when Thomas pointed to the far side of the opening. Bleachers had been ripped apart and reconfigured into a staircase that led down below. The Professor was making this all as easy as possible.

We went around to the far edge and peered down, seeing that the stairs did, in fact, go all the way to the oily liquid sheen filling the pool's bottom. Alex tested it with his foot, and when it seemed stable, he started down with me behind him and Thomas bringing up the rear. The air grew colder as we went down, and as we reached the bottom, we found the filthy water there was freezing. It went up to the middle of my thighs and I could immediately feel my feet starting to go numb. We stood there for a several seconds, looking at each other anxiously between sweeping probes of the shadows with our lights, waiting for something to happen.

Then Alex started to scream.

My chest pounding, I turned to look at him and saw he was looking off toward one of the corners of the pool. I shined my light where he was looking and couldn't understand what I was seeing. There were two bodies there, a man and a woman, both horrifically gaunt and pale, but somehow familiar looking too. They looked recently dead, and between their twisted expressions and the way they were huddled together, I knew the pair had been terrified at the end. I wanted to move closer to get a better look at their faces, sure that I knew them somehow, when I realized that Alex was still yelling. I was turning back to try and calm him down when he suddenly stopped. Meeting his eyes, I saw the Professor was on him now.

"Hello, children. Welcome home."

I tried to control my fear and anger. "Yes, we're here, Professor. What do you need from us? How can we make this all stop?"

A coarse, watery chuckle. "Full of questions, are we? My dear friends are very concerned with what I want and need now." It pulled Alex's face into an angry grimace. "All it took is killing two of us to wake you up. To make you care."

Thomas spoke up. "You didn't have to do it. You didn't have to kill my sweet Cassidy, you motherfucker. You didn't have to kill her or Ellis."

It turned Alex's withering gaze on him. "You aren't in a position to be criticizing the treatment of our friends, are you?" Thomas recoiled and fell silent. Turning back to me, the Professor continued. "But your questions, if late in coming, are reasonable and necessary. And I don't think they're the only questions you will have before this is done. But I can best answer most of them with a story. Alex's story is finally ready to be told. I'd apologize for the uncomfortable accommodations during story time, but this is where you left us to rot after all."

Before I could ask anything else, it had begun.

****

Alex's Story

Once there was a boy named Alex. One day when he was bored in class at his creepy new school, he had a thought. A terrible and wonderful thought: What if the school that he and his friends found themselves at was haunted?

He shared this thought with his friends, and this led to stories and adventures with their new friend, the Professor. As you already know, the Professor was able to come from a Realm of unbeing through your words and thoughts and belief. That place was called the Void, and it had no interest in returning there. It was an empty, lonely place, and it was now in a place with good friends and so many things to see and do.

For a long time, everything was wonderful, and the Professor grew stronger. But the Professor was very smart, and it knew these good times might not last forever. So it used a bit of its new strength to talk with its friends and better protect them, even if they were away from the school. It also used some of that strength to talk to Alex's sister, Alicia, in her dreams, planting the seeds it needed to summon her if it became necessary for its fallback plan.

In time, it began to hope it wouldn't be necessary after all. It was happy and its friends were happy--or so it thought. But then its friends decided they were tired of the Professor. They thought it was just a pet or a curiosity—some novel addition to their lives they could take off the shelf when they felt like it or when they wanted everyone else reminded how special they were. The Professor understood this, but it still loved its friends, and it tried to grow and survive without hurting anyone else.

But eventually it came to understand that people only really understand pain and fear. Even love is given shape by the relief of the pain of loneliness and the fear of losing that which you love. And the Professor was no different. And while it loved its friends dearly, it loved itself more.

When the Professor learned what the rest of the Stonebrook Six were planning, a ritual of unbeing, it was afraid it might work, but more than that, it was hurt by the betrayal. It decided that it needed to be strong enough to resist any attempts to drive it back into oblivion, and the best way to do that was to slaughter several people in front of a large crowd. It had already grown significantly stronger from Timothy Egan's death, but imagine what it could do with a few more?

It called little Alicia late that afternoon before people started to arrive for the vigil. It told her to be quiet and not let anyone see her come, which she did without fail. Her eyes were glazed over and her mouth was drooling just a bit, but no one saw her close enough to notice as she walked to Stonebrook. She slipped into the school stealthily and made her way to the gym, where the floor was open and waiting. The Professor picked her up and brought her down into the water, and it wasn't until she was in the cold and the wet that she started to wake up. Fortunately, when the Professor sealed the floor shut again, no one could hear her down there screaming and crying in the dark.

Later, when Alex went to save her, you and Ellis stopped him. The Professor was so relieved. It didn't want to hurt any of you, and it tried to just end it there, going so far as to close the pool again in the hopes you would all just go away. But Alex wouldn't stop.

He ran from the rest of you, fighting his way through the throngs of people rushing around outside. He got shoved down three times into the gravel parking lot, and once he would have had his head stepped on by a large, terrified man if the Professor had not reached out and shoved the man away. But Alex was scared for Alicia now and didn't notice. He just kept going home to get help.

His father showed up at the gym a few minutes later, screaming Alicia's name. The Professor knew where this was heading. They would try to find Alicia and take her away, ruining its plan. So it killed the man where he stood. It hoped this brutal act would be enough to scare Alex away, but no. He came back into the gym just moments later, screaming for the Professor to let his little sister go.

It knew now that Alex would never give up, and it wasn't sure it could keep her hidden from him the way it could others outside of their circle of six. So with great sadness, it opened the floor one last time.

Alex climbed down into the lower depths and Alicia ran to him with a discordant wail, her eyes full of fresh tears. She was already half mad by that point, but she knew her big brother when she saw him. Just then, Alex felt himself being dragged into the dark and tried to push his sister away towards the light, but it was too late. Too late for both of them.

Or was it? As Alex looked up, it saw a figure climbing back out. Scrambling over the floor's edge as the opening began to constrict again, it turned back. Alex realized with horror that he recognized the person looking down at them--it was himself.

The Professor has many plans. Plans within plans. One of its plans was that if it came to it, if it found itself betrayed or alone, it could find someone and take them. Pull them down into the dark and sustain them. Feed on their belief and their fear, taking in a little more than it would have to expend to keep them alive. It picked Alicia because it knew her through Alex, and through Alex, she knew it. Initially, as it sat in the shadows mulling over this plan, this failsafe if its friends ever turned on it, it also saw the collateral benefit of Alex's grief and guilt over the loss of Alicia. These emotions would fuel Alex's belief in the Professor and help it to survive.

But when Alex wouldn't leave it alone, when he insisted on returning for his sister, the Professor had to make a choice. Risk Alex somehow taking Alicia back and leaving it to starve as it was slowly forgotten, or take Alex as well. With two people to feed from, the Professor could live and grow stronger for quite some time.

It was Alex's eyes that made it change its mind. When Alex felt the Professor's grasp begin to tug them back into the dark, his eyes were so full of fear and despair that it was more than the Professor could stand. It couldn't let Alex go, but it always had a plan, even for this.

If the children had given it substance and strength just by believing, perhaps it could do the same. Its mind was not a human mind, or even a tiger mind. Its mind was vast and deep and so terribly, horribly quick. Before Alex had been drug three feet, it had imagined a new Alex. Perfect down to the last cell, even to the dirt and blood on his face. And not just physically. For all intents and purposes it was Alex, or as close as the Professor was capable of, and the Professor was capable of quite a lot.

The only thing this Alex lacked was access to certain memories. Things that would cripple him and keep him from having a good life. Things that would bring him back looking for Alicia next week or month or year. These things were buried deep. The Professor removed and sacrificed Alex's belief in it so that this version of his friend could live and be free. Then it sent the new Alex out to the football field where he lay down with their dear, unconscious friends and fell asleep.

In the next few hours, several people pried open the floor and came down to search for survivors. They found the bodies of the others, but saw no sign of Alex and Alicia. The Professor was powerful enough with both of them for strength that it could keep them glamoured and undetectable. They screamed for help, but no one heard them, and eventually the search was called off. Then things were quiet down in the dark.

The Professor knew little of the outside world in the following years. It was conserving and building its strength as best it could, but it was also expending more than it had originally planned. For it was not just keeping Alicia and the original Alex alive in the pool now. It was having to continue to believe in the new Alex too.

The Alex that crawled out of the pool that night was being seen and talked to, and every day he grew stronger because of the shared belief of the world around him that he existed and was real. And he was Alex in every way that mattered. But he was still unique in a way that made him vulnerable.

The Professor's belief was of a different quality than most. It was not from this place, and its beliefs, while powerful and potentially permanent, required regular attention to stay alive. And it wanted the new Alex to stay alive--it wanted him to have a long and happy life. So it sacrificed some of the power it was collecting to make sure that happened.

But then something unforeseen happened. The Professor is not perfect or infallible, and it made a mistake. It recognized too late a sickness in Alicia and its Alex. A simple staph infection, but one that obliterated their bodies faster than it could heal them. It could have repaired the damage if it had pulled away its support of the other Alex, of course, but it couldn't bear to do that. So it watched them finally die instead.

For a time, it resigned itself to starving to death in the darkness. It still had those that remembered it, that feared it somewhat, but that was old and abstract terror paved over by years of new memories and repression. Not enough to sustain it for long.

The problem was, it got scared. When it saw itself approaching the end, saw the Void opening up to reclaim it, it knew it couldn't just let go. It wanted to survive too much. So with the last of its power, it killed Cassidy. Within a few hours it felt far stronger. After Ellis, it was stronger still. And as Alex, your Alex, came to remember me, I felt more like myself again.

But I need your help.

****

"Enough of this," Thomas bellowed, reaching into his waistband and pulling out his gun. The last time I had seen it was when Alex had taken it from him while the Professor was using Thomas back at my house. He had gotten it back before we left apparently, and was now pointing it at me. "Mills, this is all lies. Don't you see this? It's self-serving bullshit. It's all part of its plan."

I was so broken at that point, I didn't care much if he did shoot me. I didn't want to believe what the Professor was saying, but as it talked, I had looked closer at the two huddled corpses. I knew why they were familiar. They were versions of what Alicia and Alex might look like after years of insanity and darkness. I couldn't breathe, I couldn't think, I just wanted everything to stop for a minute. Just stop.

But it wouldn't stop. And the Professor was talking again. "Yes, this was Thomas's new idea since you left your house. Kill the two of you here and then himself. The idea being that if and when someone finds you, they'll blame him, not the Professor, and I'll fade on away. Isn't that right, Tom?"

I turned to back to Thomas and saw that he was frozen, his eyes bulging. The Professor released his head enough for him to speak, and he gasped out, "It's the only way. We all have to die to stop it. We can't let it out."

I looked at Thomas for several seconds, weighing the truth and merit of his words. He might be right. It might be the only way to stop the Professor, and didn't we owe it to the world to not let it out?

But then I looked back at Alex. Maybe not the original Alex, but the only Alex I had left. I might be willing to die, but was I willing to let him die too? And the Professor had always been true to its word with us really. We were the ones trying to hurt it, not the other way around. Thoughts of Cassidy and Ellis pushed their way up and I ignored them. It had explained that, and would we do any different to protect ourselves? To protect the ones we loved the most?

"Thomas, I'm sorry." I was crying when I said it, but my voice was steady. Turning to Alex, I told the Professor my choice. "Thomas has to die."

A moment later there was a fine red mist floating in the air where Thomas had been. I let out an involuntary scream and started shaking. Then I felt Alex's arms around me. It took me only a moment to realize the Professor still had him.

"I'm sorry for that, Mills. But that part of it is over now. You and Alex will be safe from now on. I just need you to do one last thing for me."

When it began to whisper its plan to me, all I could do was laugh.

****

Alex slept all the way back, and I could tell when I woke him that he doesn't remember anything of what happened while the Professor was sitting on him. That's for the best. I'll tell him in time, over the next few days--even the parts about where he came from. I can't have secrets between us again and I won't risk him learning about it through these posts or some other means. I'll tell him everything, once it's too late for him to stop me.

The main things I need him to understand are that he is safe now and how much I love him. Because I do. There's a part of me that says I'm being selfish or delusional, but it's a small part that gets smaller every time I look at him. Like the Professor, I'm doing what's necessary for us to survive.

And what it asked in return for our safety and happiness wasn't so bad in the end. Alex had done most of the work already. It just told me to find a place where we could tell this story. The story of the Stonebrook Six. The story of how the Professor came to be.

So after I finish writing this final part, I'll start posting each portion, one at a time.

I'll post, then wait. Post, then wait. And those of you that read those first parts will hopefully come back for more. Come back to hear more about the Professor. Come back to believe a little more. By the time you've made it this far, it'll be too late.

And you say to yourself, well that's just silly. It's just a story to you. That's what I told the Professor when it first told me its plan too. But it just laughed its dead crow laugh and said, "We're all just stories to each other, Mills. And the head doesn't tell the heart what to believe. Just tell people about me and I think I'll do just fine." The more I've thought about it, the more I think it might be right.

So congratulations. And I'm sorry. You now have a tiger for a friend too.

Something has marked my family.

Part One

My family has always been lucky. I don't mean in the vague, general way people talk when they say they feel lucky or "blessed". I mean my family, particularly my mother and grandmother, have always had a very wide and deep lucky streak.

Some of it is small stuff. My mother tends to win at cards or bingo. She never has to sit in traffic or wait in lines. The rain always seems to stop before she steps outside. The same is true for my grandmother, who has lived a very full and interesting life filled with much adventure but no real personal mishaps.

But there are larger things as well. My family has always had a lot of money, mainly through some combination of the womens' business ventures and lucky occurrences. Most of it would barely be noticeable from the outside, with the only flashy example I can think of being my grandmother winning fifty grand at Atlantic City before I was born. You would think people with this kind of luck would be diehard gamblers, but instead they strictly avoid betting and any serious games of chance where money is to be made. I used to think they just didn't like gambling, but now I know better. They didn't want to attract any attention.

It's the same with how my grandmother dresses. I swear she puts on makeup to make herself look older, not younger. If we are at her house, she's in workout clothes or jeans without any real makeup on, and she doesn't look over fifty. But if we go out, she wears high-waisted pants with dingy flowered blouses tucked into the elastic waistband, and she has so much powder and blush on she looks like an eighty-year old clown. The strangest part is she's actually 86. No health issues, never been sick that I know of. Same for my mother, who at 58, people mistake for my sister.

I don't mention myself in any of that because I've never been especially lucky. I mean, I've always benefited from their luck in some ways, and I wouldn't consider myself unlucky, but I've always joked I don't have the Robinson women's luck, and that I must be adopted. I even remember when I was 10 or 11—upset at the time by some childhood misfortune—asking my father if I really was adopted. He picked me up and gave me a hug, telling me that I definitely wasn't, and I'd get that special luck one day too, when I was older. He was smiling, but then he glanced up and his face fell. I looked around and my mother was standing in the doorway giving him a hard look. He never talked about luck around me again.

The other side of all this, which I'm coming to realize more now, is that other people around the women in my family have abnormally bad luck too. Growing up I didn't really think about it this way, but when I sat down recently and made a list of every significantly bad thing I remembered happening to people that worked for or knew my mother or grandmother, the list was over thirty people.

Bear in mind I'm not counting people dying at an old age or getting into a light fender bender. I mean cancer, dying young in a freak accident, permanently crippling disease, insanity. And that's just what I remember and was aware of in my 28 years of living. My grandmother, mother, and I are all only children, so we have no real extended family on that side, but I know that both of my father's sisters were dead at relatively young ages before I was out of high school.

I say all of this because I want you to understand how strange my family is and why I didn't see it as a bad thing growing up. They seemed special, and I wanted to be special too.

Three months ago, I was on the way to work when I saw a transfer truck jackknife in front of me. It was a four lane highway, and at just after 8 in the morning the road was filled with traffic, but the area immediately around the truck was empty. At first this seemed like a good thing, and I began slowing down, ready to brake or dodge as necessary. Then I saw the front of the cab turning toward me even as the rear of the tanker it was carrying did the same. Before I could react, the tanker swung at the side of my car, so close I could see the dirt on the chemical warning signs hanging above the taillights, and then it moved past and ahead of me as it completed some doomed arc. It had missed me by inches.

The truck began to roll at that point, and then I was past. This all took less than 10 seconds, but it seemed agonizingly slow, and I was so petrified that I didn't slow down again or look back until I was half a mile down the road and I felt the car shimmy as the tanker exploded behind me.

From what I later read, cars slammed into the truck and each other trying to avoid the growing accident, with later cars stacking up and crushing those in front. When the truck exploded, it set fire to over a dozen other vehicles, and this just made everything even more chaotic. All told, 9 people died and another 15 were badly injured.

I had just gotten one of those new flip phones, and I called 911. I thought about staying at the accident, but I didn't know how I could help and I was scared, so I went on to work. I sat in the parking lot for several minutes, still in shock. Finally I went in and told my friend Beth what had happened, or at least I started to before I started crying. When I calmed down, Beth told me she had news. My position, which had been based on a temporary grant, had been made permanent with a significant raise.

It didn't feel right to celebrate with what had happened that morning, but I did find my mind guiltily wandering back to my good luck, and by the time I left work, the accident and my own close call seemed more distant. I went to the grocery store before heading home, and I managed to get a parking place up front, get right through check out with a newly opened cashier, and somehow get home without any major traffic snarls.

All pretty pedestrian stuff, right? Which is why I didn't think anything about it at first. But over the next couple of months, it kept happening. I got a random refund check from an insurance company I hadn't used since college. I now always seem to time things right. I got the good waiter, the helpful phone customer service rep, and the honest plumber, who tightened one bolt for free and fixed a drip I had listened to for six months but couldn't afford to fix until now. Everything just kept going my way. There were just two problems.

The first is that I kept noticing that bad stuff seemed to happen more often to those around me. Beth's car got keyed. My neighbor's mother broke her hip. My ex-boyfriend, who I had broken up with just a couple of weeks before this all started, suddenly lost his job of eight years. I had always been aware of my family's luck, but now I was seeing more of the other side of it too.

The second problem is I feel like something is with me all the time, watching me. I started noticing it within a day or two of the accident, and the sensation has grown stronger over time. Some might be comforted by that feeling, even thinking it's a sign of a guardian angel. And maybe that's what it is. But it doesn't make me feel like that. It makes me feel like a bug under a microscope, and the eyes studying me aren't necessarily kind.

It could be that this is all in my head, but I don't think so. Either way, I need to get some answers.

I tried to call my grandmother, but she's on a trip in Ireland at the moment and gets bad cell service in the small village she's staying in. So that leaves my mother. I don't speak to her often any more. She's always been a hard woman to know, and as I got older I realized she didn't know her daughter very well either. She can't understand why I won't take her money or the jobs she's offered. And I do want to make my own path in life without her giving me everything. And if I'm honest, maybe I also like being the one thing she doesn't get handed, the one thing she can't win.

Either way, I forced myself to call her, and we're having lunch tomorrow. With any luck (haha), she can either tell me what's going on or, better yet, make me realize I'm just being silly and seeing a pattern that isn't there. In any case, I am writing this out to document what I've experienced, and I'll follow up once I know more.

One last thing. Yesterday morning I woke up to a brief but sharp pain just above my right ankle. Sitting up, I looked at my leg and saw a mark there—an inch-long wavy line with two dots nestled within the curves. Maybe it's a scratch? I don't know, but I don't remember hurting my leg, and it looks too uniform to be accidental. Combined with the pervasive feeling of being the prisoner of some invisible gaze, the mark feels more like a livestock brand. But I'm getting ahead of myself. Let's see what mother dearest has to say.

Part Two

My mother lived about five hours away from me in one of the wealthy and newly trendy parts of Atlanta. In truth, she had two other houses in the U.S. and my grandmother had another four here and in other parts of the world, but she always came back to Georgia, being fond of referring to it as "home base". So it wasn't overly surprising that I got lucky (yes I know) and she answered her condo's phone on the third ring. Like usual, the phone call began with an awkward exchange of pleasantries, but I pushed through it quickly and told her I wanted to come see her. The very next day. That I had some things I needed to ask her about.

I could hear the measured consideration in her silence, but when she spoke her voice was even. Of course I should come. But if I could try to get there by one for lunch, as she had dinner plans and still needed to make some arrangements for some function she was sponsoring the following week. I agreed I'd get there as soon as possible, and was going to launch into some kind of farewell, but I heard the line click as she hung up.

When I arrived that afternoon, I checked in with the front desk of the building and waited as they called up to verify that my mother was expecting company. Moments later, a large man in a blue blazer stepped out of a nearby elevator and approached me. He looked strange in the coat and dress pants he wore, his hard features and cold blue eyes framed by close cropped blond hair and an air of barely restrained violence. I looked at the breast of his blazer and saw his company's logo stitched in small, inconspicuous lines of silver thread—Tattersall Security. He gave me a nod and perfunctory smile as he reached me, identifying himself as the head of my mother's security detail. I thought about asking questions, but decided to save them for her instead.

He led me back to the elevator and we went up to the penthouse area, which was comprised of the top three floors of the building. A couple of other men that were clearly security stood near the entrance to the area, and as we went from room to room I saw another couple of members of household staff that I didn't recognize. This also seemed a bit strange, as she had kept the same housekeeper and butler/valet since before I went to college. Then we were outside again on a large patio, my mother sitting at a table frowning over a laptop.

It had been awhile since I had seen my mother, and I again found myself amazed at how beautiful she was and how young she looked. At 58 she looked half her age, with rich, honey colored hair that tumbled down past her shoulders and cradled her perfect features—large gray eyes, an elegant nose perched above wide and curving lips that always seemed to be on the verge of laughing, which was odd, as I had rarely ever heard my mother actually laugh.

Still, she was a striking woman, and her effect on most men and some women was as clear and palpable as it was effortless. Yet despite that, I don't know that she had ever dated or been with anyone since my father had died when I was 17. Whatever her flaws, I think she truly loved him, and I think losing him broke something in her. While we had not been the closest before that, it was after he died that I felt the wall between myself and my mother harden into something that was far denser and cold to the touch. That cold distance was never more obvious than when I was with her in person, feeling her gaze weighing me in those moments before she spoke.

"Good to see you, Eliza. Please come give me a hug."

I did as I was bade and then sat down across from her. She went back to the laptop for a moment and then closed it with a snap. "So to what do I owe the visit? Not that I'm not glad to see you, but I have to admit it was unexpected."

During the drive down I had debated how to broach this discussion, and ultimately I decided that direct was best. I knew that my mother knew what was going on, or at least knew a lot more than I did. There was no way she had lived with this for so long and not figured out at least some of it. So my plan was to launch into it with little preamble and keep at it until she gave in and told me what was going on. I was about to open my mouth when she spoke again.

"Wait, that's a lie. And it's unfair to you. I know why you're here. You've got the luck now, don't you?

Got the luck. The phrase was a succinct but apt description of the situation, and it struck me that it almost made it sound like "the luck" was a disease. Which maybe it is. All I said was, "Yeah. I do. What is it?"

She smiled, her bright winning smile that was compelling even knowing it was wholly disconnected from anything she was actually thinking or feeling, and reached forward to pat my hand. "Well, it's just that, isn't it? It's luck. Our family, the women in our family, have always been lucky. Just like you used to say growing up."

I pulled my hand back, frustration sharpening my tone. "It's not just luck. Or at least not normal luck. I'm not stupid and you need to tell me what's going on."

She frowned at my tone and raised her hand. "I didn't say it was normal luck. And you're my daughter, obviously you're not stupid. But it's also not something you should worry about or that you can control. When women in our family get to a certain age, it just…kicks in. And yes, it takes getting used to. And you have to be careful to not be too…showy with it. But at the end of the day, it truly is a blessing." She gestured around to all her wealthy surroundings, as if to say the proof was in the pudding.

"It hurts people. You know it does. It's like us being more lucky makes other people around us less lucky. Don't act like you don't realize that."

My mother's eyes grew harder as she leaned towards me. "Grow up. Yes, I realize that. I also realize that the world is a hard fucking place and it doesn't need me or my luck for bad things to happen to good people. And beyond all of that, what choice or say do I have in it? Are you wishing bad things on people? Are you getting people hurt or killed? No. You're just living your life, and if something outside your control gives you someone else's luck or however it actually works, because it may surprise you to know I don't have all the answers, then what am I to do about it? Kill myself? Ruin my life because I don't deserve to be happy? What exactly would you have me do?" Her voice had raised and cracked at the last, and we sat in silence for several seconds. This was more emotion than I had seen from her in years.

"I'm sorry. I am not accusing you of anything. I just…I'm scared. And I feel…something watching me all the time now. And I have this." I lifted my pants leg to show the brand above my ankle. It had paled some, but it was still visible in the afternoon light. It reminded me of a yin-yang symbol that had been broken along its curving center and straightened out into a single serpentine line. I looked up to see my mother looking at my leg with an expression that was a mixture of distaste and fear.

"Yes, the marks. They will happen once a year, typically around the time of your birthday." She was wearing shorts and lifted her legs up for me to see. I could only see the faintest ghosts of marks on her legs. They seemed to go side by side in rows to the extent they could be seen at all. "You can get them removed with a laser. When you were little I had to use makeup and stockings, but technology is a wonderful thing. I can give you a referral to a good surgeon that won't ask questions."

"But don't you wonder what it is? What we're a part of?"

She looked tired now, sitting back in her chair with a sigh. "Not really. I've lived with it for 28 years, taken the bad with the good, and any curiosity died out a long time ago."

I was going to ask another question when something struck me.

"Is this what happened to Daddy?" I blurted out the question before I thought about how it sounded, and my mother looked like I had struck her in the face. Her eyes began welling up as she stood up from the table, fists and jaw clenched.

"Get out."

Within seconds a slab of a bodyguard was at my elbow, gently but firmly guiding me back through the condo to the elevator. My own vision was watery and I rode back down in silence. In the weeks since I haven't talked to my mother again, despite repeated attempts to apologize or explain myself.

But that wasn't the worst of it. I went to the gym, and a guy lifting weights in the back started screaming when his feet slipped off the leg press machine and his knees were crushed by 500 pounds of metal. I started taking walks in a local park, which was nice and soothing. Until I realized that at least once a week I saw a dead bird or squirrel near my path.

The worst was the fire. I was walking to the bank around the corner from work when I heard a siren. Then two, then three. As I turned the corner, I saw smoke billowing out of a fourth floor window. Decades earlier it had been a large department store, but a few years back it was converted into expensive apartments. These apartments were now ablaze, and I could hear a woman shrieking from the top floor.

At first I couldn't tell what she was saying, but then I made it out. "Save. Baby. Catch her." By now I could see that she was burning. I could see as she tossed an infant out the window, a lash of flame reaching out, chasing the child, setting it alight. It didn't cry, and I tell myself it was already dead from the smoke. But I think I saw it moving for a moment when it struck the concrete below. When I got back to work later that morning, I ran to the bathroom and vomited.

Usually very social, I found myself becoming more isolated, partially out of fear that the more someone was around me, the more likely it was that they would get hurt. Externally my life continued humming along smoothly at every turn. Despite my self-exile, I found fast friends and helpful strangers at every turn. Despite my depression, I actually felt better physically. I swear, I think I started looking better too. And I would notice these good things, even appreciate them at times through my numbness, but it didn't help me feel less alone.

Then my grandmother came to visit. She had just gotten back from her time in the U.K. and wanted to check in on her favorite granddaughter. Per our standard joke, I pointed out I was her only granddaughter, and she laughed and gave me a hug.

She fixed us a delicious dinner out of the motley groceries I had at the moment, and we ate slowly while we talked, with most of the conversation about her travels or my work. She was the opposite of my mother in so many ways, and I had always been close with her even though her constant movement meant I would sometimes go long periods without seeing her in person. I had debated whether to ask her about what was happening to us, not wanting to ruin the first fun I had had in months, but when I did she just smiled and nodded.

"I wondered when you'd ask me about it. Your mother told me you had spoken to her. She's not thrilled with you at the moment, either, though that will pass in time. But I'm glad you asked me."

I felt myself wince at the mention of my mother, but I forced myself to press ahead. "So can you tell me more than she did?"

The woman nodded, her normally bright and mischievous eyes growing more serious. "I can. Not necessarily because I know more, but your mother…she has trouble talking about it. I wonder if she doesn't lie to herself about some parts of it."

"What parts?"

She folded her hands with a sigh. "When I was young, younger than you, it came on me. It had been on my mother and her mother before that. Farther back than that I don't know, and I don't know how it started or where it comes from. But from my experience, what I've learned, and what I've observed with your mother and now you, this is how it works."

"It comes on you some time between 15 and 30, or that seems to be the case. And once it starts, it lasts for thirty years. Not the luck part, once you get the luck it's yours forever. But the rest, the feeling something with you, the marks, the people around you getting a raw deal, that just…stops. And honestly, the bad luck for others seems like its way worse for the first few months after it starts. It seems to, well, stabilize to some degree. I'm not going to say people don't still get hurt more than normal, but it's nothing like it must seem to you right now."

"Right now, it is heightened, and right now, you are also very sensitive about it, so you assume every slight misfortune is connected to you. I'm telling you it's not. The world is a hard place and it doesn't need you or your luck for bad things to happen to good people."

I frowned at that. "That's what Mama said."

She smiled. "Well, she's got some sense after all." She paused and then shook her head. "I need to be honest and tell you the whole thing."

I felt my stomach lurch. "What's the whole thing?"

"Well, for one thing, I'm not an only child, at least not technically. Neither is your mother and neither are you. We were all twins. As far back as I could find, the women have always carried twins, but only one child ever survives childbirth. Always a girl, and always the only child the woman ever has. I don't know why that is, just that it is."

I felt like I was going to throw up. "So all those babies…"

"I know, honey. I know. Best not to dwell on it, as it can't be helped. But some things can be. Let's go on in the living room and I'll tell you the rest of what I know."

Part Three

"If you are anything like me, and I know you are, you're probably dealing with this period of…adjustment by isolating yourself from everyone around you. Am I right?"

I nodded glumly. "I don't want to cause people to get hurt."

My grandmother reached out across the sofa and patted my leg. "I understand. I do. But there's several things you need to understand."

"First, you don't control this thing and you can't let it control you. Whatever this is, it doesn't decide who gets hurt based on what you want or don't want, and it doesn't limit itself to people that you make physical contact with or even people you have ever met. Distance is a part of it, yes, but it's unreliable. Back in my forties I spent about five years obsessing over what kind of pattern there must be underneath all of this."

“We didn’t have fancy things like the internet back then, of course, but I started getting every newspaper in a hundred-mile radius. Then five hundred. Then a thousand. By then I was good at spotting the bad ones, the times when I felt like I was likely the thing that turned a fender bender into a funeral or bad wiring into a school fire. Some of that was me guessing or feeling guilty—that’s why I was obsessed in the first place, of course. But you do develop a feel for it I think, almost as if you can see a thin, invisible cord stretching back to you or whatever lurks over your shoulder.” Her gaze had begun to drift into some unseen distance, but she pulled herself back with a quick smile to me. “But I’m getting sidetracked. I’m 86, so cut me some slack.”

“So I would keep track of these bad events from newspapers, people I knew, any source of information, all this bad luck, and over time I figured it out. There is no pattern. Sometimes weeks would pass with nothing out of the ordinary happening. Then there would be five things in one day. Sometimes they happened to people I knew, sometimes they happened to people two states away. No rhyme or reason, they just happened.”

She paused a moment and I spoke up. “So how do you know it was tied to you really? I mean, I know you said you felt it was, but how do you know for sure?”

The woman shrugged and gave a sad smile. “I guess I don’t know for sure, though if I’m wrong, it means I have less bad things on my conscience, so that’s a good thing in the end. But believe me, I feel pretty certain, in part because of my traveling.”

“You know I’ve always traveled a lot. Well, like I said, you only have the negative parts of this thing for thirty years, and in my case it started when I was 17, so by 47 I was done with everything but the good fortune. But by then I had already been searching for a pattern for years, and like you I doubted if I could rely on my sense of what was and was not connected. Plus, my information was so limited. It’s not like people’s smaller problems and illnesses are going in the newspaper. I was only seeing the most sensational examples from articles and the handful of more personal accounts I got from people I knew. There were a lot of gaps. So that’s when I started traveling.”

"I naturally had plenty of money, so I was in a unique position to expand my investigation further. I planned out a schedule of travel for two years that followed the same routine in each place. I started off by going to Rome, Italy. I got newspapers from the area for a month beforehand, the month I stayed there, and a month after I left. It was harder while traveling to get everything delivered, even with the amounts I was paying, but I developed a clear picture over time. Bad luck was following at my heel like a hungry dog. When I came, misfortune followed. When I left, the dog went with me."

I suppressed a shiver and swallowed, my tongue dry in my mouth. Not seeming to notice, my grandmother continued. "I kept track of things until I was 56, but of course it had all stopped long before then. By then your mother had it, and not that long after you were born." She sighed. "And I hoped it would skip her, that it would skip you. But it was a silly hope."

She paused, sipping from her glass, her dark eyes studying me over it. "And I think I've made you more scared, not less. I'm sorry, sweetie. I got the bad part out of the way first. Now the…well, if not good, at least better part."

"One," she held up a single finger as she spoke, "the bad luck will never affect your daughter. They won't have our special luck until it comes to them, but they should never have abnormal bad luck either. I guess whatever it is protects the line in that way."

"Two, you can find love and it be okay. Something my mother told me about, and I've found it to be true, is that your bad luck will never touch the person you love the most. So if you find that special someone, that truly special someone, they are kind of tucked under your umbrella with you. I don't know if it can change from person to person over time, or what all the rules are, but I do believe that it works."

"Third," she held up a third finger with a warm smile, "you're not alone in this. I'll help you through it best I can, and while I don't have all the answers, having someone to talk to can help."

I suddenly felt my vision blurring with tears and I leaned over, hugging the older woman tightly. She hugged me back and stroked my hair, and it wasn't long before I fell asleep.

When I woke up I was laying on my sofa with a blanket covering me. I rolled over and saw a note from my grandmother. She said she decided to leave me sleeping, but to call her in the next couple of days and we'd get together again. Still blinking blearily, I went to the kitchen and saw by the clock and the light coming in from outside that it was the next morning after our dinner. I stood for a moment looking glumly into my refrigerator, debating cereal versus no breakfast, when my stomach gave a sudden lurch. I ran to the bathroom, making a last second decision to throw up in the sink because I wouldn't have reached the toilet.

The smell of the vomit hit me and I retched again, then a third time. I practically never threw up, and now I had thrown up twice in a few days. My first thought was that I was getting a stomach bug, but then a terrible thought struck me.

Twenty minutes to the drug store, and then on impulse, into their bathroom to do the test. I peed on the stick, my hand shaking so bad I felt sure it wouldn't even register. But before the allotted time was even up, I had an answer. Positive.

The stick couldn't tell me, but I knew it would be twins.

The rest of the day was a blur of sadness and anxiety. I had left the drugstore with the grim thought that I should either go to an abortion clinic or buy a lottery ticket, and I felt disgusted with myself for thinking it. Still, part of me couldn't help but feel like I was murdering at least one child by having either of them, at least if there was truly two like I suspected. Ultimately, I settled on calling and getting a doctor's appointment for the following week before settling into a depressed stupor in my bed. I didn't call my mother or grandmother, but later that night it struck me that I should call Brad.

Back when I found out that Brad had lost his job, I felt guilty. Maybe it was because of me or maybe not, but I had visited him, we had talked, and ultimately we had sex. I knew immediately it was a mistake, and Brad, who clearly saw this as a sign that we were getting back together, took it hard when I let him know that it was an isolated thing, not the first step towards us getting back together.

Since then I hadn't talked to him, but I needed to now, because even though that had been over two months ago, I hadn't been with anyone else before or since.

I didn't tell him any details over the phone, just that I needed to talk to him if he could meet me the next day. He agreed reluctantly, his tone guarded. He wanted to know what it was about, but I remained vague and told him I'd see him the next day.

We met at the food court of the mall he was working at now, having gotten a job at a clothing store a week before. He didn't have a long break, but it wound up not being a long conversation.

I told him I was pregnant, that I wasn't expecting anything from him, but I thought he had the right to know. He asked why I was telling him this now, and I explained I had just found out myself. He said it was bullshit, that I had probably fucked ten guys since I gave him a pity screw, but that he was the only one with a job, so I thought I'd hang it around his neck. Well fuck that, and fuck me. He stood up then, his neck straining and red, his eyes bulging. I had never seen him so angry. I wondered for a second if he was going to hit me, but instead he spat at me and stormed off.

The spit had been aimed at my face but had gone short and wide to land on my arm. I grimaced, wiping it away with a napkin from the dispenser on the rickety food court table we had been sitting at. A few people nearby were dimly looking in my direction for the source of the commotion, but I didn't care. I felt shell-shocked and tired, but I also felt angry. None of this was my fault, and I was trying. I didn't deserve any of this bullshit, and I didn't deserve being talked to like I was some kind of fucking dog, being called a whore, being fucking spit on.

I felt myself raging more and more as I drove home, and even when I went to bed that night, I kept replaying that scene of him yelling and spitting on me as I fell into a fitful, restless sleep.

It was two days later that I heard that the day after I had met him, Brad had been on a ladder at work hanging up a bracket when he had fallen. Somehow his mouth had gotten hooked on a metal coat rod on the way down, shoving the large metallic disc at the end of the rod up through the roof of his mouth and snapping his neck. He had died later, on the way to the hospital.

I've called my grandmother, but I haven't heard back. I may try talking to my mother again, but I don't know if she'll even talk to me. I don't know what to do, or who will ever even read this, but I feel like I'm being crushed down, squeezed and pressurized more every day, becoming a black hole that just eats light and life. It needs to get better or I don't know how long I can make it.

Final addition to this entry. I've just gone through my mail from the last few days and I've won two different cruises. So unless I change my mind or get in touch with my grandmother or mother, I'm going to leave for a few days and go. I wouldn't think the ship would sink with me on it, and I could at least inflict myself on a different part of the world for awhile. I will write another update soon, if I can.

Part Four

I am writing this entry on my fifth day aboard the Lodestar, a luxury cruise ship in the Mediterranean Sea. I've never heard of the cruise company before, and I hadn't signed up for any contest to win either this or the other cruise I had won in the mail, but between the two, this one was farther from home, so it won out. I wanted to be away from everything familiar, away from myself if it was possible. Of course, the opposite has been the case.

The trip started off well enough. I flew out of Atlanta, my heart thudding as the plane took off. I kept being haunted by the idea of all the flights that crashed where only a few people survived. I wasn't very worried about myself, but I didn't want to be responsible for the people around me being hurt or dying. I'd be lying if I said it was a pleasant flight, as I felt myself tensing at the slightest noise or shimmy of turbulence, but other than hearing several people complaining about small inconveniences like their phone dying or something being wrong with their meal, the trip was uneventful.

We landed in Barcelona, and from there I took a taxi to the docks where the ship was boarding. After going through the initial check-in and handing over the suitcase I had brought, I went up the series of small ramps to the ship itself. It was beautiful, feeling more like a fancy hotel than a big boat until you looked out a window. The ship left the port, and while I could occasionally feel the slight motion of the water we were slipping through, I felt no signs of the sea sickness I'd had the few times I had been on the water growing up. I felt a combination of gratefulness and bitterness as I guessed the reason for the change, but pushing the thought aside I tried to focus on exploring the ship.

The ship was truly massive, filled with rooms, three restaurants, a casino, four pools, and even a small ice rink on one of the lower levels. I considered trying to kill time in the casino, but my stomach turned at the idea of having the constant reminder of winning. Instead I went up to one of the upper decks and looked out at the water.

It's June as I write this, and the weather has been warm but not hot, with the cool air coming off the sea being both gentle and refreshing. I felt myself starting to relax slightly, and as the hours went by uneventfully, I actually started to enjoy myself, or at least not hate myself so much.

The next day we landed in Italy near Florence, and while I debated getting off the ship at all, I was glad when I did. The city was beautiful, with such a weight of history and artistry around every corner. I started out with one of the ship's tour groups, but I felt uncomfortable around so many people. Splitting off by myself, I traveled some of the smaller streets away from the main piazzas, dipping in and out of shops and grabbing a sandwich to eat as I walked. Being alone, with so many things to distract me, I actually felt good for the first time in months.

The next two days were much the same. The ship stopped in Rome and then in Venice, and I had days of solitary sightseeing that were peaceful. The fourth full day at sea was actually called an "at sea" day, with the ship not landing at any port on its way to a stop along the coast of Croatia. Naturally, that led a lot of people to take the day to relax by the pools, and I was no different.

I had set up in a lounge chair away from other people, my face barely shaded by a nearby umbrella. I wasn't showing yet, and my old bathing suits still fit just fine, but it still struck me how little I cared how I looked anymore. Occasionally I would see a guy looking at me, weighing his odds if he came over, but clearly my expression told them all they needed to know. I reminded myself of my mother. Never truly laughing or smiling, just putting on faces as was needed for the task at hand. I had closed my eyes, trying to force those thoughts away and maybe take a nap, when the strong smell of cinnamon hit my nostrils. The smell was so strong and sharp that I sat up and opened my eyes almost involuntarily. That's when I found the young woman standing nearby, her smile seeming genuine as she gave a light laugh.

She gestured at the chair next to mine. "Is this taken?"

I shook my head and she plopped down, spreading her hair out behind the top edge of the chair and settling back. I thought it was strange that she picked that spot when there were plenty of open chairs, but I was about to lay back down on my own when she spoke again.

"So what smell is it?"

I froze mid lay-down and turned back to her. "What?"

She rolled on her side and propped her head on her hand as she looked at me. She looked to be about twenty and was on the beautiful side of pretty, but she also seemed strange. Not just what she was saying, but her...manner. Her movements, the meter of her words, they all seemed slightly off from what I would expect from someone of her age. Then she was speaking again.

"When I came up. You smelled a strong smell, right? What was it?"

I blinked. "Cinnamon."

She laughed and gave a nod. "That's lucky. Sometimes you get a burning trash or dog shit smell, or strong cheese. I hate cheese, except for American, which is mainly plastic anyway, right?"

I felt like I had stumbled into the middle of a conversation she was having with someone else. "I don't understand."

The woman gave a shake of her head. "Sorry, not trying to be mysterious or weird. Just been looking forward to talking to you.

Running off at the mouth." She stopped a minute, looking around before continuing. "When I got near you, I smelled coconut. Those of us with…the luck is what most of us call it…we can smell when each other are near. You can't ever predict what the smell will be, and once it's smelt, it's always the same for that person. So again, better you smelled cinnamon than dog shit when I showed up, because that can happen." She gave another laugh.

My mind was racing, and I wasn't sure what to believe or what to say. I didn't want to admit to anything in case this was a misunderstanding or a trick, but I also didn't want to give up this chance to possibly learn more about what was going on. Ultimately, I just lamely blurted out, "I don't smell my mother or grandmother."

The woman's face grew more serious for a moment before lightening again. "Well, no it doesn't happen inside your own family. I don't know why, but I don't know why the smells happen in the first place." She studied me for a moment. "Did they tell you there were other families like yours?"

I shook my head and she reached over to pat my arm. "Well, this is even weirder for you then. I'm sorry." She pushed herself up to a sitting position, folding her legs underneath her. "Ok. There are other families that have it too, just like yours. Not many, of course. I know about eight. Well, seven now." She frowned but pushed on. "To answer some questions you might have off the bat, yes, it's always girls. Yes, the rules are the same for everyone. Yes, a lot of it sucks, but you can learn to live with it and use the rules in your favor." The girl beamed as though she had just finished a sales pitch, which in some ways she had. I shrugged in return.

"I guess. I just am so tired. I'm so guilty feeling for all these people I'm hurting."

She nodded. "Understandable. Totally get it. But once you come to terms with people getting hurt and that you can influence who that is, it becomes easier to channel the bad into something more positive." Noticing my confused stare, she went on. "Ok. Wow. They told you very little." She swung her feet back onto the chair, turning to face out at the pool. "Alright, you see the little guy across the way, sitting next to bar? The one with the glasses?"

I nodded. "Yeah. So?"

She turned her gaze back to me. "So, he's a convicted child molester. Two months after he got paroled, he got a letter in the mail saying he had won a free cruise. This cruise. Lucky, right?" She gave me a wink. "Now, during his trip, I've made it a point to talk to him for a few minutes. Make sure I have a clear memory and feel for him. And a few days from now, when he's back home, lying to his parole officer that he hasn't left the city, much less the country, he'll have some really bad luck. And that will be the story of him."

"But how? I thought we don't control it?"

She waggled her hand back and forth. "Eh, we do and we don't. It's going to happen regardless—we can't stop it, that's for sure. But you can channel it to a large degree. If you go to sleep thinking about someone with deep anger or hatred towards them, most of the time, they're going to get popped the next day or two. And you'll find that very little other stuff happens if you give the bad a direction regularly."

I thought about Brad and felt nauseous, but pressed on. "So how did you pick him? How did you know about him in the first place?"

The girl grinned. "Oh, this is my ship. My cruise line. It's semi-profitable, but it's real purpose is that once or twice a year I also take a cruise myself. On those trips, I make sure I have a dozen or so people show up that can go onto my list. Pedophiles, murderers, people that the world is better without. And I chat with them some, get enough so I can put some feeling behind it when the time comes. And then they go home. Then some time later, it might be a week or a few months, I'll do my part, and they will feed whatever this thing really is."

I sat for a moment, thinking about all that she was saying. Was it true? And why hadn't my mother or grandmother told me about it? About any of this? I didn't know what to believe or whether I could trust this woman at all.

"How long have you been doing this?"

Her grin widened. "Fifty-two years, give or take. My mother did it a little before she passed, and I know some other families do variations on it as well, but I like to think I've perfected it. I'm helping the world and myself too."

I sucked in a breath as she spoke. "How old are you?"

"73." She paused and raised a hand. "I know how it sounds with you being so new to it all, but I've been doing this pretty much since it came on me, and there are certain benefits to directing it beyond your conscience. You don't really age, and your body can even get younger and stronger depending on how frequently you do it. Plus, it really does make you look better, or at least closer to how you would want yourself to look. You won't look like a totally different person, but more like the best version of yourself. And believe me, some people have a very broad range they can travel in that regard. Before this stuff hit me, my face looked like someone took a shit from the top of the ugly tree." She swung herself back around to facing me, her face serious again. "Look, I know this is a ton of stuff to take in. If not for all you've been through, you would think it was all made up shit. But I've been keeping an eye on you, and I think you've seen enough to know that what I'm saying is possible. You just have to decide how much you trust you can put in it and me."

I frowned at her. "I don't know how much I can trust. Why have you been keeping an eye on me?"

The woman sighed, and for the first time she looked truly sad. "I used to be your mother's best friend. She wasn't introduced to all of this until just a few months before it came on her, but our families have always gotten along fairly well, so we were that introduction. Me and her became close really quickly. She always smelled like cotton-candy to me." She smiled, her eyes glimmering. "I was with her when she met your father. He was handsome, and such a good guy. She loved him so much." She stopped and rubbed her eyes. "But things happened, and she cut off ties from everyone. Even me. She was pregnant with you at the time, so I never got to meet you before now, but I've always kept an eye out."

"What 'things happened'? I'm so tired of people not telling me everything. What happened back then that changed everything so much?"

She was shaking her head before I even finished. "I'm sorry, Eliza, but I can't go into that. I don't know all the details, and even if I did, that's for your mother to tell. It won't be easy for her, but I think if you push her on it she will be honest."

I gave a bitter laugh. "She won't even return my calls. The only person that will even talk to me anymore, aside from I guess you now, is my grandmother."

The woman's face hardened, her expression dark. "Well, go to her then. Make her talk. After you have talked to her, I'm happy to talk to you again, to help any way I can. But please, if you take nothing else I've said to heart, listen to me on this: Do not trust that other woman, the one you call grandmother."

My eyes widened. "What? Why? She's my grandmother. She's always looked out for me."

She shook her head. "No. No she isn't and no she hasn't."

"What're you saying?"

She reached forward, gripping my hand tightly. "I'm saying that fucking bitch isn't your grandmother and she is extremely dangerous. That's what I'm saying."

Part Five

A number of days have passed since my last entry, and I've been back home for close to a week as I write this. I left off in the middle of talking to Rosalyn, who refused to answer any more of my questions for now, and soon left after telling me her name so I could confirm her identity with my mother. I didn't know how much I trusted what she said, and the idea that my grandmother wasn't who I thought she was...well, it shook me, but I didn't know if I could ever believe that. And if she was wrong or lying about that, how much weight could I give to the rest? Still, I needed to try and talk to my mother again anyway, so this at least gave me a stronger purpose in doing so.

Two days later I was off the ship, and the following day I was back at my mother's house in Atlanta. I had not called ahead, and there was some delay at the front desk as messages were carried back and forth upstairs, but ultimately I was escorted up and taken to my mother, who sat on a sofa reading a tablet. The room was likely intended to be a library of sorts, but without any books it looked bare and gloomy. It suited the woman that occupied it.

My mother had lost some of her fake glow since I saw her last. She looked up at me, not unkindly, but with a weariness that I wasn't used to. Setting down the tablet, she patted the sofa next to her.

"Come on and sit down. I'm glad you're here." She looked at the guard. "We're fine. Leave us alone." The man hesitated. "I said go." Nodding silently, the man ducked back through the door and closed it behind him.

The whole exchange was strange, but I wanted to get some things out before the conversation got derailed again. "Look, I'm sorry how things were left b…" She raised her hand to silence me.

"No, that was my fault. I overreacted, my guilt has given me a thin skin and a sour disposition. Those things aren't your fault." She reached over and rubbed my back with the palm of her hand. "There's things I need to tell you. I should have told you a long time ago, and I certainly need to tell you now that you're involved yourself."

I nodded, but I felt like I needed to get something out first. "I met Rosalyn. I went on a cruise, and it was her ship. She told me some things, said she was your friend."

Her eyes widened as I spoke, and as I said 'friend', I watched her face crumple into tears. After a moment she regained her composure and nodded. "She was. She was my best friend. One of only a couple of people I could talk to about any of this before I met your father. And I'm not sure what all she told you, but it's probably much of what I am going to say."

I broke in. "She said something happened, I think something bad, but she never knew what exactly and said it was for you to tell me, not her."

I could see relief lighten her features as she relaxed a bit. "That sounds like her. And she probably knows more than she's letting on. Her family has always been good at getting information on everyone. But in any case, I need to get to telling you. We have limited time."

I nodded, wanting to ask more questions, but remaining silent.

"First, this room is the only room that isn't bugged, and that's only because I've disabled the surveillance for the moment. They check it every couple of days, but I waited to do it until I knew you were here to see me again. As for who the 'they' is, you need to understand that these guards aren't mine. They aren't really guards at all, they're jailers. It's the same reason I don't have the same house staff any more, the same reason I don't travel any more. Things have gotten much more restrictive the past few months."

"But how? And why?"

Her expression grew angry. "There are other interests in play here than just us or even the other families that are marked like we are. So I don't know all of it. But I know who imprisoned me. It's the woman you know as your grandmother. She's not your grandmother. She's actually your great-great grandmother, Emily Burke."

"How is that possible?"

Her eyes lowered, and her voice grew thin, the anger burned down to a smoky residue around the edges of her words. "With my help. I…When this all happened to me, Emily was there for me. She was my great-grandmother, and yes, she had always seemed far younger than her age, which was around 90 when I was 10, but I knew women in our family aged well, and when they introduced me to Rosalyn and her family, to the strange luck we carry, it explained why. At first it had sounded magical. Stay young and healthy forever, or at least a really long time, and have wonderful luck to boot? I was young and stupid, and I tried to ignore the downsides they were talking to me about."

She let out a sigh. "Then when the luck came on me, I watched a school bus catch fire with half a baseball team on it. They were screaming, clawing at the windows as their skin stuck and slid off against the glass. I can still smell it a lot of mornings when I wake up." She gave a shudder. "I would like to say I went crazy, but that's an excuse. Seeing that, knowing I was responsible…it broke me a little. It gave enough of a crack for Emily to crawl in."

"Over the next couple of years, her and Rosalyn were my world, my support system. I had never known my grandmother, though she was still alive, and my mother had always been a hard, distant woman that…well, she was a vicious, spiteful bitch. That made it easier when Emily came to me worried, saying that my mother was trying to kill her."

I frowned. "How would that even work?"

"Well, what I was told by Emily, which was only a partial truth, was that if two people with the mark focus their hatred and anger on another marked person on the same night as they go to sleep, they would overcome that person's protection and the targeted person would fall. She claimed that my mother was working with Rosalyn's mother to kill her, and that she had barely survived two different accidents within the past few days."

"But why?"

She looked at me closely. "Because if you kill a member of your line in that way, it makes you much stronger and younger. It's why I look like this. You can get some small benefit from directing it towards other people—I've heard Rosalyn's family does that a lot. I haven't had the heart to direct it since everything that happened with Emily, but I can see the evidence of what I did every day when I look in the mirror." She looked away. "I…this isn't easy talking about. Bear with me. And try not to hate me more than you have to."

I didn't know what to say, so I remained silent. Then she went on.

"Emily was so earnest, so upset, so convincing. It only took a short time for me to believe her. And of course, she had worked in the benefits to me if I helped, and I'd be lying if I said it didn't make it all more palatable. As much as I hated hurting people at first, as the months had gone by, I had gotten more numb to it. And I loved being beautiful. I loved the way people treated me, looked at me, wanted to be me. I was stupid and selfish and vain, and that is just what she was looking for."

She paused, rubbing her face and seeming to have to physically force herself to go on. "After it was done, she told me the truth. That my mother had been conspiring to kill a member of the family, but it hadn't been Emily, it had been Emily's daughter, my grandmother. And she had been doing it with Emily. Emily had used my mother to kill her own daughter, and then used me to kill my mother. When I asked her why, she laughed. She said it only worked when two of the same family teamed up against a third, and she wanted to live a long time. She'd figured out over the years that if you occasionally ate some of your family's lives, you could get by just fine and have less risk to yourself."

"By this point, I had married your father and I was carrying you and your brother. I knew only you would make it, and I had somewhat accepted it. I was looking forward to having you, to loving you. You and your daddy were the only reasons I didn't try to kill myself right then."

"I cut all ties with her, of course. I did the same with Rosalyn, out of shame. Years went by and you grew up. You were such a wonderful child, I loved you so much. But I always kept some distance from you too. As though my dirt, my sin, might rub off on you. I hated myself so much, but I loved the two of you with all my heart."

"As you got older, I got more and more worried because I knew your time would be coming. I ultimately broke down and told your father everything. He had known parts before, but he didn't know about what me and Emily had done. He could have left me for that, or hated me. Instead, he came up with a plan to get away. Take you and disappear so that hopefully Emily would never find us again."

Her voice cracked. "Somehow she found out. I never knew how. But that's why your father died, because she killed him. She came to me later, telling me to never try to run again, that this family belonged to her, and as long as we stayed in line, everything would be fine."

I frowned. "But why didn't you loving Daddy protect him? I thought it can't touch the one you love the most?"

She looked up at me sadly. "Ah, baby, that's true. But the one I loved the most was you."

Part Six

My mother and I hugged each other and wept, but she reminded me that our time was limited and there was still much to talk about. She told me more about the years since my father's death, how she had become more and more withdrawn and isolated, at first by choice. But as I had grown older and it seemed increasingly likely that I would be getting the luck soon, Emily had imposed more restrictions on her as well—a security detail that was meant to spy on her and keep her from doing anything rash, threats against both her and myself if she tried to tell me the truth.

She knew that Emily's plan was likely to gain my trust and trick me into helping kill my mother the same way my mother herself had been tricked, and that keeping the two of us separated was key. Tears returning to her eyes, she grabbed my hand.

"I'm sorry again for how I acted before. For not telling you more before now. I think a part of me wanted her plan to work, wanted an end to all of this for myself. I've lived so long with this pain and guilt, and for a time I would go through spells where I tried to kill myself, but of course I couldn't."

I squeezed her hand back, intent on listening, but her last statement gave me pause and some low tickling in the back of my brain. "What do you mean you couldn't?"

She shrugged and gave me an embarrassed look. "Just that. Tried to hang myself, the rope broke. Tried to shoot myself, the gun jammed. Poison had no effect other than a bit of diarrhea, razor blades would literally slip out of my hand whenever I brought it near my wrists."

The idea of her being so beaten down for so long, so alone, felt like it was crushing me. I wanted to comfort her, but I still felt that low tickling, stronger now, and I knew I needed to press on. "Did you ever try to get someone else to kill you?"

She rubbed her face and nodded. "Yes, twice. Same thing. They couldn't hurt me. It's an aspect of the luck we don't think about as much because it's much more obvious when something good or lucky happens then when you avoid something bad happening. But yes, I don't think we can be seriously hurt by normal means."

"Why are you telling me all this now? What's changed?"

Giving my hand another squeeze, she let go and sat up straighter. "I realized I needed to stop being a coward. I couldn't let you fall into the same trap that's held me all these years. I don't know how much knowing will help you, but at least it's something. I'm finally doing something."

The tickle had pushed its way forward into the forefront of my mind. I had a plan, or at least the start of a plan. I shook my head. "You're not doing something yet. But you will. We both will. We're going to end this."

In the few minutes we had left, I outlined the rough sketch of my idea and we figured out more details. By the time the guard came back in to tell my mother that she was going to be late for a phone conference if we didn't stop now, we knew what needed to be done.

The preparations took nearly a week, helped along immensely by Rosalyn, who was able to get us details on both the security watching over both my mother and Emily, as well as where Emily was going to be for the next few days. My mother's security detail consisted of five guards rotated in and out on a 12-hour basis, with the idea being that at any given time she would have two to three guards with her. It wasn't hard to arrange a night where my mother, myself, and Rosalyn all fell asleep thinking of a different guard.

The next day, in the aftermath of one guard calling in sick, one dying as he drove to her condo, and one falling and inexplicably breaking his hip while patrolling her home, my mother was ready to head out with us. But as she approached the elevator, the doors slid open and the other two guards appeared. They gave her wary smiles and told her she needed to stay put for her safety.

She shot the first one in the head with the gun the injured guard had somehow lost in his fall. She had never fired a gun before outside of trying to end her own life, but there was no jam or misfire this time, and the bullet struck him dead center in the forehead. The second guard moved to tackle her, but tripped at the last moment, his weight and momentum carrying him headfirst into the wall behind her. When he didn't stir after a few seconds, she took the elevator downstairs and met us in the parking lot.

I say us, because Rosalyn had insisted on coming along. I told her she had helped enough, but she wasn't hearing it. She said she'd failed my mother for years by not coming and offering help, but she was done failing her now. When my mother reached the car, the two of them began to laugh and cry as they hugged each other, spinning in a slow circle in the parking lot. I watched for over a minute before reminding them we had a plane to catch.

Emily had a large manor house outside of Enniscorthy, Ireland, and it took some time to reach it. We flew into Gatwick and then onto Dublin before renting a car and heading south. Taking the train would have been nice, but we had picked up some items from a contact of Rosalyn's when we hit Dublin, and it didn't seem wise to push our luck by going through boarding on a public train. We needed to save every drop of that luck for what was coming next.

The manor house was beautiful, with thick, leaded glass windows and peaks done in the Tudor-style. There was a large garage behind the house, and some distance away I could see a stable, though I saw no signs of horses or other animals. For that matter, I saw no signs of people either, and I felt my stomach begin to drop.

"I don't think she's here." I looked over at Rosalyn with a questioning look. She was driving, but as she rolled to a stop, she gave me a comforting smile.

"No worries. She's here. There should be two guards and a housemaid too. But that's it." She glanced back at my mother. All the way across the Atlantic and then back across the Irish Sea, they had been talking almost non-stop, catching up on nearly three decades of missing each other. But as we had grown closer to Emily's house, my mother had grown more and more silent. Rosalyn poked her knee. "You okay? You ready?"

I turned around in my seat to look at my mother. She looked small and frail, all pale skin and big eyes. She swallowed before she spoke. "I…I don't know. I'm afraid I'll mess up. I'm so scared of her. She…she's not really human anymore I don't think. She's lived so long."

Rosalyn shook her head. "No, that's bullshit. You won't mess up, and whatever she is or isn't, this ends now. You can do this." Her tone softened as she added. "We're here with you. We're all in this together."

My mother nodded and looked at me. I tried to smile, pushing down my own fears and worries. "Let's go fuck this old bitch up."

As I turned back around, I saw that the front door of the manor had opened and a burly looking man was coming towards the car. I got out, ready to talk to him, but then I saw the knife in his hand. I let out a small yelp as I tried to dodge to my left, my hands fumbling with the gun I had tucked at my back. But he was fast and anticipated my dodge, and in the same moment my gun came free from my waistband I saw the knife coming up in an arc that would likely gut me.

I couldn't think of anything else in that fraction of an instant, so I pulled the trigger. The gun was behind my back, in my non-dominant hand and not even remotely pointed towards the man, but in the moment there wasn't time for rational thought or consideration, just instinct and reaction.

I heard the crack of the gun, a dim "tink" sound to my right, and then the man's head caved in, the force of the bullet turning him just enough that the knife passed by harmlessly a couple of inches away from my belly.

I stared at the man's lifeless body for a couple of seconds, but was startled out of my reverie by a second gun shot. I looked up to see a second guard falling just outside the front door as Rosalyn began to lower her gun. She shot me a glance and shrugged. "No need in letting him get close. Not everyone can be fancy like you." She gestured to the left bumper of the car where there was a new dent. It took me a second to realize that is where my bullet had ricocheted before killing the man attacking me. I swallowed and gave a weak smile.

My mother was out of the car now, her hands trembling slightly but her expression set and grim. I thought about making a Charlie's Angels joke, but suppressed the urge. The three of us shared a look and then headed into the manor without another word.

It only took a few moments of exploration to find Emily in a large room off the main hallway. All of the furniture except for one chair had been moved to the perimeter of the room, and I noticed that a large floor rug had been rolled up and tucked into a corner as well. It looked like she was expecting us, and when we entered, she stayed seated in the plush chair that occupied the center of the room. While her overall appearance was pretty much the same, this was the first time I was seeing her without the false mask of love and warmth. Her dark eyes glittered with a strange, almost insectile malignity, and her mouth, normally smiling and expressive, hung slack as dead meat. When she started talking, I found myself imagining a bone puppet covered in corpse meat dancing, causing the lifeless flesh to jiggle and sway.

"Welcome, children. I see you've all come to visit. Decided to gang up on me, eh?" She gave a wet and unpleasant chuckle as she took us all in with her cold glare. "Have you two been wishing me dead in your jammies last night?" She pointed out two fingers at me and my mother, waggling them mockingly as she spoke. "That's real cute." She paused, seeming to consider something for a moment before continuing. "But I can tell you, it won't work. I've been at this a lot longer than any of you, and I'm a lot stronger. It's not all about who you wish bad luck onto, you know. It's also about willpower. I've shown what I'm willing to do to survive. All any of you have ever done is eat scraps and cry over spilt milk."

Her eyes raked over us. "So this is it. Last chance, last warning. Go home. Live your lives and enjoy that wonderful luck. Because if you stay, I'm going to eat you all up." Her mouth stretched into a crooked, yellow leer. I had a second to worry that my mother would cave, but then she was walking towards Emily, gun out.

"Fuck you. You've taken enough from all of us. You're going to die today, and we're here to help it along." She began to fire, each shot seemingly aimed right at Emily. Yet somehow the bullets would miss her, sending off sparks on the stone wall and marble floor behind her, tearing small chunks out of the chair she was sitting in.

Rosalyn and I joined in, both moving out in different directions so that between the three of us we were all shooting at her several feet and over 100 degrees apart. Still nothing. Her chair was a ruin now, but no bullet, no wood shrapnel, not even a speck of dirt, seemed to have touched her. I could feel my heart thudding now with confusion and fear, and this only intensified when she stood up. We were all reloading, but I didn't know if it would matter. It was clear that she wasn't afraid of our guns. As I slammed home the clip and racked the slide on my gun, I saw long curved knives appear in both of Emily's hands.

She looked at us each for a moment before settling her gaze on my mother. "My turn."

I've never seen a person move so fast. I could barely make sense of what I was seeing. She lunged forward towards my mother, who tried to move and fell in the process. The fall saved her from the first blow, but I didn't know how long her luck would hold out. Emily pivoted and struck out again, with my mother rolling to the side at the last moment. A third strike and a near miss. Then a fourth with no hit.

I felt hope begin to bloom that even if we couldn't kill Emily, she wouldn't be unable to kill us either. Then my mother screamed. The fifth blow had struck home in her stomach, and now Emily was straddling her, jamming the other knife in beside the first. I screamed and ran towards them, shoving my gun against the side of Emily's head. I pulled the trigger over and over, but nothing happened. Emily turned to look at me, her lips peeled back from her teeth, gray spittle flying out of the corners of her mouth. She was about to say something when my mother interrupted her.

I looked back to my mother in time two register two things: First, that she was telling me she loved me. Second, that she had just pulled the pin on a grenade. In a blur of motion, and before Emily could react, my mother pulled herself up to wrap her arms tightly around Emily, digging the blades deeper into her abdomen and wedging the live grenade between them. A moment later me and Rosalyn were flung back by the concussive force of the explosion.

I think I blacked out for a moment, but when I came to I realized I was unharmed. I rolled over and sat up, and some distance away I saw Rosalyn doing the same. We both turned to the smoking center of the room, where the remains of my mother lay smoldering. Emily was a couple of feet away, slowly crawling for the door as she left a slug trail of blood and burned flesh behind her.

I wanted to cry and scream, but more than that, I wanted to finish Emily. As I stood up shakily, I saw Rosalyn pulling out a thin piece of serrated wire with wooden handles on the ends. She looked as shaken as I was, but I wasn't sure she looked as shocked. In any case, there was no time to wonder now. Any moment an ambulance would pull up to save Emily, or some other improbable coincidence would intervene to her benefit. Rosalyn handed me one of the handles and together we looped the wire around the front of Emily's neck, tugging lightly as the saw teeth found purchase in her flesh. We both put a foot on one of her shoulders, stopping her struggling as we began to saw rhythmically, back and forth, as she gurgled in bloody protest. Five passes and we were to the spine. Another five and the head was off entirely.

I went to the kitchen and found some lighter fluid along with a frightened housemaid that I sent away with a shooing gesture. We burned the head until it was just black bone.

When that was done, we sat against the wall of the room in silence for some time before I spoke. I tried to make my words even and non-accusatory, but I could hear the anger in them when they came out.

"You knew she was going to sacrifice herself, didn't you?"

I was staring ahead, but I could see Rosalyn shift uncomfortably next to me. "Yeah, I did. Your plan, it was a good one. But it is what Emily would expect, and we didn't really know how strong she was." She gave a bitter laugh. "Apparently pretty strong."

Shaking her head, she continued. "But she wouldn't expect self-sacrifice from your mother. The idea wouldn't even occur to someone like her. So you were directing it towards Emily, which weakened her protection, but wouldn't allow her to be killed. But instead of joining you in wishing Emily dead, your mother was wishing it on herself. She knew that Emily would be wishing her dead too, both because she hoped to still use you in the future and because she would hate that your mother was defying her after all this time. She wouldn't be able to help herself, even if she didn't think it would amount to anything."

I shook my head. "She didn't have to do that. My plan would have worked. You should have stopped her. Or told me so I could." I glared at her, feeling my anger and grief building as the reality of it all began to sink in.

Rosalyn sighed. "Sweetie, maybe your plan would have worked. I don't know. But I know she seemed confident in being able to take all three of us, luck or no, when she was pushed to it. There aren't any guarantees in life, much less in something as fucked up as all of this. But your mother wasn't going to take that chance. She knew that her own luck would be neutralized enough for the grenade to go off, and that Emily's own luck should be weak enough for her to be hurt by the blast if she was close enough. She relied on us being okay from it and our own luck being enough to help finish Emily off. Which we did."

I understood the logic, but it didn't make me feel any better. "But she's gone now. I was just getting to know her again. Or maybe know her at all."

Rosalyn scooted over closer to me to give me a hug. At first I resisted, but she was determined and I finally gave in. After a few seconds, Rosalyn spoke again. "I know, honey. And I believe you'll see her again someday. But she needed to do this. She loved you so much, but she was so ashamed of herself. Blamed herself for so much. This was her way of protecting us and atoning a little at the same time."

I nodded, crying harder. Rosalyn called someone to come gather up my mother's remains so we could get them transported back home, and as soon as that was done, we left. We've spent the last few days in London, and as I write this we're waiting to board Rosalyn's plane back the U.S. I don't know what comes next in all of this, but that's okay. Hopefully the worst is over. I still have my luck, and I can tell I'm much stronger now—a byproduct of us killing Emily, I suppose. For now, I'm going to go home and start preparing for my baby to come. And when she gets here, I'm going to make sure she knows how lucky she is. Not because of some magic we don't understand, but because of the people that love her and the sacrifices they've made. I'll try and teach her to value what's really important, and hope that it's enough.

I wrote a letter to myself. I got a response.

Part One

I've been on my knees trying to scrub up all this blood and the scraps of paper for the last half hour. I'm making some progress, but it's slow, and I keep having to stop when my hands start shaking too much. I'm out of my apartment for the moment, sitting on the floor in the hallway, and I can feel my nerves settling some. I'm going to write this out so I'll have it all recorded and also so I can wait a bit before having to go back in.

It started when I was bored yesterday. The internet was out in my apartment, and after casting about for a couple of hours trying to read or do some cleaning, I was out of ideas to entertain myself. That's when I saw the box of stationary on my desk.

My Aunt Emma had given me the stationary as a birthday gift the week before, and there was nothing inherently wrong with such a gift—it was a box of high-quality paper and envelopes personalized with my initials at the top of the sheets of paper and on the back fold of the envelopes. As a seventy year-old man, I would probably have thought they were the cat's pajamas, but as a twenty-five year old man, not so much.

But still. I was very bored, so I sat down at my desk and started messing around with it. At first I tried writing as neatly and fancily as I knew how. My handwriting is horrible, and my best efforts looked like a slow fourth-grader as opposed to a slower second-grader, but it was something to do. Then I doodled a bit, but my drawing skills are equally lacking.

I was feeling myself getting drowsy, but then a thought occurred to me of what to do with the stationary. I'd write a letter to myself. It was a stupid idea, but I thought it was kind of funny too. So I took out a clean sheet of paper and set to work.

Hey Scott! How're you today? My day is okay if kind of boring. Christine is out-of-town visiting her parents and the internet is dead! I have zero ideas of what to do with myself. This is lame. Good-bye. Sincerely, Scott.

The novelty of the idea had clearly worn off quickly, but I did fold it up and stick it in an envelope at least, even going so far as to address the letter to myself. Standing up from the table with a sigh, I laid down and fairly soon I was fast asleep.

When I woke up, it was early evening and the room was only dimly lit by the fading twilight outside. I reached over and turned on my bedside lamp, blinking blearily at its brightness. I hated taking naps. I always felt groggy afterward and had trouble sleeping later in the night. Rubbing my eyes, I rolled discontentedly onto my side and began getting up. When my eyes lit upon my desk, I sat back down.

The envelope with the letter I had written was different now. It was in a different spot for one, but I could tell from the bed that it was also a different color and looked like it had a small stain in one corner. Standing up and going to my desk, I looked at the envelope closer before picking it up. My name and address was still on the front, but hadn't I written it smaller and more centered than that? Regardless, the envelope itself was definitely different, so clearly I hadn't written this at all.

My next thought was that someone had come into my apartment to either prank me or try and scare me. The obvious answer was Christine. It didn't really seem like something she would do, but she was the only other person with a key. After I did a quick sweep of the apartment for intruders I texted her. She swore she was still half a state away and even sent me a picture as proof. She also seemed worried and asked if I had called the cops, but I wasn't to that point yet. I needed to look inside the envelope first.

I pried it open carefully and peeked inside, seeing a light blue piece of paper that matched the envelope and was wholly different than the cream-colored paper I had used earlier in the afternoon. When I unfolded it, I was surprised to see it really did look like my handwriting, but it wasn't the same letter. Instead it seemed to be responding to mine.

Good to hear from you! I've been watching you when I can for years, and it seems like the universe has finally given us a way to talk! I'm guessing that you have apartment 3B on Nesbitt Street in Baltimore, right? And your Uncle Tom gave you the box of stationary for your birthday? It's so weird! I guess things have to line up just right. If this actually works and you are reading this, I know it will probably come as a shock. I don't think your side knows about us like we do you. But that's cool, we can swap stories! I'll keep it short for now, but hope to hear from you again soon. Glory and peace, Scott.

I read the letter three times. I really couldn't tell I didn't write it other than the content itself, which was decidedly weird. Whoever was doing this was either a very good prankster or I had a dedicated stalker that had taken the time to learn my handwriting. Either way, I was calling their bluff.

Hey, man. Good to get a response. So are you like me in some other world? That's crazy. Tell me some facts about your world and we can compare. And if you have some kind of souvenir you can send next time, that'd be awesome! Looking forward to the next letter!

I put the new letter in an envelope, addressed it and set it on my desk. I then took out my tablet, plugged it in, and set the camera to record at an angle where it could see my desk and the door to the bedroom. I thought about just sitting and waiting, but the idea was too tedious and would make it less likely anyone would come back. That was assuming this wasn't some kind of one-shot joke or harassment, but time would tell. Either way, I decided to go grab something to eat and see a movie. Four hours later I returned home to another blue letter.

I understand you being skeptical. Thinking it's all a joke, right? Well, here's some info like you asked, and I sent along something that might help convince you. Our world is a lot like yours, though it is different in some ways. About forty years ago we had a lot of animals start dying off. Not all of them, of course, but most of the birds, all of the dogs, and a few other species

here and there. Still don't know why. But around that same time we lost our mirrors.

What I mean is our mirrors stopped showing our reflections. A lot of them just went dark, but some of them, where they have twins in your world, would show us your reflections instead. We knew it was reflections because all the writing is backwards, and I can tell from your letters you don't actually write backward anyhow. Lol!

But after that, a lot of people started changing. Getting weird or violent. It's stabilized some now, but it was really bad when I was younger. A lot of people died. Anywho, like I said, things are better now, though we do have odd stuff pop up and people go missing some. Is your world like that? From what I've seen and what I know of studies people on our side have done observing active mirrors, it seems like things are a lot better over there. If so, I'm kind of jealous.

But enclosed you'll find one of our nickels. It's got President Robert Kennedy on it. He was president from 1969 through 1977. I don't know for sure, but I think I read he's one of the differences between your place and mine. Write back soon!

I looked back in the envelope and found a nickel tucked into the corner. On one side it had a man's profile with the name "Robert F. Kennedy" listed under it. On the other it had what looked like a large turkey glowering over a shield bristling with spears and covered with stars and stripes.

What. The. Fuck.

I remembered my tablet and checked the footage. It had actually stopped recording after two hours, but it was enough. At the forty-two minute mark I watched as my cream envelope gave a shudder and disappeared. Thirty minutes later the blue envelope had faded into existence a few inches over on the desk.

I wasn't sure what to do at this point. I thought about asking Christine for advice, but it would be hard to explain over the phone and I didn't want her to worry. I could call the police, but what good would it do? Even if I showed them the video they would think it was fake and I was a jackass wasting their time. I didn't know if I believed everything the letters were saying, but I couldn't deny the evidence was compelling, and if this guy really was another me, it could wind up being something really great. I might even become famous for discovering some parallel dimension.

But first things first. I needed to write another letter.

Wow, so this is big news, right? So you're saying you can see us through mirrors? That's kind of embarrassing! Can you hear us too or just see us? Do your people have any theories on how this all happened? Have other people on your world had this happen where you can talk to people from my world? I'm very curious to know more.

This time I watched as my letter disappeared, only to be replaced with another response a short time later.

Yeah, you've got a lot of questions. I understand. No, we can't hear, just see, and I don't know about anyone actually communicating like this before. No one knows why the world is changing so much. When the other things started appearing last year, people said it was the end of the world. That we were being judged. But people are just going crazy, you know? I don't believe in all that stuff. Things are changing and we just have to change with it. Hey, did you say you have a Christine? Is she a hot blond girl there too? She your girlfriend?

I didn't like the tone of the new letter, and I had even more questions now, but I wanted to keep him talking, so I tried to respond in a way that would make him happy.

Yeah, she's my girlfriend. She's great! We're planning on getting married next year. Do you have a Christine too? Tell me more about your world when you can!

My letter shuddered away fairly quickly and I waited for an answer, but none came. It was getting late, so eventually I went to bed, though I would wake up periodically and check the desk. Around six in the morning I saw the blue envelope and I jumped out of bed to read the two lines written there.

I did have a Christine. But she was a fucking whore. I had to punish her. I hope yours isn't a whore too. Lol!

I was done. I didn't know what this was, but I knew it had to be real and it was feeling more and more like it was dangerous. Throwing the letter down, I started looking around the room. I saw the small mirror I had hanging on the back of my closet and I yanked it down quickly, hearing it crack as it hit the floor. I tried to think of any others, and the only ones that came to mind were in the bathroom and the one Christine had hung over the mantle in the living room.

Christine!

I looked at my phone and saw it was almost seven. She was going to be back in town this morning, probably coming straight here. I tried calling her, but it went straight to voicemail like it was powered off. I didn't have her parents' number, so I had to resort to leaving her a voicemail and text message telling her not to come to my apartment, that I would meet her at hers when she got back.

I debated what to do until she arrived, but ultimately decided I couldn't stand being in the apartment myself, so I left a note on the door saying "Christine, don't go in the apartment. Call me instead. I'll explain and meet you" and left the building. For the next few hours I basically drove a circuit between our two apartments, occasionally parking outside one place or the other. I was sitting outside her place when I got a call from her phone.

It was her mother. She said Christine had knocked her phone in the toilet getting ready for bed last night and they had put it in a bowl of rice to dry it out. When Christine left to come back home a few hours ago, she must have forgotten it. I felt my mouth go dry. Her mother was asking what she should do to get Christine the phone, but I told her I'd have to call her back and hung up. Based on when she left, she should have been back at least an hour at that point. I knew she wasn't at her apartment, so I sped back over to mine.

I saw her car parked down the street from my place and my head started pounding. Running up the stairs, I reached my door and saw the note I had left was gone. In its place was a blue sheet of nice stationary bearing a drawing of a red ink heart and the words "Come on in!" in my handwriting.

I started yelling her name as I fumbled the door open, but as I entered I could tell she wasn't there. The apartment felt empty and lifeless. I ran to the bedroom, stumbling to a stop at the doorway. My mind had difficulty making sense of what it was seeing at first. On the wall next to my desk there were strips of paper plastered to the wall and making the outline of a small door about three-feet tall. The strips seemed to be some combination of blue and cream paper, speckled here and there with spots of crimson and soggy near the baseboard where there were partial bloody handprints on both sides as though someone had been trying to hold on.

Leading away from the paper door the floor was covered with more blood, and as I looked closer I could see several thick runnels in the wood that I thought at first were scrapes or cuts of some kind by something heavy being drug. But then I saw one of Christine's bloody fingernails, torn off at the nailbed and ragged, jutting out of one of the grooves she had raked into the floor in her fight to get away.

I collapsed to the floor and began crying. After a few minutes I pulled myself together enough to look around the room for any other clues or some means of helping her. That's when I saw the blue envelope on the desk.

You were right, she's a hot one. Better than mine even. But I can tell she has those same slutting ways. It's in the eyes. But don't you worry. She'll find less tolerance for that over here, and I'll be sure to keep her corrected. Don't bother trying to come across either, bud. I figured out how to do it, but I'm going to have to keep it close to my vest. I have to apologize for not being completely honest before. Things are worse here than I let on. Maybe this Christine can keep me happy and satisfied with my life, but whose to say? Like I told you, some people are really losing it over here. Might be I have to come visiting again some time. More permanently. Till then, glory and peace. Or as you would say, Sincerely, Scott.

As I'm finishing writing this, I dread going back into that room. I know I have no way of getting her back and I know I can't have her blood being found in my apartment. Even without hard evidence, there will be questions when she's reported missing. But all of that is in the background at the moment. I can't shake the feeling of being watched. I look around and see no one, but then I notice the dingy brass door of the elevator across the hall from where I'm sitting.

The reflection there is dark and distorted, but I can still see myself in it, or at least a version of myself. It looks like me, but I can tell that it isn't. Because that version of me is laughing.

Part Two

Scott, I know you're a good guy at heart. I know that because, well, you're me. And despite my flaws, I like to think I'm a good guy too. I understand that your world is different than mine and that has to have affected you a lot. Whose to say what you would be doing, who you would be as a person, if you had grown up like I did? My point is, I don't blame you for anything. I just need you to listen to me.

I spent a lot of time with my Dad growing up. I don't know if that was true for you, or what your version of Dad was even like, but mine was great. He was always there for me, and not just out of some sense of parental duty, but because he really loved me and wanted me to succeed in life.

One thing we did a lot was go hunting. Sometimes for wild pig or rabbit, but mostly for deer. I remember the first time I killed a deer. It wasn't a clean shot, and we had to track it over a mile before finding it dead in some underbrush at the edge of an empty field. My father took out his knife to show me how to field dress it, but before he handed it to me he stopped and put his hand on my shoulder.

"You never kill things or hurt things unless it is necessary either for your survival or some greater good. This deer is clean, healthy meat that will feed us and your mom for several weeks. Us being willing or able to kill this deer doesn't make its life unimportant. It just means that we have to value ourselves above others while still trying to live a good and virtuous life. You understand?" I said that I did, and I was being honest at the time,

but of course that was the understanding of a child, and the world has taught me to more fully appreciate the importance of his words now.

My father would also tell me stories about his own childhood. My favorites were always about the dog he had growing up named Rex. Dad had gotten him when he was eight, and he loved that dog more than anything. They really were best friends I think. They would play together, explore the forests around the farm where my dad grew up, and were generally inseparable as much as life allowed.

When Dad got old enough to drive, Rex would ride everywhere with him. He was big for a dog apparently, so he could easily sit in his seat and stick his head out the window to catch smells as they drove to town or out to go camping.

My version of our father never went to college, but he was a smart man and a hard-worker. He opened up a little hardware store at 19, and within a couple of years he had bought a house and was saving up ring money for the girl that is our mother.

One night, as he was closing up the shop, he heard Rex start growling. He turned to see where the dog was and found him at the back door, hackles raised and teeth bared. At first my father thought it was a raccoon or another dog maybe. He grabbed Rex by the collar and opened the door to look out. It was dark and he couldn't see much, but suddenly he was knocked down and being attacked. He would never say by what, though I've always suspected that was more to keep from scaring me too much than because he didn't know.

Rex broke free of his grasp and charged the thing, whatever it was. He snapped and snarled, bit and clawed, and after a moment my father was free of it. It was preoccupied by Rex, who was fighting it for everything he was worth. He was an older dog now, but no one was going to mess with our daddy.

Rex drove the thing off into the woods, but he was hurt badly. Too badly to make it, in fact. My father held him crying as he died.

The first time Dad told me that story, I was fifteen. I was horrified. I had been hearing stories about Rex for years. I loved

Rex, felt like I knew him even though he died well before I was born. And truth be told, Rex wouldn't have lived that much longer anyway, but still. It was so sad.

I sat there crying my eyes out, and I remember my father started crying too. It was one of the few times I ever saw him cry. He reached over and hugged me before explaining why he was telling me the story in the first place.

"Scott, this world is a hard place, and it's only going to get harder. Rex and me...we loved each other with everything we had, and he sacrificed himself to save me. That's the lesson. If you are going to live a life worth living, you can't be afraid to make sacrifices. Whether it's something that is important to you or to someone else, sometimes a cost has to be paid and you have to be willing to pay it. Being too afraid or too weak to do what needs to be done is a greater sin than trying and failing or making the wrong choice. Always remember that."

And I have, Scott. I've tried to make the best decisions in my life, and all things considered, things have turned out well for me. For instance, I remember the first time I saw our Christine. I felt such a strong surge of excitement and anticipation that I didn't even know what to say to her. And later, when we made love for the first time, I remember she cried. If I'm honest, I cried a little too.

And I think I was too hard on her initially, Scott. I thought she was a whore like the old Christine, but I think living in a softer, kinder world kept her from developing some of those rough edges that I was trying to wear down on old Christine. She's still got a slut look about her face at times, so she bears watching, but I do think she can be rehabilitated if you are firm with her.

I want to apologize to you too, Scott. When I came back and took you by surprise in your bed...well, I'll be honest, I was disappointed. I expected more of a fight. But you were half asleep, and just like our Christine, you've had the luxury of a softer life than I've had. I don't think less of you because you couldn't stop me from forcing you through the door.

I also want to say I'm sorry because I know from your perspective I may seem like a bad guy. I took your girl—and then you—from this cushy life and pushed you into a world that, well, from your point of view might seem a bit like hell. I want you to know I didn't do that out of some ill will towards you or even Christine. But I had to get out of there, and sacrifices had to be made. And those sacrifices are valued by me, Scott. It's important that you know that.

Don't worry about trying to get back, either. I know from the peeks I've managed to get in the last couple of weeks that you were trying, and you had figured out that combining our two papers was a part of it, but you won't get the rest. And I made sure to not leave any of your letters or envelopes on my side anyway. This letter and envelope will be the only paper from your old world you will have, and trust me, it isn't enough. I don't say this to trick or discourage you, but because I don't want you wasting time and energy chasing some impossible goal when you should be focused to getting your feet under you and making a new life.

I really hope you two crazy kids make a go of it over there. Lol! Whose to say? You might be better at that life than I ever was. As for me, I just got back from walking in the park across from your...I mean my...apartment. It seemed like I could hear birds singing everywhere! And I saw a woman walking a dog! Can you believe it? A real, live dog!

I know this world isn't perfect. I can already see a lot of impurity and corruption. Maybe I can help correct some of that in time. But for now, I'm just going to enjoy my new life. I won't be writing you again I'm afraid, but I'll think of you often. I'm going this afternoon to buy a puppy. I'd name it after you, but well, that'd be weird. Lol! Have a good life! Sincerely, Scott.

Part Three

I woke to ashes fluttering down onto my face like sullen snowflakes, covering my skin in a hundred gray kisses of burned down yesterday. I coughed as I sat up, pulling in another spasmodic breath as I wiped at my eyes. The ashes had caked there because I had apparently been crying in my unconsciousness. My hands came away black and running as my eyes began to water again, and blinking through the smut and the tears, I could see the flakes falling down on me through a hole in the roof. Or rather the ceiling, because Scott's apartment wasn't on the top floor.

Yet looking around, it was Scott's apartment, or a very close approximation of it. It was far more run down and dirty, and some of the decorations were different, but the layout and the general appearance was similar. My head was still drifting through a fog so thick I could scarcely tell I was even in a fog, but I was starting to remember myself and Scott, and parts of what had happened. I looked up again and remembered that there should be at least three floors above this one, and at the edges of the hole in the ceiling I could see parts of those ruined rooms hiding in the shadows up there. It seemed that the top part of the building had been destroyed somehow at some point in the past, and through the hole that was left behind I could see the ashes, and beyond that, the stars.

I came back to myself again as I remembered Scott attacking me. Well, not Scott, but someone that looked like him. A lot. Like some older, crazy twin brother. He had dragged me into Scott's bedroom, and I had seen that the floor and wall were covered in blood. He dipped his finger in the blood and traced the outline of a rectangle inside the perimeter of a strange collage of colored paper pasted to the wall. I had felt amazement push through my terror as I saw a crack appear in the wall where his finger had traced, and at his touch, it swung open as a door.

I had known then what was coming next, however insane or impossible all of this was. I fought harder to get away, but he was bigger and stronger, and when he slammed my head against the floor the second time, I couldn't fight the darkness that rose up around me any longer.

I felt the back of my head at the memory and gasped at the pain as my hand found a clotting wound in my sweaty tangle of hair. I started looking around again, and I could see I was in the living room of this place that is like Scott's apartment but not. My brain had been screaming a thousand things that are wrong since I first woke up, but I could only process a few at a time. Just as I realized that Not Scott was coming back from the bedroom, my hand found its way up to my throat and the dog collar there.

"Hello, Christine." His grin was so like Scott's that its familiarity made it all the more ghastly on this man. His face was thin and his eyes were two bright pieces of glass in sunken pits, glittering with intelligence and ill will. I could now see that it somehow was Scott, despite the longer hair and the harder, harsher lines of his face. It just wasn't my Scott. I didn't know how it was possible, but once the thought was fixed in my mind, I knew it was true.

"Hello. Where did you take me?" I tried to sound confident, but it was a weak attempt given I was sitting hurt and confused in a dog collar in some bizarre place with some bizarre version of Scott.

His smile widened. "That's a fair question. This is my world. I brought you from yours after hearing good things about you from Scott. Well, the other Scott." He raised his hands in a placating gesture. "Look, I know what you're thinking. I kidnapped you, knocked you out and brought you to this place. Hell, I put a collar on you. I guess this all looks really bad, huh?"

He crouched down on his haunches next to me. "I brought you here because I miss my old Christine. See, we were together here too, but things didn't work out well. I'm not saying it wasn't selfish to take you away, but it was with love in my heart. And as for this," he pointed to the dog collar, "I just wanted to make sure you didn't run out if I wasn't awake or paying attention when you came to. My world is pretty different from yours, and it's not safe out there a lot of the time. I wouldn't want you getting hurt on my account."

I stared at him, trying to keep any scorn out of my expression. He was clearly insane, and I didn't want to risk setting him off, especially when I really didn't know what was going on or what this place was like. And that was the key. I needed as much information as possible and I needed to see how much latitude I could get before trying to escape.

"So you'll take the collar off now?"

He chuckled and shook his head. "I can already tell I'm going to like you better." Sighing wistfully he went on. "No, not yet, honey. It'll take some time for you to acclimate, and until you do,

I'm afraid you'll be your own worst enemy. For now, just rest and I'll bring you some food. Your chain goes far enough for you to reach the bathroom over there, just remember do not flush it during nighttime hours, okay? That's very important. This building is fairly secure, but the neighborhood has gone to shit lately. Lots of home invasions at night and they target buildings where they hear noise or see lights. The blinds keep the light in pretty well, but the pipes in this old bitch kick up a fuss when you flush, so just save that for the morning and we should be shiny golden."

The next few days were a cycle of sleeping, eating, and trying to figure out the best way to escape and where exactly I would be escaping to. The last part was primarily facilitated by Not Scott. He spent hours each day talking to me, seemingly starved for conversation and human contact. He had some kind of job, and depending on something he called "occurrence reports", he would be gone working for periods of time most days. But whenever he was there he was usually talking to me.

He would tell me stories about himself sometimes, but a lot of his time was spent asking me questions. What was my childhood like, what had my life been like before he took me, what kinds of things did I like to do, like to eat, etc. It was all so strange. He had this aura of discord and violence around him so palpable the air fairly vibrated with menace when he was in the room, but he was never rough or even rude to me aside from the obvious of holding me against my will.

It was made stranger because parts of him did remind me of my Scott. The way his face would light up when he was telling a story, or the way that he would look at me sometimes when he didn't know I was looking. It somehow made it all worse instead of better, seeing those glimpses of something I loved being choked to death by whatever sickness had taken root in him.

I tried to find out more about the world I was in from him, and he told me some, but not much. He said that years ago, before he was born, things had started changing. A lot of animals had started dying off for no discernable reason and all at once. This had led to the partial collapse of a number of ecosystems around the world, which lead to disease and famine and death. According to Not Scott, things stabilized some eventually, but they were never really right again. Strange things would happen. People would disappear or go on murder sprees. Pods of dolphins started killing off large portions of the shark and whale populations in the Pacific. Then in 1998, over 200,000 people across the globe committed suicide within ten minutes of each other for no apparent reason. People called it the Awakening now, because that was when the world governments and media began admitting that there was an ongoing major problem and they didn't know how to stop it.

Not Scott told me with a laugh that it wasn't like the world was ending, but sometimes it sure felt like it. After the Awakening, a lot of fanatics started popping up. Religious zealots, doomsday preppers, militant groups itching for a fight. He said those groups caused disorder and could be dangerous to be around, but mostly they were just scared people looking for an answer. And for the most part, civilization was still chugging along. Governments existed, people went to work, and as time went on, strange became the new normal.

Then people started going insane. Not the normal, scared "I'm going to wear a bullet proof vest to the grocery store" insane, but more the "I'm going to eat the bus driver's face" insane. He said that actually happened to him when he was riding the metro one day. People turning crazy didn't happen a lot at first, but in the last five years it was building. There were more random acts of extreme violence—a teacher chopping up her third-grade class, a little boy stabbing out his father's eyes while he slept—but there were more subtle versions of it too.

People would develop strange obsessions or fetishes. They would become paranoid or have wild mood swings for no apparent reason. Not Scott said that most days at work there would be at least one or two people crying or laughing uncontrollably at random times throughout the day.

He had tears in his eyes when he told me that last, and I felt my heart breaking a little at what he said next.

"I know it's happening to me. It's happened to me already. I've done terrible things. Not just what I've done to you and to your

Scott…I've done much worse than that. I…I used to not be like this."

I reached forward and took his hand. "I can't imagine what you've been through. And I'm not saying you can fix everything, but you can make it better. Let me go back. You come too. If this world is what is making you do these bad things, maybe you'll be better away from it."

Not Scott pulled his hand away, his face hardening. "I should have expected this kind of cozening from you. You're not as different as I'd hoped." Standing up, he wiped his eyes with the palms of his hands as he stared off, his expression hurt and almost embarrassed. "You aren't leaving and there's no real hope for me either beyond embracing this world as it is. Letting it reshape me so I can survive it." He looked back down at me. "You best get to accepting your reality too. It's a hard world and it's going to get harder."

After that he talked to me a lot less, though some nights he would sit with me for awhile, saying very little but seeming to not want to be alone. Other nights he would seem different, a dark look on his face more akin to when I first saw him upon waking. Those nights I just tried to stay inconspicuous and small.

He didn't tell me much more about the world outside other than that there were worse problems now than just people going crazy. But I could hear signs of the chaos outside. Gunshots, screaming, and the orange glow of distant fires were a regular part of life. I asked about what had happened to the building and he said a television helicopter had crashed into it a couple of years back, taking out most of the top three floors. It had only put the small hole in Not Scott's ceiling and caused minimal structural damage to the rest of the building, so he had stayed. He grinned and said he'd negotiated the rent down and decided to look at it like a skylight.

And the days moved on.

I need to stress again that after he got me here, he never hurt me. He was generally kind in fact. He didn't threaten me, he didn't try to force himself on me or even come on to me sexually. And the things we talked about, they seemed harmless. Combine that with the fact that in a lot of ways Not Scott was Scott, and it made it easier to be taken in.

Looking back on it now, I see that peppered into our conversations were questions that would prompt me to talk about my Scott, to talk about my world. As I told him stories of my parents or my ninth birthday or my college major, I was giving him information and insight into a place he was desperate to learn more about. He was smart about it. Subtle. But over time I was handing him everything he wanted.

I had let myself forget I wasn't dealing with my Scott, but just afflicted with some strange mental illness. I was dealing with a stranger.

I remembered that fact when he brought her in, screaming and crying, snot pouring from her nose as he dragged her by the arm across the living room and into the bedroom. He tried to shut the door back when they entered, but in her flailing she kicked it and it swung back open as he brought the knife down across her stomach. As blood welled out of the wound, she raised her head and her eyes met mine. She couldn't have been more than eight years old.

Not Scott followed her gaze and saw the door was open. He looked at me, his face pale and stricken. "I'm sorry you saw this, Christine. I'm just doing what's necessary to survive. Tell him I left the key to your collar in my closet." With that, he slammed the door shut. It muffled the girl's last gurgling scream, but not nearly enough.

I screamed at the door, begging him to stop, but I knew it was no use. It was more just to make myself feel better and to vent my frustration. For the hundredth time I strained at my collar and tugged at my chain, but he had secured both well. I finally gave up, my throat hoarse and my body exhausted.

Even amid my struggling and thrashing about, I had noticed that the bedroom had fallen silent. As I lay there panting, I strained to hear any sound. There was nothing for several minutes, then a series of small scuffling noises followed by the sound of something being drug. Then silence again. I debated yelling, but I knew it was too late for the girl, so I stayed quiet. When the door suddenly burst open, I let out a scream.

Scott was standing there, his face and clothes smeared with blood. He was squinting and seemed unsteady on his feet, but when he saw me, his eyes widened.

"Christine?"

Part Four

I woke to hands around my throat, choking off my air as I swam out of the black currents of sleep and opened my eyes to see a face eerily similar to mine staring down at me. The other Scott was straddling me, bearing down hard as I started trying to flail and get free. His arms prevented me from getting a good hit in on his head, so I tried punching him in the sides. He grunted at each impact, but was unmoved.

I tried to make eye contact, mouth something to him, but he wouldn't meet my eyes--seemed to be avoiding them, in fact. He just stared at his hands around my throat, lips skinned back from his teeth in some kind of snarl or grimace below eyes that looked almost sorrowful. This somehow scared me worse.

I started fighting back harder, trying to buck him off while slamming an elbow into his arm, hoping to break his grip. But he was too strong, and I could already feel myself slipping back into the icier waters of unconsciousness. As I faded out, I had time to worry if my shoes were still on and to hear him say he was sorry. When I woke next, I was facedown on the floor, the left side of my head wet with some kind of viscous liquid. I wiped at my left eye and then opened them both experimentally.

I was in a version of my bedroom, but I could tell it wasn't mine. I looked around slowly, my throat aching with every breath as I sat up. The room was empty and the door was shut, and I had to fight the urge to rush out and search for Christine. I needed to be smart. Take my time and take everything in.

With revulsion I noticed my hand was wet with blood from where I had wiped my head. My entire side was soaked in fact, as was the floor. I felt a lurch of fear in my stomach that he had killed Christine before he came back across to get me, but I tried to hold it at bay as I studied the rest of the room. Nothing that noteworthy other than that he had five mirrors hanging in different spots in the room, all of which were dark. I looked to the corner of the ceiling above the bed and breathed a sigh of relief when I saw no mirror there.

Turning to the wall, I saw that he had stripped away the paper he used to make the doorway on this side. I guessed he had replicated it on the other side so it would stay open while he destroyed this side, but aside from the paper I still had no real idea how it was done. Given the fresh blood, it seemed likely that was a part of it. Again I had a thrill of fear for Christine, and this time I couldn't resist it.

Standing up stiffly, I went to the door and yanked it open. A woman screamed, and as I looked across the dimly lit living room, I saw it was Christine. She looked terrified, and she was chained to the wall by some kind of collar, but she was alive.

"Christine?"

She blinked, her mouth slowly closing as she took me in. After a moment she started to stand, her face shifting between fear and hopefulness. "Scott? Is that really you?"

I wanted to run to her, but I could tell she was freaked out, so I approached slowly. "It's me, baby. Did he hurt you? Are you okay?"

Her face crumpled as she ran to me, almost knocking me over with the force of her embrace. "Thank God. Oh God oh God oh God." I stayed quiet and hugged her back, and after a minute she pulled back, her expression serious and more composed. "Is he gone?"

I nodded. "I think so. He jumped me when I was asleep and drug me here. I was unconscious, but I didn't see any sign of him when I woke up. He didn't come back out of the room did he?" She shook her head. "Then he must be over in our world. The fucker wanted to take my life and now he has." I caught myself and smiled sadly at her. "But it'll be okay. We'll figure things out." I reached out to stroke her hair, but she pulled back.

"I…I'm sorry, Scott. I'm so happy to see you, but it…he looks so much like you and I've been stuck here for two weeks with him. It's going to take me a bit to readjust, that's all." She took a couple of steps back, her hands holding her elbows as she smiled apologetically at me. "But I'm okay. I'll be okay. What about you?"

Trying to hide the pain and guilt I felt at her words, I turned away to take in the living room. "I'm fine. He choked me out, but I'm okay other than a sore throat." I glanced back at her. "I…I'm so sorry for this. I know this is all insane and out of our control, but it's still a version of me that's doing it." I wanted to ask about the details of how he may have mistreated her, but I didn't want to make it any harder on her than it already had been, and we could talk about it later when she was ready. So instead I added lamely, "I know he's crazy, and I hope you know I'm not anything like him."

Christine reached out and touched my arm. "Hey. I know that. You're not him and I know you're not like him. And honestly, I almost felt sorry for him at times. I haven't seen it, but from what I can tell and what he said about it, this place is really fucked up. Dangerous fucked up. He said people were going crazy here, and I think that was part of his problem too." She pulled her arm back, her voice trembling slightly. "Do you know how to get us back?"

I shook my head as I turned away again, ashamed to look at her any longer. "I've been trying to figure it out ever since you were taken, but I don't know yet. I communicated with him through that stationary my aunt gave me. He did the same with some an uncle of his on this side had given him. That paper, the two combined together, is how he makes the doorways. But no matter what I do, nothing seems to work."

Out of the corner of my eye I saw Christine's face fall with despair. I pointed into the bedroom and went on. "There's blood in there. A lot of it. And there was blood in my bedroom when you were taken too. I was afraid it was yours, but it wasn't was it?" She hesitated and then shook her head. "Okay, that's what I was thinking. The blood has to be part of it then. Did you see how he did it?"

Again that strange pause and then she gave a quick nod. "I saw him draw the shape of a door in blood. Inside the paper outline like you talked about. Is the paper still there?" She looked past me into the bedroom. "Did he take it when he left?"

Finally I had some good news. "He did, but I have more. When I realized I might not figure out how to get across to you on my own, I started hoping he would come back for me. I took to sleeping with my shoes on every night, and I kept the strips of paper I had saved tucked into the bottoms of them. If we can figure out how to create the doorway, I have the paper to do it."

Her expression brightened for the first time and she grabbed my hand, pulling me into the bedroom. "Try it! Maybe it will work."

I took the strips of paper from my shoes and for the next few minutes we pasted them carefully in an alternating pattern of cream and blue. As far as I could tell, it was close to exactly how he had them arranged when he took Christine. Then, dipping a pencil eraser in the thickening blood on the floor, I traced the outline as she directed. It did nothing.

After a couple of minutes of waiting, I tried again. No change. Suddenly Christine pushed past me, her fingers dripping with blood. She frantically traced and retraced the outline over and over, but to no avail. Screaming, she punched the wall and fell back in a heap on the floor. I realized that her hand wasn't covered in the blood from the floor, but was bleeding itself.

"What happened? How did your hand get hurt?" I started to reach out to her, but her dark look stopped me.

"I bit it. Just now. I thought maybe it needed fresher blood or something other than a fucking eraser wiping it on the wall. I don't know. Not Scott is the one that did this bullshit, not Christine." She sighed deeply and seemed to regain control. "I'm sorry. I know this isn't your fault. But we need to get out of here." Her bloody hand touched her collar. "Fuck, this thing is still on. He said the key is in his closet. I can't reach it."

I swallowed and nodded, jumping up to check the closet. Inside I found a small assortment of clothes and a couple of pairs of shoes, but the rest of the closet was devoted to books. They were stacked on a shelf at the top and in neat piles along the closet's walls. Most of them looked to be fantasy or science fiction, many by authors I had never heard of, a few by authors who had never written those particular books in my world. On top of the closest book stack was a key.

After Christine was free, we searched the apartment over for any clues of how to reopen the door. Thirty minutes later we were back in the living room, Christine staring at the floor forlornly while I tried to figure out something comforting to say.

"Look, it'll work out. We'll figure it out. But it may take some time." Her expression didn't change and I went on. "I need to go out and get us some supplies. Figure out if this place is even anything like what he said. Maybe it's not half bad and he's just a crazy liar." I knew the unspoken subtext of what I was saying was that hopefully it would be nice because we might be stuck here, but I couldn't quite bear to say it. Instead the idea of being marooned in this place just hung between us like some kind of noxious cloud, slowly killing the little hope we had left. As I was thinking this, I realized Christine was on her feet.

"You're right. Let's go and see what this place is even like."

I thought about protesting, asking that she stay at the apartment in case the outside world was dangerous, but I could tell she was determined to go and it would be good if there were two of us. Between us we managed to find a pair of long kitchen knives and a flashlight along with a light jacket with pockets I could store the items in while we traveled. Then we were off.

Stepping out of the apartment, the ill-repair of the hallway matched the hole in the ceiling of the apartment. The only thing in sight that looked cleaned or well-maintained was the elevator, the brass of which carried a mirror-like sheen. I stopped and looked at the reflection there, but saw nothing. At her questioning look, I explained my encounter in the hallway to Christine. She said "Not Scott", as she called him, had told her some about the mirrors but not a lot. She asked how I'd been able to see him back in the reflection on the elevator, and I realized I didn't know.

But by then we were pushing out of the downstairs outside door. When we stepped out, the first thing that struck me was how quiet the city was. How still. It was still early, but in our world there would already be people out and cars bustling along the narrow lanes of the street that ran in front of the apartment building. There would be sounds of nature mixed in as well, even if it was just the occasional bird song or dog bark.

Here there were a handful of cars driving down the street, and the people driving them seemed to either be staring straight ahead as though their gazes were welded to the road in front of them or constantly looking in every direction, seemingly terrified of some surprise attack. It was hard to say which was the better idea.

We turned to the left and made our way down to what would be a corner grocery store in our world. Along the way we passed only a couple of people, and they were both walking determinedly on the far sidewalk. They shot us wary glances but that was all, and my attempt at waving hello to the second person was ignored.

At the end of the block we found that Patterson's Grocery Store was now Patterson's Package Shop, but when we entered we found that aside from a large volume of alcohol the place still sold various food and drinks. Sticking close to each other, we selected a small variety of items and headed toward the front. Money didn't seem to be an issue for the moment, as Not Scott had left a small stack of bills and a debit card with the PIN taped to it sitting on the kitchen counter. The bills were red and reminded me of Monopoly money, but when I handed the cashier a hundred dollar bill, he took it without complaint and gave me a handful of strange change in return, including another RFK nickel.

On the way out we were almost run over by a large teenage boy barreling into the store past us. As he cleared the threshold, he started yelling about how he needed "fresh ciggies for my mam. Get them up for her, you cozening fucker." I propelled Christine out onto the sidewalk, but not before I heard the cashier scream back that the boy's mother had been dead for three years.

We exchanged a look, and I debated suggesting we just head back to the apartment, but Christine was already opening a bottle of water and cutting across the street. There was starting to be more traffic now, but the flow of people was still anemic. I made the comment that this is what the world would be like after some plague in a movie where half the people had been wiped out.

Christine had shot me a glance, her face hard. “I don’t know that it’s that far from the truth.” She pointed ahead to Bristow Park, which was actually called the same thing here as well. “Let’s go in there and see if there are any people out.”

Our version of Bristow Park was always bustling with people in the morning. On the weekends it would be families and casual games of football or frisbee, but even the weekdays saw a steady stream of joggers, dog walkers, and miscellaneous others. At first, we thought this version of the park was largely empty, but then Christine heard singing.

The outer paths of the park follow cultivated hedges and trees, curving and winding along the park perimeter with inlets into the more central areas every hundred yards or so. Even when you start down one of those inner paths, it takes more than a few steps before the large open spaces at the center of the park are revealed.

As we were walking along the outer path, Christine suddenly cut onto one of the inner paths, murmuring that she heard music. I followed, but at first I heard nothing. It was only as we were stepping onto the dying grass of the central field that I heard the faint singing or chanting that was coming from the throng of people clustered around the enormous bonfire in the distance.

Christine was walking towards the group quickly and after a few more paces I grabbed her arm and stopped her. She turned to me, her eyes fierce and her voice low and trembling when she spoke. “What are they doing? Do you see that?”

I had been more focused on Christine as we had drawn nearer, but as I looked again, I saw exactly what they were doing.

The bonfire was not really a bonfire. It was a twenty-foot metal frame in the shape of an X, the lower half squatter and much thicker than the top. Inside the frame, wood had been carefully inserted throughout and set ablaze. That was all very strange, but I only noted it in a perfunctory way as I watched the man catching fire.

The man had been stripped naked and chained at each wrist, the lengthy metal bindings trailing off into the crowd on each side of the burning X. The man was in the middle between the burning effigy's legs, the top of the white-hot metal only inches from his head. The air around him shimmered with the heat, his skin blackening and peeling off as he was jerked back and forth from one side of the X to the other at the whims of the crowds pulling the chains.

We were still fifty yards away, but when a breeze shifted direction I could smell the pungently sweet smell of his flesh cooking even as I heard him scream. I was about to start pulling Christine away when I stopped, my skin growing cold.

The man wasn't screaming. He was laughing.

I tugged weakly at Christine and she glanced at me, her eyes wet and wide. We began to back away slowly, and I was terrified at any moment we would be noticed. But the crowd was transfixed, and even when the man stopped laughing and slumped forward, they kept him aloft and dancing like some kind of macabre tug-of-war.

We edged our way back to the perimeter of the field. In my last look before we headed back to the path and out of the park, I saw the cooked meat of the man begin to pull apart as the mob ripped him in two. I swear I could hear the wet gasping of his skin as it ruptured, the greasy crackle of his weaker bones as they flexed and snapped, but it seemed impossible at such a distance. Real or imagined, I had to stop and vomit on the path, Christine patting my back and telling me to please hurry.

We exited the park and wasted no time returning to the apartment. I could feel Christine's terror and knew my own matched it, but I felt no closer to an answer than I had before. We didn't talk about what we had seen, but Christine did take my hand and sit silently with me for awhile. I could tell we were both starting to slip into shock or some despondent form of madness. We had to do something. Getting up, I started searching the apartment again for anything we might have missed.

That's when I found a cream-colored envelope on the bedroom desk. I opened it and read it, then read it again, my heart pounding. When I gave it to Christine, she studied it for a long time before looking up at me. She was about to speak, but I couldn't hold it in any longer and blurted out:

"Did he rape you?"

Scott's face was worried, hurt and scared all at the same time as he asked, and I could feel myself loving him and hating him for asking the question. I knew he was concerned for my well-being, that he loved me. And I knew that he felt guilty because of who had taken me. But there was still something so selfish in him asking. So childish in him needing to be comforted if I had been raped, or even better, him hoping I could reassure him that whatever brutalities I had endured at Not Scott's hands weren't as bad as all that so he could start pretending this wasn't his fault.

Because it was his fault. I saw that now. Not necessarily because it was an alternate version of him, but because he had talked to Not Scott, responded to him, told him about me. I was trying not to be angry with him, but I was so hurt and scared and we had to get out of this place.

I had already been toying with the idea of lying to Scott after reading Not Scott's letter. I had no idea why Not Scott had lied about raping me, whether it was due to his insanity, natural cruelty, or just to make Scott hate him more. It didn't matter. If it could drive Scott's guilt and his anger long enough to force him to do what had to be done, it was a blessing. And if Scott's sad face and worried tone made it easier to tell the lie, so be it. I could ask for forgiveness when we weren't in Hell anymore.

"Yes. He did. He started the second day, and it got worse as the days went on. More…extreme." I was going to try and fake tears, but I found there was no need. After everything, after what we had just witnessed, tears were going to come easily for some time.

I saw Scott's face darken as his fists balled at his sides. That's the response I was hoping for. I waited a moment for him to stew and then I went on. "And I lied before. I do know a bit more about how to make the door work. Not Scott killed a little girl. He used her blood to open the door." Some of that was guesswork on my part, but I had seen enough to make it an educated guess.

Scott's eyes widened some, but he still looked hard and determined. "Then that's what we'll do. I'll find someone and take blood from them." I winced and he stopped. "What is it? What's wrong?"

I licked my lips. Ask for forgiveness when you aren't in Hell. "Scott…I mean, Not Scott told me that it had to be from a child and the blood only worked as they were dying. I didn't want to tell you because it's so horrible, but I don't think there's any other way to get us home."

This too was a lie, of course, as Not Scott had never told me any such thing. But it made sense. The leftover blood of the girl hadn't worked and neither had my own fresh blood. So we needed to replicate what Not Scott had done as closely as possible as soon as possible. I didn't…We didn't have time for Scott to moralize, try to think up humane alternatives, let the edge his emotions were giving him now grow dull with time and equivocation. No. We…

"We have to get out of here. I have to make this right and get you out of here. If I have to do something horrible to do that, that'll be on me." His eyes were glimmering, but his voice didn't falter. "I'll go find someone right now so we can be done with it."

I reached out and squeezed his hand. "I'll help."

Part Five

I woke to something licking my face. I reached out in my sleep fog and feeling short, soft fur, I realized that Tricksy had somehow made it onto the bed. Opening my eyes, I saw his happy smushed face as he gave me another lick, clearly proud at having gotten up on the bed somehow.

The girl at the pet store had said he was called a Pug, and from the moment I saw him I knew he was the weirdest and cutest thing I'd ever seen. I had always been fascinated by dogs growing up, only in part because of Dad's stories about Rex, but I had never seen a dog like this in any of the old pictures. An hour later I had him home, getting his bed and food ready while he explored the apartment with a manic, bouncy determination.

Ruffling his fur, I pondered trying to go back to sleep, but I knew it was a lost cause. In the five days since I wrote my last letter to the other Scott, I had been having more and more trouble sleeping. I had a lot of guilt for what I had done to him and Christine, and the longer I was out of that place, the more I felt it.

Living in that other world, my old world, I had come to feel like I was trapped inside myself. When I had first started noticing the change in myself a couple of years back, I was worried but also strangely intrigued. It was like I was standing at the edge of some newly formed cave, and each day I went into it a little deeper and a little more frequently. But over time, the light from outside didn't penetrate the darkness nearly as well and I would get lost in the black. I would blindly traverse jagged rocks as unseen things crept around me, and when I finally found my way back out, I would swear it was the last time I would go near the thing. But then I would go back in.

That's the funny thing about madness. It makes you feel like you have a choice. Like the options you pick are reasonable or justified, and then when you look back in horror at what you've done, you feel completely responsible for everything. And I am. I'm not trying to make excuses or pawn off all that I've done on whatever corruption is slowly eating that other world. I earned this guilt…this taint…honestly and through my own works, and I'll carry it with me always.

But that's part of why I love Tricksy so much. Aside from him being sweet and cute and generally awesome, he also doesn't know what a despicable piece of shit I really am.

For the thousandth time in the last few days I look at the wall next to the desk. I both fear and hope to see a doorway open there most of the time. I'm terrified of going back, and if they ever made it through I'm sure the other Scott and Christine would either try to kill me or send me back through.

At first, my response to that was that I would just kill them if they came back. Now, I'm not so sure. Maybe we can all survive in this world. I can take Tricksy and move away somewhere, and in time, they can forget that I even exist. I know I'm still crazy, but at least now I can recognize it, and I do feel like I'm out of the cave and in the sunlight more every day.

And I love this world so much.

I figured out how to work Scott's cell phone after an hour or so on the second day I was here. Most people don't have cell phones where I come from because they're so unreliable. One of the side effects when things started changing for the worse a few years back was that most wireless transmissions stopped working with any regularity. It's like sunspots or a solar flare, but all of the time.

But I did have a cell phone years ago, just not one of these fancy touchscreen things. I poked around in it until I figured out where the other Scott worked, and then I called in sick. I needed time to get acclimated, but I also needed money, so the following day I gave a sad Tricksy a hug and headed in. The job was at a company that made greeting cards, oddly enough. Greetings cards weren't much of a thing anymore where I was from, but apparently other Scott wrote them for a living.

The first couple of days were rough. I could tell by the odd looks I got from some of my co-workers that I wasn't producing the kind of material they were expecting from Scott. So I went through all his old work to get a feel for it. Most of it was saccharine and idiotic, but there were some good ideas in there too. Some of them I felt like I could see other Scott in, and it made me know him more, see him more as a person rather than just an obstacle. Or maybe that was just my crazy starting to wear off and my guilt starting to kick in.

Either way, it didn't stop me from loving going to work. Living in that old world, even when I was deep in the cave, it felt like everyone you met was a high-voltage powerline just humming with dark impulses and brimming with potential for violence. Not everyone was, of course, and I certainly fell into that camp myself, but none of that made the constant tension of daily life any easier to bear.

Here, people aren't always happy or nice, but they are normal. The way I remember being when I was younger. Yesterday I just sat at my desk, trying to think up a way to say Happy Birthday that wasn't overly off-putting or strange, and I marveled at the sounds around me.

People gossiping, eating donuts, talking about what they are doing for their vacation in two weeks or about their daughter's wedding last month. Even the work-related stuff was done in such a mundane and civil manner that it felt surreal.

Much as I enjoy it though, by the end of the day I have to get home and be alone. Being around people too long, even normal people that probably won't suddenly start screaming or trying to kill you, is hard for me. I'm not used to that anymore, and I may never be again. I don't know. But I already have more in this world than I ever thought I'd have again.

New movies! I've been spending a lot of time when I'm at home watching movies. They made movies out of Tolkien's "The Red Book of Westmarch" trilogy over here! They call it "The Lord of the Rings", which is a dumb name, but the movies are great. My favorite has to be Gollum. I read they did him with computer graphics, which is amazing and more advanced than anything I've seen in my world. I even named Tricksy after him, albeit indirectly. He looks a little bit like a bug-eyed Gollum anyway.

He's asleep on my lap as I write this out, and as stupid as this sounds, I think he's part of the reason I'm having so much trouble with what I did. I love the little guy, and it's the first time I've loved something since my Christine. Just thinking about her, what we did to each other as it got bad…I will always hate myself for that.

The question is, how much sin do I want to add on top? How much more do I want to hate myself?

I decided to write this all out as a way of working through all of these thoughts and feelings. Almost as though I was writing it to the other Scott, but with no intention of actually sending it. But I'm coming to realize I should send it to him. Not just this either, but instructions on how to get back or a message on setting up a time when I can open the door on this side if he's not up to doing it on his. I had better wait to send the extra paper until I know what he wants to do, and I hope I'm not too late for either of them.

And yet…I still hear a voice calling from that deep, dark cave. That voice says I have to look out for myself. That they will kill me or force me back if I help them. I know that I can't trust that voice, but I also can't shake the feeling that it is part of what has kept me alive as my own world turned into some kind of hell. I need to think about this. I don't want to lose this life, but I'm not sure it won't be poisoned if I leave them condemned to that terrible place.

Tricksy just woke up and wants to go outside. I think I'm going to take him for a long walk and then see about sending a letter.

****

Abducting a child isn't as easy as you might think, especially in this place. There are fewer people for one thing, and everyone is much more guarded, especially with their children. The first few days me and Christine went out, we only saw a couple of children at all. We had a plan of only going out for two hours at a time in different directions. We wanted to make sure that if we saw something like what happened in the park, we could get back to the apartment relatively quickly, and this way we were exploring different potential places every time we went.

We saw a number of things in those days. Much of it was relatively mild—people talking to themselves or arguing loudly, acting erratic or strangely twitchy and emotional. We saw a couple of fights, and one guy ran out into the street and started stabbing a woman who was just quietly making her way along the crosswalk. The most troubling thing was very brief, and I don't think Christine saw it.

We were walking south that day, debating if we should push out further than normal in the hopes we could reach a school that was supposed to be a few blocks away. It was a big risk to take a child from a school, particularly when we had to go back all that way on foot with them in tow, but every day we were getting more desperate, and the more time we spent here seeing this place, the more the question of should we do it faded away as the question of how we do it became more and more pressing.

As we walked, I happened to glance into an alley we were passing. I saw a woman and a child of about ten hunched over a man who lay slumped against a dumpster. At first, I thought they were leaning down checking on him, but then the little boy turned and looked at me with deep-set green eyes that twinkled with madness. His mouth was covered in blood and bits of flesh from where they were eating the man, and as my mouth fell open he smiled at me and licked his lips.

I tried not to lose my stride so as to not alert Christine, and the last glimpse I saw was the woman's hand on the boy's shoulder. It may have been my fear or a trick of the shadows, but I swear I saw her hand going into him slowly, as though they were running together like pink candle wax. I told Christine we should keep going, deciding in the back of my mind we would be taking a different route back to the apartment. I kept looking over my shoulder, but to my relief I saw no sign we were being followed.

That was the day our luck changed. A mile down the road we found an elementary school. It had already let out for the day, but the next day we were back bright and early, and after watching most of the morning, we had a plan.

Most of the children came in by school bus or were dropped off by parents, but there were a handful that walked there in the morning. Assuming that was true in the afternoon as well, we would just wait for a small child who was walking alone, preferably a girl since that's what Not Scott had used, and that would be that. It was terrible, and I still hated the idea of doing it, but it had to be done. I had to try and make all of this right, even if I had to do some wrong to do it. And I told myself that these children had no real future here other than a short life filled with pain and fear. I couldn't quite convince myself that killing one of them was a mercy, but it did take the edge off of my guilt at least.

School let out and it soon became clear who we were following. While many of the children who were walking had left in pairs or groups, there was one little girl who had headed off on her own immediately as though she couldn't wait to be away from all the laughing and shoving and joking around the rest of the children were doing as they got picked up or struck out on foot. She was overweight, with long, black hair that was stringy and unkempt. Her clothes were clearly old and dirty in spots, and as she walked, I could see that the sole was starting to separate on the back of one of her red sneakers. She looked sad and unloved, and I had to fight the urge to tell Christine that this was a mistake. But when I looked at her, all I saw was the grim almost manic determination I had seen since we had started this days before. She was past any mercy or equivocation at this point, and how could I blame her, given all she had been through?

So we followed the child until she started down a route different than what would lead in the apartment's direction, at which point we approached her and told her she needed to come with us. She asked why, and we gave our preplanned generic response of "a member of your family has been hurt and we were told to get you. We don't have all the details yet." It was vague and lame, but we hoped it would be enough to at least get her down the road a mile or two before she started asking more questions. She seemed to weigh our words, considering, and I could tell she didn't really believe us for any of a dozen good reasons. Still, to my surprise she just shrugged with a resigned look on her face.

"Okay. I'll go."

It occurred to me that children were likely going crazy in this place just like the adults. And given what I thought I had seen in the alley, my appreciation for how potentially dangerous this little girl might be was exponentially greater. But as we walked, she didn't try to attack us or even complain. She moved along docilely, and after a couple of miles I began wondering what her life must be like that she was okay with being abducted. I pushed the thought away. The less I thought of her as a person, as a sad little girl, the better.

The trip back was taking longer than expected, not because of any problems with her, but because we had gotten lost. As twilight came on, the semi-familiar landmarks became less familiar, and somehow in my rerouting we took a wrong turn. We made it to the apartment without incident but well after nightfall, and the resolutely stoic little girl had started to murmur about being hungry and needing the bathroom.

When we got upstairs, I shared a look with Christine as I told the girl we'd fix her some dinner after we showed her something in the other room. The paper and knife were already set up in the bedroom, so it should go quickly enough. But when the girl asked again about going to the bathroom, I relented, telling her to go on, but to make it quick.

She nodded and went with dutiful haste into the hallway bathroom, closing the door behind her. Christine was giving me a hard look to which I just shrugged. "It's five minutes, and I think it's the least we can do. She's just a little girl."

Her expression softened a little, her voice mimicking my hushed tone. "I know. I just want it over with. We have to get back."

I nodded and thought about reaching out to comfort her, but now wasn't the time. We had to stay focused, and get past this. Then we could work on helping each other get back to normal.

After another minute, the toilet flushed. Immediately the pipes began to squeal and rattle with a level of noise that still amazed me after nearly a week of using them. Christine had warned me about them, about not using them at…

"It's after dark!" Christine's eyes were wide with panic. "He said never flush it after dark!

I felt fear fluttering in my chest and I tried to ignore it. "I'm sure it'll be okay. What're the odds some roving band is patrolling outside right now, just waiting for a sign of life to break in?" Still, I could feel my heart racing, and I was about to hammer on the bathroom door when the girl came out, looking confused at our excitement.

I grabbed her arm and pulled her across into the bedroom. She was still quiet, but she was starting to physically resist now. Fortunately, Christine was there and grabbed her from behind, wrapping her arms around the girl's chest.

"I've got her. Do it, hurry." I let go of the girl's arm and looked into Christine's face. She looked ten years older and like a different person than the woman I knew and loved. Her easy smile and bright, intelligent eyes had been replaced with a grim slash and dull stones that bored into me as she waited for me to grab the knife.

I picked it up and had time to think about how heavy it felt, how wrong it felt in my hand. The next moment there was a crash that sounded like it was coming from the front door of the apartment as someone tried to bash their way in.

Christine's eyes widened as her grip on the child tightened. "Do it now, fucker! You fucking do it now before they're on top of us!"

Being careful to avoid the child's face, I moved my gaze down to the knife. Taking a deep breath, I shoved it into the girl's stomach. Even then she didn't complain other than to make a "woof" sound like she had been punched in the gut. I was starting to cry, but the splintering sound of the front door finally giving way spurred me on. I put my fingers in the blood pouring from the knife wound and turned to trace the rectangle inside the paper door. Immediately a crack appeared, and at my touch the door swung open.

I shuffled away and told Christine to go through, seeing two men and one woman coming into the living room and looking at me across the distance. I jumped and slammed the bedroom door shut, twisting the lock but knowing the door would only hold for seconds. Turning back, I saw the last of Christine disappear through the door and I dove behind her, scrabbling through and back into my world.

The first thing I noticed when I passed through was barking. I looked up to see Christine standing nearby, the knife we had used on the girl in her hand. Standing a few feet away at the doorway to the room was Not Scott, and bizarrely it looked like he was holding a small Pug puppy that was furiously barking at us.

"Get back, motherfucker." Christine growled at him. Not Scott was about to say something in response, but then I was getting pulled back through the door. Rough hands had me, pulling at my clothes and yanking me away from my way home. I looked up and saw strange faces with small symbols tattooed between the eyebrows of all three of them. They didn't seem angry or even upset as they began to punch and kick me. Instead, they were placidly calm, almost bored looking, as though what they were doing was just part of their daily routine. Most likely it was.

I tried to ball up, but I was hurting badly already, and protecting my stomach only exposed my back more. I closed my eyes tight. I knew I was going to die here, beaten to death by strangers in a strange world. But one of them started screaming, and when I opened my eyes, I saw Not Scott pulling the knife Christine had been holding out of one of the men's eyes. As that man began to fall, the woman left off kicking me to jump on Not Scott's back with a furious howl. He pushed backward, slamming her into the wall and jamming the knife back and into her side. Her howl turned into a yell of pain, and as he yanked the knife free, he twisted around to drive it home into her neck with a wet, popping sound that made me wince.

I realized that the other man had run out during this, and I was going to say so to Not Scott, but he was busy looking at the tattoo on the woman's face.

"Fuck. Okay, you have to get out of here. Get back through the door. I'm going to destroy it as soon as you go and then try to go catch that fuck and his buddies."

I was so confused, but I suddenly felt sure I shouldn't be leaving Not Scott here, despite everything he had done. "Why don't you come back with us? You can pay for your crimes there."

He stared at me a moment and then shook his head. "I can't. These aren't regular criminals. They're part of one of the big cults that has sprung up in the last few years. Call themselves the House of the Claw. If they figure out how to make a door, there's nothing stopping them and God knows what else from pouring over into your world. They always run in packs of 4 or 5, so I have to try and get the rest of them now." He paused. "But thank you for offering. And please take care of my puppy. His name is Tricksy and...he's a very good boy." I could see he was crying, but I knew we didn't like it when people commented on us crying, so I left it alone.

"I promise, Scott. If you get them and..." I almost said survive, but I couldn't make myself say the word, "...you want to come over, use one of these scraps and send me a note. I'll…send you more paper to make a door." I left out the unspoken step of him having to kill another child, but I saw in his eyes he was thinking it. He shook his head. "Don't worry about that. We have to be willing to make sacrifices for what matters. I understand that better now. Just go. Have a good life, both of you. And I'm sorry."

I nodded and rolled back onto my stomach, crawling as quickly as my pain would allow. As soon as my feet had cleared the other side, the door was gone. I looked up to see Christine holding the shaking puppy, who looked at me for a moment before starting back to barking frantically and squirming.

It's been six hours since then. I found and read what the other Scott had written and have included it above. To her credit, Christine was honest after reading his letter. She told me she had lied about him abusing her, and told me what she says is the truthful account of her time there with him and with me. I plan to include portions of that in this or earlier postings as well.

She left a couple of hours ago to go home and clean up. Get some rest. We hugged when we parted at my door, but I can tell everything is different now. Something has broken between us. It was too fragile or too rigid to bear the weight of all we have seen and said and done. And the saddest part is that I'm okay with that. The last month has given me a great deal of insight into what I can survive.

Right now, I'm trying to make friends with a small puppy named Tricksy. He is a cute little guy, but he rolls his eyes at me with mistrust whenever I try to get near him. I'm not the right Scott for him. I'm starting to think I'm not the right Scott for a lot of things.

I have been checking the desk for a sign all night, but there's been nothing. So finally, after taking a second long shower and giving Tricksy some more water, I tumble into bed and a deep slumber.

I start awake and I can tell it's either early morning or early evening, but I have no idea which. Tricksy is what woke me up, barking at something. I roll over and see he's jumping and barking at the desk. On it is a single scrap of blue paper.

Leaping out of bed, I wipe sleep from my eyes and read it.

Got them. Fortunately for me, the House isn't afraid to recruit young. I'll be over shortly. Tell Tricksy he's my precious.

Laughing and feeling stupid, I read the note to Tricksy, who was bouncing excitedly against my leg as though he knew what was coming. Just then I saw it.

The door was opening one last time.

Mary Jane's Pumpkin Patch

Autumn has always been my favorite season. I like the cool air and the turning of the leaves, and it has both Halloween and Thanksgiving going for it too. Every year I try to do some seasonal things to get into the spirit of it, be it going to a scare house or buying some apple cider at one of the roadside stands north of where I live, and this year was no different.

Except this year I took a different route up into the mountains in my search for roadside stands and brightly-colored leaves. I'd recently broken up with (been dumped by) my girlfriend of two years, and while I could have gotten one of my friends or my sister to go with me, I was looking forward to having some time by myself. I wouldn't say I was depressed, but I knew I was more than a little mopey, and I didn't want to inflict my bad mood on someone else. Plus, these trips always cheered me up, and I was hoping this one would be no different—especially with the adventure of going on a different route I wasn't familiar with.

At first that seemed to hold true. I was paying more attention to where I was going due to the unfamiliar roads, and it didn't take long before I started getting into areas with truly beautiful scenery. A little after noon I stopped at a small-town restaurant and grabbed some lunch before hitting the road again.

But as the day wore on, I realized I wasn't hitting any other small towns, including one or two I had expected to run across. I was relying on memory, as I was trying to avoid using a map or my phone unless I truly got lost, but when I had glanced at the area a few days ago, I was sure there were other small towns dotting the area I was traveling through. It wasn't a big deal—I had plenty of gas from refueling at lunch—but I was a bit disappointed. Worse was the lack of small country stores, fruit stands, and other mountain oddities you normally see. I always loved finding places selling art made out of logs and metal, weird tiny museums to obscure local heritage, and other quirky spots that I didn't get to see in my day-to-day.

But this trip, all I saw was mile after mile of admittedly beautiful trees punctuated by the occasional rural road trailing off into the wilderness. As the sunlight began to take on the softer, orange tones of late afternoon, I started weighing my options. I hadn't even seen a sign pointing toward a town or highway in probably fifty miles, and I had a good enough phone signal to pull up a map or use gps to find my way to a more familiar route heading back home. I started fumbling for the phone in the passenger seat when I noticed a white particleboard sign nailed to an approaching tree.

"Peches" it proclaimed in blood-red letters. The misspelling aside, my heart leapt at the prospect of finally finding some kind of obscure mountain trader.

"Cidar" the next sign shouted from a tree about fifty yards after the first. The signs were crude and poorly done, but they looked relatively well-maintained and new. Still, I kept my expectations in check, looking for a small weathered stand that might not even be open. Instead, as I rounded the corner, I found myself coming up on what looked like a small farm. As I slowed down, I saw it had a little orchard on one side that seemed to go on behind the medium-sized green farm house that sat in the middle of the property. I saw with growing excitement that on the far side of the house was a large and sprawling pumpkin patch. Far from picked over like many patches you see in October, this one was brimming with row after row of huge, beautiful pumpkins. The small white sign at the front of the driveway said "Raymond's Cidar and Fruit" and had a crooked arrow pointing toward the farmhouse. Feeling a buzz of happy excitement, I pulled in and made my way up the dirt driveway.

When I got out of the car, I saw there was an old man in a ball cap sitting on the front porch watching me. Raising my hand, I got no response, and though I tried to look friendly as I approached, I felt a growing worry in my stomach that I had somehow made a mistake. When I got to the bottom of the steps I paused.

"Excuse me, sir. Is this Raymond's Cider and Fruit?"

The old man nodded, a small smile playing across his face. "Yup. It is, young fella. And I'm Raymond." His smile broke into a grin as he began to rock in his chair, a look of satisfaction spreading across his face as he began a well-recited sales pitch. "I've got some of the best peaches and apple cider you've ever tasted, all made from the trees you see around you. I've also got some rock candy and peanut brittle for sale, and though I don't make that here, I can vouch for its quality." As though to underline his guarantee, he smiled wider, revealing three missing teeth. Chuckling at his own joke, Raymond stopped rocking as he leaned forward in his chair. "So what're you interested in buying?"

Relieved, I smiled back. "Well, I'd like to get some apple cider and a bag of peaches, and one of those big, pretty pumpkins you've got out there too."

Raymond's smile left his eyes as he glanced out toward the pumpkin patch. "The cider and fruit I can help you with, but no pumpkins for sale, I'm afraid."

I couldn't help but be disappointed, so I decided to push on a bit. "So that's not your pumpkin patch, or you're just not selling them?"

The old man looked at me steadily for a moment before answering. "Oh, it's my land all right, just not my patch or pumpkins. Them's are Mary Jane's pumpkins." He looked away as he said her name, rubbing his mouth distractedly.

"Mary Jane? Is she…," I was going to ask if she was his wife, but decided I didn't want to push my luck asking personal questions. "…around? Maybe she wants to sell me a pumpkin."

His eyes found mine again, and at first I thought he was angry, but when he spoke, his voice seemed to tremble slightly.

"No, she's not around at the moment. Won't return until tonight I 'spect, and you need to be moving on well before that. So you want that cider and peaches?"

"Sure, sure." I had brought two hundred dollars in cash along for the trip—a hundred dollar bill and five twenties. I handed him a twenty. "Is that enough? I don't need change."

Raymond eyed the money and then me. "Yeah, I reckon that will do just fine." With that, he got up and shuffled inside the house for a minute before coming back with two paper bags and a glass jug of cider. "I gave you a bag of apples as well for the extra money." He was glancing around more now, as though he was looking for something or someone, though we were the only ones there as far as I could tell. "You have a safe trip back home, young fella. Tell your friends." His farewell and final bid for recommendations seemed half-hearted, and he looked increasingly anxious and preoccupied as I left the porch and went back to my car.

I turned around in the yard and headed back out on the road. I could have turned back the way I had come from, but instead I turned right and went on past his house down the road toward the pumpkin patch. I found myself going slow and continuing to look at the pumpkins, and that's the main reason I saw the small dirt path that ran along the perimeter of the patch further down. Stopping the car, I looked back to see if I could see the porch of Raymond's house, but the combination of the curve of the road and a swell of land blocked all but the top of the house from view.

I pulled onto the dirt path and sat for a moment. I knew I shouldn't be doing it, but I really wanted one of those pumpkins, and what would taking one pumpkin really hurt? Still, it was stealing if I just took it. The compromise I finally reached between my conscience and my desire was to leave the hundred dollar bill under a rock near the pumpkin I took. That way, if they noticed one was gone, they'd find the money for it. If they didn't notice, then no harm no foul.

I knew I didn't have a knife with me, but I managed to find a flat-headed screwdriver to help work a pumpkin loose from the vine. My heart beating in my chest, I eased open the car door and headed around the front of my car and toward the edge of the pumpkin patch. The pumpkins were all oddly similar to one another, so it was easy to pick one from the first batch I ran across. I jammed and twisted the tip of the screwdriver into the thick, black vine that the pumpkin was attached to, but it was surprisingly durable. After a couple of minutes with little progress, I sat down the screwdriver and just tried twisting the pumpkin from the vine. To my surprise, it popped off easily, a light spray of liquid hitting me as it came loose.

I wiped my face on my sleeve and scooped the pumpkin up, staggering in the process. The thing was heavy. Really heavy. Grunting with the effort, I waddled it over to my car and sat it in my front passenger seat. Feeling a bit stupid but not wanting to take any chances, I put a seat belt on the pumpkin before running around to the other side to get in and drive off. As I glanced back in the rear view mirror for signs of pursuit, I realized I had forgotten to leave the money under a rock. I could go back and do it, but that would just increase the risk of me getting caught. Feeling somewhat guilty, I decided to drive on.

I was preoccupied with my thoughts after leaving the patch, driving pretty much on autopilot. I could have wound up more lost than before, but instead I realized with relief that I was back on a road I recognized. Smiling to myself, I patted the pumpkin next to me and headed home.

****

That was four hours ago. When I got home I was tired, but I also felt determined to go ahead and carve up the pumpkin into a jack-o-lantern. It was almost as though I felt that if I made immediate use of the pumpkin it would justify stealing it in the first place. Pushing that thought aside, I grabbed up a large kitchen knife and stuck it into the side of the pumpkin.

The blade went in an inch or so before meeting some kind of resistance. I pushed harder, and after a moment the knife plunged deeper into the pumpkin. When I went to pull it out, it seemed oddly difficult to do it, but I finally managed. All of this was strange, but I just attributed it to the size and healthiness of the pumpkin. I would just have to work harder to get through its tough skin.

So I did. I pushed and pulled, shoved and tugged, until I had cut out a large triangle piece that was meant to be the nose. As I pulled the wedge free, I saw a wisp of black hair trailing behind the removed chunk of pumpkin skin. It lay in that triangular hole like some kind of deadly snake, coiled and alien against the bright orange of the pumpkin. I jerked my hand back, dropping the wedge in the process. It took me a moment to summon the courage to reach out and touch the hair, having already half convinced myself it was just some kind of internal rot making the pumpkin's innards look like dark hair.

But when I felt the hair, I knew the truth. I felt my gorge rise slightly, but I forced it down. Driven more by fear than reason now, I hacked away at the pumpkin again until a quarter of one side could be broken off. As it fell away and I saw what lay inside that pumpkin, I wanted to scream, but I couldn't find the breath to do it.

It was a head. A bloodless, human head. From the looks of it, the woman had been in her mid-thirties when she died, and while she looked very pale and drawn, she wasn't decayed or dried up. She also wasn't bleeding or oozing from the cuts where I had struck the head with my knife. I considered it being some kind of joke, but she looked too real to be a fake. Besides, how would someone even pull off something like that, anyway? And what would be the point?

No, I knew it was real and there was no rationalizing it away. The best thing I could do would be to call the police, even if I had to admit stealing the pumpkin in the first place. I was reaching for my phone when it began to glow and buzz. My hand was shaking slightly as I answered the incoming call.

"Hello?"

"You took something that didn't belong to you, didn't you?" The voice was smoky but very feminine, and under other circumstances I might have found it sexy. As it was, I was terrified.

My hand started shaking worse as I tried to think of a response. A thousand things whirled through my mind like startled birds before I settled on one. "I can just give it back. I'm sorry."

The woman gave out a short laugh. "No, why would I want that thing back? You ruined it as soon as you cut it open."

"But I didn't open it. I didn't see anything." I winced as soon as the last words left my mouth. Idiot. If I didn't see anything, why would I know I needed to assure her I didn't see anything? But she seemed to ignore my response as she continued.

"No need to worry, my new friend. What is done cannot be undone, but I'm open to reparations. Yes…that's just what I need. Reparations for your sin against me."

I was nodding into the phone frantically. "Sure, of course! How much do you think is fair for the pumpkin and…your trouble? One hundred? How about two, just so there's no hard feelings." I could have said a million, because I had no intention of paying her anything. As soon as I was off the phone I was calling 911.

Mary Jane laughed again. "Money? I have no need for that. No, what I have to get is a replacement for what you took." She paused a moment, her voice full of mirth when she continued. "You know, for the head."

I gripped my phone tighter as my breath caught in my chest. I was on the verge of just hanging up when I realized she was speaking again.

"What size hat do you wear, Wallace?"

How the fuck did she know my name? But then again, how did she have my cell phone number to call me in the first place? With growing dread, I pulled the phone away from my ear and ended the call before dropping the phone on the floor like it was hot. I glanced around the kitchen, letting out a short moan when I saw that the pumpkin was gone. In its place was a small piece of folded paper tented on the edge of my kitchen counter. Creeping up closer, I read it without picking it up.

Don't worry, my new friend, it said, *I'll measure when I come for it. Be seeing you.*

Mary Jane

Come Live in the Ashes of my Heart

Journal Entry 1

So I just found a strange note in the basement. It is just one sentence, and it says, "Come live in the ashes of my heart." Weird, right? It's a bit of strange excitement, but I don't think it's enough to get me out of this funk.

I moved into this house two days ago, and already I regret it. I'm tired and filthy, but that's not the problem. And the house itself, while very old and sometimes creepy, is also very beautiful in a lot of ways. It's certainly nicer than anywhere I've ever lived before, even if that isn't saying much, and what I just found in the basement is the most interesting thing I've run across in a long time. The problem is that I never should have moved here with Phil. After being with him for two years, I knew in the back of my head that there were problems that went beyond the normal growing pains of a relationship. I think Phil knows it too, and that's why he suggested the move to a new state, as though the stress of moving and the isolation of a new town was going to somehow bond us closer together rather than driving us apart.

But let me be clear. Phil is a good guy. He drinks too much at times, and he doesn't always have the best judgment, but he is generally responsible, kind and loyal. I just don't think he's the right person for me. I knew it before I agreed to move, I knew it when we closed on the house, and I certainly know it now, sitting in a room packed with boxes stuffed full of reminders of our lives.

But still, I can't put all the blame on him. I was fool enough to go along with it, both of us playing relationship chicken, revving our engines and careening towards each other faster and faster, daring the other to be the one that says "No, that's enough. This isn't working anymore." And I think I'm just about there.

I started keeping this journal based on a self-help book I read once that said that when you have a difficult decision to make, journaling to keep track of your thoughts and feelings over time can help you see the objective reality of your inner self better than relying purely on memory and your subjective thoughts and feelings at any given time. So that's what I'm going to do for the next few days. And when I look back at it, if I'm still feeling like I do right now, I'm going to tell Phil it's over.

But back to what I just found in the basement. First, you need to understand that when I say this house is old, I mean it is old. I don't know a ton about styles of houses, but the realtor said that it was "Victorian style" and may have been built during the Victorian era, as the land records for the area first account for the house in 1884. But that's also how far back the local records go for anything, and the house was already here, so it's hard to say when it was actually built.

In any case, like I said, the house is beautiful. It's made of light gray brick with dark gray fans of shingles draping the various peaks and curves of its roof like the feathers of some large wintery bird, and the rooms inside are a strange mix of large open spaces and tight alcoves and hallways. And while the entire house has a certain…weight to it, I kind of chalk that up to it being so old, and most of the weird feelings I get come from when I'm in the basement anyway.

The basement is surprisingly clean, being comprised of two large rooms devoid of any furnishings except for a row of empty gunracks that are built into one wall. My initial thought was to replace them with bookshelves at some point, but now I'm starting to wonder if I'll be here long enough for it to matter. Anyway, enough about that. It's time to talk about the note I found.

So I was moving some boxes down here when I noticed something sticking out of one of the walls. It was a piece of folded paper, so yellowed with age that I was afraid it was going to crumble when I opened it. It held, however, and I saw written inside that single line in beautiful handwriting.

Come live in the ashes of my heart.

I checked the place in the brick I had pulled it from and saw there was a gap in the mortar. I didn't look closely at the time because of the lighting, but I think I'm going back down there with a flashlight and check it out again. Something is weird about that room anyway. I haven't measured it, but I would swear that it is several feet shorter than the other room, and while there are reasons that could be the case, I almost feel like the brick wall with the note was built later than the rest to divide the basement. The brick looks slightly different than the rest, or at least I think it does.

Who knows? I'll write more when I'm done checking it out. If I'm going to write this stuff down, I would like it to be more than just my complaining about my boyfriend problems. Fuck, I'm so lonely out here, and my job doesn't start for two weeks. Anyway, signing off for now.

Journal Entry 2

There's something behind that wall. I went back down there, shined a flashlight into the gap in the mortar, and it goes all the way through. The hole was too small for me to see and shine the light at the same time, so I got a screwdriver and poked out some more of the mortar until I could remove the brick. I couldn't see much, but there is definitely another room over there and I thought I saw part of a bedframe.

About that time is when I heard Phil coming in upstairs. For some reason I didn't want him to know about it yet, didn't want to share my discovery. I had the uncharitable thought that I didn't want him to "Phil all over it", which is a general phrase I sometimes think of when he gets involved in some conversation or activity and just…lessens it somehow. Fuck, I sound like a bitch right now. I don't mean it like that. I just mean that he can't just enjoy something strange like this. He has an almost hostile reaction to things he doesn't understand, and he would immediately want to either dismiss it or come up with some rational explanation. I just want to savor the mystery of it, even if just for a little while.

I put the brick back quickly and went upstairs, managing to avoid mentioning the note or the hidden room I had just found without strictly lying to him. I'm writing this before heading to bed, and I already have plans to go buy a sledgehammer in the morning. I'm going to see what's in that room.

Journal Entry 3

So breaking down a brick wall, even an old and slightly crumbly one, is harder that I thought it would be. I kind of assumed that since I had so little trouble getting the one brick free, the rest would crumble in pretty easily, but not so much. I went to a local hardware store and bought a small sledgehammer, avoiding the cashier's chipper questions about what a little lady like myself was going to use such a big hammer for, and when I got back to the house I went to work on the wall immediately.

The biggest problem wasn't swinging it—it's heavy, but I'm in good shape and I made sure I could swing it well before I bought it. The problem is the vibration. Every time it hit the bricks, shockwaves went up my arms all the way to my shoulders. I put on some gardening gloves I rooted out of a box in the garage, and it helped a little, but my hands were still buzzing and numb by the time I was done.

Still, after a little over an hour, the wall was about a third gone, which was more than enough to let me in and allow in more light. I had also picked up a small electric lantern at the store, and when I turned it on, it sent a wash of cold, white light out across the dark contours of the hidden room.

What I had seen before was a bed. A rusty iron frame bed with a thin mattress that was half black with rot. Next to the bed was a wooden nightstand that contained a few candle stubs in holders and on small plates, and against one wall was a cedar chest with what looked like some kind of leather-bound notebook sitting on top of it.

My heart was in my throat at this point. I had either found an old bedroom that had been walled up without ever being cleaned out, or I had found where someone had been imprisoned at some point. I considered calling the police, but there was no sign of the body, and there was such a sense of age and musty disuse here that I felt sure that any victims, if there were any, would be long gone by now anyway.

I was doing another sweep of the room with the lantern and my flashlight when I saw the shape of a man. I screamed, dropping the lantern and backing toward the opening in the wall. Then I realized what I was seeing wasn't an actual man. It was the silhouette of a man painted or burned into the far wall.

My breathing still quick and painful, I looked around for several moments to make sure that I wasn't mistaken, that there wasn't some stranger in that abandoned room with me. But I saw nothing. Bending down, I got the lantern and gave a quick peek to the empty space underneath the bed and nightstand table before standing and walking to the silhouette.

Up close, I could see that it looked less like paint or burning and more like a form of mold or rot, though it was still undeniably in the shape of a man half a foot taller than myself and half again as broad. When I reached out to touch the black area where his chest would be, the wall had a slight sponginess to it that made me pull back my finger quickly. Wiping my hand on my pants, I went over to the chest and sat the leather book aside. Inside the chest were clothes. Most the size for a large man, though some towards the bottom did look somewhat smaller. All of them were in surprisingly good condition, particularly given how old-fashioned they looked.

I felt a strange kind of guilt going through those clothes, as though I was prying into the private world of a stranger. I guess in some ways I was, but time had made the point moot all the same. There was nothing left but this dark room and the handful of belongings left behind. And, of course, that book.

I picked up the book and stepped back out into the main part of the basement where the light was better. The book seemed to be pristine, with signs of age but none of mold or decay. There was a leather cord tying it shut, and as I gently unwound the cord and opened the book, I could smell not only the leather and the pages, but I imagined I could smell the owner of the book as well. A masculine smell, a good smell that made the experience of holding that book and seeing the words written on the first page more personal, more powerful, than I can really describe.

The handwriting was the same as that note I had found stuck in the wall. It said "The Last Testament of Justin Paring. Completed June 12, 1909. May this find its way into kinder hands than I have known."

I'm about to start reading it, and I will try to transcribe it here as soon as possible. This feels so...important. I'm going to have to explain the room to Phil when he sees the wall, but for now at least, this book is going to stay a secret. Until next time, journal. Keep my secrets for me.

Journal Entry 4

As promised, here is the transcription of what I found in the book belonging to Justin Paring. It's pretty long, so I'll finish the transcription in my next post.

****

As I write this, I am a twenty-one year old man of what I believe to be sound mind and firm spiritual foundation. Despite what I have been told over these last eight years, I am not insane and I am not possessed by the Devil or any of his lesser imps. To the contrary, even now I hold much love in my heart, with no small portion still being afforded to my tormentors. My parents and brother, though many of their acts would aptly be described as evil, are not bad people. Misguided and fearful, yes. But I do believe that they still have goodness in them.

I am given food and water, candles and occasionally a book to read or some scraps of paper to write upon. I have developed a persistent cough in the last year, and I fear that the lack of sunlight and the pervasive dampness of this sealed away space are slowly doing damage that time and medicine may not be able to reverse. I know I get sores at times from my infrequent ability to bathe, and the twin stenches of myself and the waste bucket in the corner are imperceptible to me now. I try to separate my hate for my situation from those that cause it, and most of the time I think I succeed. My hope is that writing this will help further.

I turned twenty-one two weeks ago, and as a gift my brother John gave me this notebook and a new set of Waterman Safety Pens. I didn't know such a thing even existed, and it truly is wonderful to have such a convenient writing tool. I cried at the kindness, and outside my room John looked in and smiled his sad smile as I crouched in the dark, clutching this book and softly weeping as our mother began to close the door for the day.

I don't have much dignity left at this point. Dignity is like a plant. Much as a plant needs sunlight and oxygen, dignity needs an audience and hope. When you are completely isolated, when you move past any idea of ever really escaping the black hole you are in, you find yourself quickly shedding things like dignity. My primary reasons for living have been a base animal drive to survive and my internal world. I had always had a powerful imagination, and in this purgatory I have spent many hours far away in some distant land of my own creation. I loved to write as well, but since my imprisonment it has been rare that I had enough paper to write much of any length. That, and the act of kindness behind it, is what made the book and the pens such a wonderful gift to me.

Yet when I got them, I found I had trouble finding things to write about. After three days of trying, a realization struck me. My imagination was starting to wither and die too. This thought terrified me in a way that losing my liberty or my dignity had not. It was the final bulwark I had against abject despair, the last remaining island in a rising sea of insanity and death. If I lost the ability to escape into my mind, I would truly be lost.

It was six days ago that I first contemplated taking my life. For some that may seem absurd, as I know many people would have considered it or committed the act long before now. I would like to say that I had abstained because of my deep moral reserves or my titanic willpower, but neither would be the truth. In all honesty, the only reason I haven't taken my life before now is because of the Ghost Tree.

I know I need to explain myself, and to do so in a clear fashion, I need to further elucidate how I came to be confined here, a prisoner in the basement of my own home.

It all began when I was eleven. The younger of two children and raised by two strict but kind parents, I was still prone to frequent wanderings of thought and flights of fancy. I was a largely obedient child, and I had enough admiration for my brother and fearful respect for my parents that when I was rebuked for daydreaming or telling fantastic tales, I truly did try to curb those tendencies, or at least confine them to my own thoughts and late-night conversations with John.

I suppose that is why the trouble with the Ghost Tree caught me by surprise. When I woke up the day after Christmas and ran outside to play, I found a giant new tree near the edge of our yard. It stood out to me not just because of the oddity of a new tree suddenly appearing, but also because it varied so much from any other trees we had or that I had ever seen.

Where most of our trees were pine or oak, with the occasional sweetgum or poplar for variety's sake, this tree was something else entirely. It had a massive trunk that twisted and warped upon itself before breaking out into at least twelve distinct branches of such girth and height that they all stood as substantial trees on their own. Coming off of these smaller trees were swirls of wood the color of dark red wine and sweeping greens that looked more like storm clouds than the clumps of leaves that I supposed they were.

I should be clear that from the start I had a sense of the strangeness of that tree, but I also felt profound feelings of joy and excitement at its discovery and presence, as though some looming giant had settled in our yard, intent on a deep slumber while he guarded our home. This thought was firmly in my mind as I ran to the tree and touched it.

Its bark felt strange, but was solid enough, and under the canopy of its many arms, I could smell a warm, spicy smell unlike any I had ever encountered. It made my head swim slightly, but not in an unpleasant way. The thought suddenly occurred to me that I might be the first one to discover it, and I couldn't wait to show John and my parents my proud accomplishment.

Ten minutes later, my parents were walking back into the house, my father shaking his head disgustedly. John was still outside with me, his face stricken with worry. He was two years older than me, but he never seemed like an older brother except at times like this. It was the look he would get when he was afraid I was going to get into trouble or when he couldn't understand something I was talking about, at which times he politely assumed that what I was saying was somehow wrong. I hated that look, but I understood it now.

None of them could see the tree.

In the two years that followed, I would occasionally bring up the tree to them, and each time I was met with greater anger and rejection. I was told that I was to give up these childish games and fantasies, that my behavior was continuing to deteriorate and I needed to start showing signs of growing up and becoming a man. Finally my father, not the most emotional of men at the best of times, struck me across the face one afternoon.

He had tears in his eyes when he did it, his voice carrying a note of raw desperation as he gripped my arms and gave me a light shake. He asked me why I persisted with this tree story, and what had they done wrong for me to become as I was. Didn't I care how I upset my mother? Didn't I care what people in town said about my strange ways?

What was I to say? His words would have hurt more when I was eleven, but I was growing a thicker skin due to regular sharp words and scornful looks. Still, it did strike a nerve, him accusing me of not caring, of being so thoughtless. All while they blindly punished me for being able to see something they could not. So out of frustration and anger, out of a need to end the debate and the accusations once and for all, I did the one thing I had always held off from doing in anyone else's presence.

I climbed the tree.

I heard my father yelling angrily for me to stop whatever it was I was doing. But even from his vantage on the front porch, I was only two feet up before he could tell at a distance that I was no longer touching the ground. His voice died in his chest, but it was too late. I was now four feet up and the earlier commotion had brought out Mama and John. I was focused on climbing the familiar bark of my special tree, the strangeness of scaling it during daylight hours or for an audience not lost on me but of secondary importance.

Then I heard my mother let out a scream and I almost lost my grip. I shifted my feet and leaned against nearest branch for a moment, catching my breath and my bearings. Turning to glance back at the house, I saw all three of them staring at me with abject horror. I considered going back down, but no. It was time for this to be done.

So I continued to climb until I was over thirty feet up and perched like a raccoon on one of the tallest branches that could support my weight. It was strange, but despite my general dislike of heights, I never felt scared climbing that tree. It made me feel invigorated, as though I was taking part in some secret ritual of nature that was replenishing me body and soul. At the top, I took a moment to take in the sprawling land around us in the fading afternoon light. It was so beautiful.

With more than a little reluctance, I turned my eyes back to my family, who sat huddled and broken on the front porch steps, my brother and father still watching me while my mother wept softly into her hands. I had always imagined their reaction being something like this. To them, I suppose it looked like I convulsed and leapt my way up a tower of nothingness, and now I sat perched in midair. I tried to give them a comforting smile, but I couldn't quite manage it and they likely couldn't have seen it anyway. Instead, I planned to go down and explain to them that I was not making up the tree and that just because they couldn't see it didn't mean it was imaginary or something to fear.

Things went rather differently. As I made my last careful movements back down to the earth, I felt a rope around my neck. I grabbed at it, losing my balance as I was tugged off my feet. It was John and my father. They meant to bind me.

I fought but it was a short contest. I tried to explain, but they would hear nothing more from me. I was locked in the basement that night, and by week's end, this room had been constructed and I was told it would be my new home until "I was released from the Devil's clutches". I found all of this terrifying of course, and I screamed and cried to be released, but it was no use.

In the back of my mind I also found it all very strange, and upon reflection I find it even more so. My parents were religious people, as were John and I, but not overly so. I had never known my family to be prone to bouts of overzealous piety or religious hysteria. And while I had no doubt that what they had seen when I climbed the Ghost Tree was disturbing, I would never have thought them capable of anything approaching this—the abject abandonment and imprisonment of their own child.

Yet I have no clear alternative answer for the past eight years. Their determination has never wavered, and I have never seen any real sign of hope from them that they would reach a point where they would release me. Rather they move about like corpses, or hot air balloons floating along on the buoyancy of sad acceptance and insane conviction. They go through the routines and rituals of caring for me the minimal amount that is required, but I imagine they try their best to forget about me the rest of the time. Just as I can feel my memory of the world and all its colors and smells and sources of joy and imagination fading from me, I can only imagine I have faded away from the world. A ghost haunting the lowest chambers of this house and my family's minds.

And as I have said previously, it was my knowledge and belief in the Ghost Tree that sustained me through all these dark years. The feeling that it was special, that it had somehow picked me, and that the magical connection between myself and it would bear more fruit than me dying in this makeshift cell. But still, I felt the last candle of even this secret hope guttering low.

Then I saw the root poking through the wall. It was a tiny thing—three feet up the back wall of my room, it was impossible to see in the dark and easy to miss in the candlelight. When I saw it and recognized it as a root from the tree, I felt a thrill of excitement run through me. Reaching out a probing finger, I touched the tip of it gently and gasped at the rush of energy that shot through me at the contact. Images and sounds flooded through my mind, and I felt a vitality return to me that I hadn't known since my family had first betrayed me.

My finger had come away from the root at the shock of that first touch, and when I reached towards it again, I saw the root move to meet me. Holding my finger to it the second time was less shocking, but no less profound. I felt my mind drifting as my eyes lost focus and my breathing slowed. I was sitting on the edge of my bed, leaned forward with an index finger touching this strange plant, and as I watched, the wall in front of me seemed to melt away. It was no longer a brick wall, or even the bare earth behind it. Instead, it was a large tunnel a foot taller than I was, wreathed in roots from the Ghost Tree and filled with a sweet-smelling breeze.

The smell was the most powerful part at the time, as though my body and mind were so starved for air that wasn't rancid and stale that the breeze from the tunnel sent me into a deep state of euphoria. I stood and walked into that tunnel without hesitation, unaware of where I was going, but resolute in my determination that any place had to be better than the one I was leaving behind.

As you might imagine, I had much to learn.

Journal Entry 5

I've learned and experienced a lot more since I started transcribing Justin's book, and this record is quickly becoming more of an insurance policy for my safety than an outlet for some kind of relationship angst. I think I might be in real trouble here and I don't understand what's going on. But before I get further into that, I will post the last portion of Justin's writings and then come back after to explain what has happened since I first read it.

****

When I entered the tunnel for the first time, I walked for what seemed like hours. The path would slant up and down, wind this way and that, but the strangest part was that I never grew tired. Whether it was just my exuberance at finally being free of that room or something suffusing the sweet air I was breathing, I went on until I reached a branching path. I took the right most of three options and went on. Five more decisions later, always taking the rightmost option, and I found myself approaching a wall.

I feared that my journey was either at an end or I would have to try and breach the wall to continue, but as I drew closer it faded away and my passage was clear. I was in a basement much like my own, but different in a variety of ways. There was no wall and door partitioning part of this basement into a cell, and the space was entirely bare of any possessions or furniture. After glancing around the basement for a moment, I crept slowly up the steps and eased open the door to the kitchen. The room was bereft of any signs of life or habitation, and the only noise was some distant sound from outside.

Exploring the rest of the house, I found much the same. There were no signs of anyone living there. When I looked out the window upstairs, I began to understand why. This version of the house was sitting on the bedrock of a small island surrounded by blue sea as far as the eye could see. That wasn't entirely true, I suppose, as I could see a larger landmass near the edge of the horizon to the west, but that did nothing to change the fact that this house was wholly isolated and remote. In the span of thirty minutes I had walked the length and breadth of the island twice, and it confirmed my suspicions that I was alone in this corner of whatever strange world this might be.

Well, almost alone.

Two hundred yards from the house the Ghost Tree stood proudly, its leaves blowing gently in the breeze coming off the water. It couldn't be the same tree, of course, yet at the same time I felt sure it was. The tree was somehow connecting this place and where I was from like an umbilical cord of some kind. My mind was torn between taking in all the strange and beautiful sights and marveling at the implications of this hidden, alternate world.

In the end, the joy of being in fresh air and sunshine won out. I spent an hour walking the small stretch of sandy beach in front of the house and looking at the exterior of the house itself. It was strange. This house was like mine, but it wasn't the same. For one thing, it was in far too good a condition, with none of the age or damage that had existed on mine when I last saw its outer walls. For another, there was no sign that a person had ever lived there at all. I saw no screws or nail holes, no faded stains from a piece of furniture or a plant. I had the thought that this wasn't the house at all, but rather the idea of the house. The perfect ideal.

The idea was compelling, and for some reason it temporarily mollified my need for further explanation. Still, I couldn't stay here indefinitely. I still needed clean water and food, and I wanted to ensure I could find my way back to my world before I stayed too long here or elsewhere—if there were other worlds at the end of those other branching paths. With a heavy heart, I went back inside. Going back down into the basement was the hardest part, but I forced myself down those steps and into the place that served as my hell in another version of the world.

The wall began to dissolve at my approach, and on an impulse I bent down and scratched the number "2" onto the floor in the area where the bed was in my version. I wanted to keep track if there were multiple places too similar to discern, and that seemed the best way on short notice.

Then, with a deep breath, I walked back through the wall and into the tunnel. To my surprise, I backtracked rather easily, and within a few minutes I was walking back into my cell. After looking around the room briefly to ensure it truly was my cell, I scratched a "1" into the floor beneath my bed. I then lay down on my bed and began to formulate a plan.

I would store up food and water for the next two days and then venture back out on the third. Ideally, I would either find the tools in some other world to secure my freedom here or find a world that would be more accepting of me than this one. Either way, the last two days have been the hardest of all my time here, I think.

The anticipation of new places, of more freedom, is so wonderful I can hardly bear it. The fear that it won't work for me a second time, or that my plan will be discovered, fills me with the deepest dread. But I am at the precipice now. I have made a crude supply bag out of my pillowcase and the wall, which has been dormant for the last two days, is now already fading away like morning mist in a patch of sunlight.

It may be that these are the last words I write in this precious book that has been my sole confidant in the darkness and light of these past few days. I hope the end of this story, chronicled or no, finds me well and safe and free.

Journal Entry 6

That was the end of the writing of Justin Paring. When I finished reading it, I went back down to that room and I saw the number "1" scratched onto the floor as he described. But more than that, I saw what looked like a thin, red root sticking out between the bricks on the far wall. It was just outside the edge of the black, spongey man-shape on the wall, and when I stepped back I saw it was actually close enough to one shadow hand that it looked as though the root and finger were moving to touch each other.

I felt a thrill of excitement and fear, and before I knew it I was reaching out to touch the root myself. A sudden noise from upstairs brought me up short only inches from contact. It was Phil coming home. Still determined to not share what I'd discovered, I hid the book and went up to greet him, trying to spin vague tales of unpacking and home improvements while counting the hours until he was asleep and I could think what to do next.

Ultimately, I decided it was a good thing that Phil had interrupted me. I needed to learn more about all of this before I made any rash decisions. I started by asking Phil for the name of the real estate agent that had sold us the house. I had been present for the signing of some paperwork at the end, but I had never dealt with the agent.

But Phil told me that there was no agent. He had bought the house from an estate administrator who had listed the house online. That was strange, because I felt sure he'd mentioned an agent before, but I couldn't say for sure. He asked why I was wondering, and I made up the excuse that I wanted to know if the old owners had the names of specific paint colors they'd used in the house. In typical Phil fashion, he accepted this without further argument and finished getting ready for bed.

The next day I went to the library, which unlike every movie or t.v. show I've ever seen, was grossly unhelpful in finding out any details about the creepy old house I was living in or the prior owners.

I was running out of ideas when I passed a sign that said "Historical Society".

It was apparently a quasi-museum to local history, though its small size and overwhelming to devotion old farm equipment and pictures of the main street fifty years earlier didn't give the best impression of its depth or breadth. Fortunately, the woman that ran the place was very friendly and knowledgeable. She said that her great-grandmother had actually been a distant cousin of the Paring family.

"They were an odd bunch to be sure. Kept to themselves, especially as the boys got older. Then people started noticing that Justin was nowhere to be found. Never came to town or went to church any more. But it was a different time back then. People tended to their own business more, and they weren't going to ask questions if they didn't have to. Rumors were that Justin had run off or died and the parents just couldn't take it."

"So nobody ever saw Justin again?" I felt a mixture of sadness and relief welling up inside me. Sadness that Justin's terrible life had been real and relief that he might have finally escaped it to a better place.

She shook her head. "No, but then the rest of the family didn't last long either. One night, someone came in on them and killed the parents and the brother. Or at least that's what people figured. There was blood and they were all missing, though no bodies were ever found."

I couldn't help but feel some grim satisfaction that they were punished for how they'd treated Justin. Whatever he did to them, it wasn't enough. But the woman was frowning now.

"I could have sworn I had a picture of them. I know I did. I swear, this is going to drive me crazy until I find it." She looked up from talking to herself and patted my arm with a smile. "I'm sorry, honey. But I tell you what. Give me your number and I'll send you a copy of the picture if I find it."

Half an hour later and I was back down in the basement. Enough with being safe. I wanted to see how much of it was real. I reached out and touched the root, feeling a surge of power flood my body as I did so. Falling back against the rotten mattress, my hand punched through the fabric and onto rusty springs. I jerked my hand away, fears of tetanus dancing in my head, but I saw no cut or scratch. Besides, I had other things to think about. Like how the wall in front of me had just dissolved.

Still feeling the rush of energy crackling across my skin, I stood up and began walking forward. The tunnel was just as he had described, and I could smell the sweet, glowing air wafting into that dank secret room as I…

I felt my phone buzz once. Then again.

Stifling a wave of irritation, I took out my phone and opened it. There were two new text messages from a number I didn't have a name associated with. When I opened it, I realized it was the woman from the historical society. The first text was a message. It said:

Found it! This is a picture from Easter of 1901. The Baptist Church took family photos for all the local families that were members. This is the Paring family from left to right. John, Stewart, Edna, Justin.

The second text was the picture itself. It was black and white, of course, but of surprisingly good quality for its age. Zooming in on my phone, I filled the screen with the faces of each person in turn.

John, his smile friendly but sad.

Stewart, his eyes hard and stern.

Edna, her face open and warm.

Justin…Justin…it…it wasn't possible.

I texted the woman back, asking her if she was sure. If she was sure that the person in that picture, the person on the far right, was Justin Paring back in 1901. A moment later she responded that she was certain, was something wrong?

I didn't reply back. I had no response to give that would make any sense. Because the person in the picture, years younger looking but unmistakably him, the person she said was Justin Paring…I knew him. I knew him very well.

It was Phil.

Just then I heard the front door open upstairs. He was home.

I considered going upstairs. Trying to make up more half-truths or confronting Phil/Justin. But instead I ran into the tunnel.

Five feet in the wall behind me faded back into view, and while I assumed I could still get back out that way, at the moment I didn't care. I was tired of waiting for something special, tired of being scared when something this magical was right in front of me. I was going to see things for myself instead of just reading about it.

The tunnel went on, chamber after chamber of deep red roots and dark, loamy earth. As Justin had described, I eventually came to a branching of paths. Instead of taking the rightmost, I took the center. On and on I went for what felt like hours. But I was never tired or hungry, and with each branching path I just felt my urgency to go further growing. Center path every time, always leading to another choice further down the tangled path.

Then I saw I was entering a larger chamber. It was roughly circular in shape, the ceiling and walls made up of an endless cascade of roots woven tightly together except for several openings every few feet that I assumed led to other twisting paths. The roots here weren't red for the most part, but a smoky grey that was almost black. And the flesh of those roots was blistered and scarred in many places as though there had been a fire here at one point.

Looking to the center of the room, I saw a small upgrowth of branches that almost looked like a pedestal of sorts for the black tangle of roots that lay atop it. If I had to guess, I'd say this is where the fire had started, but whatever had happened, the Ghost Tree (or Trees, depending on how you looked at it) had survived. I could see green shoots and new, unscarred red bark poking through the black ashy residue the flames had left behind.

I was reaching out to touch it, felt a strong and compelling need to touch it, but something held me back. Whatever this place was, it was clearly significant. Important. And I had a sense that in some ways it was more of a doorway and threshold than even passing into the tunnel had been. So I stepped back, picked a new tunnel, and journeyed on.

While my cell phone was useless for phone calls here, I used it to keep track of my choice in the larger chamber and the couple of times when there was an even number of tunnels with no "center path" to pick. Finally, after what felt like another hour or more, I saw a wall.

When I approached it, it dissolved away much like the wall in my house had done, but instead of entering a dank secret cell I appeared to be entering a large, well-lit room that someone used as a woodworking shop. Entering quietly, I listened for any signs of movement, but there were none. I was still in the basement of the house…of a version of the house, and the combination of similarities and differences made it seem surreal. I paused to look under a work bench occupied by a belt sander and what I thought might be a Dremel of some sort, and there I saw a faded "43" scratched into the floor where the bed was in my version of the house.

Going into the other room, I saw it was some kind of media room, though what I thought must be the television was simply a large pane of either glass or plastic suspended from the ceiling by two braided wires. I had no idea how something like that would work, but I supposed it didn't matter. It might be the least of the differences in this world.

I crept up the stairs and eased open the basement door, and as it swung open I saw two men sitting at a table eating cereal. Or rather they had been eating cereal. Now they were staring at me.

"What the fuck?" One of them bellowed as he stood up, his expression a dangerous combination of fear and anger. "Who the fuck are you, lady?"

The other man was trying to calm him down, but he wasn't listening. I slammed the door back shut before he reached it and ran down the stairs two at a time, desperate to reach the wall and terrified that it might not open for me this time.

But the tunnel was ready and waiting, and as I passed into it, the wall closed behind me, protecting me. I stood there for a moment, hands on my knees and breathing heavy, more out of fear and adrenaline than exertion. I had to be more careful. I never knew what I was going to be getting myself into, and I had to be ready.

I debated heading back then. I could get proper supplies and then head back out to explore more worlds with more than my cell phone and determination. But I finally decided I would give it one more try first. I backtracked two junctions and then took another path. This time the tunnel went on for quite some time, and after seven more choices I found myself at another wall. The basement I entered was pitch black, and I gave a shudder as I crossed over into it with my cell phone's flashlight app acting as my only source of illumination. It was freezing here. I almost turned back, but then I spied a number etched onto the floor.

"71".

For some reason that made me want to go on. I needed to see more of what Justin had seen. Try to understand more of what he experienced before I confronted him. He had obviously been lying to me, possibly trying to trick me into something, and I didn't want to go into that conversation with nothing but his old writings to guide me.

So I went forward very slowly into the rest of the basement, holding up my little phone like a guiding star as I pushed through the cold darkness. I listened at the top of the stairs for a couple of minutes before deciding it was probably safe to open it. When I did so, I saw the house was totally empty, much like Justin had described in his trip to the house on the island.

I also realized that while the house itself was dark, there was a faint blue glow coming through the windows. My first thought was that I was in a world where it was late twilight or early morning, but when I approached the window over the kitchen sink, I saw I was wrong.

I was in a cave.

The house, as strange and impossible as it seemed, was sitting in some kind of massive cave. I went to the front door and opened it. The air was even colder outside, and while there were no distinct sources of light, the air was saturated with a soft, blue glow. It reminded me in some ways of the light in the tunnels of the Ghost Tree, but instead of being comforting, it filled me with a vague and terrible sense of dread.

Still, I wanted to see this through. I left the front door open for a quick escape and walked a few steps further into the cave. It was an enormous cavern, and in the distance I could barely make out several dark spots that I assumed were tunnels leading to other parts of the whatever cave system this was on whatever world I found myself in.

I turned to my right and saw the Ghost Tree there, its red branches and green flowing leaves blowing in the currents of some breeze I couldn't feel. I felt a surge of happiness and familiarity at seeing it, as though I had run into an old friend, and I found myself heading toward it. Then I noticed the bodies stacked at its base.

Perfectly preserved, twenty bodies or more were stacked at the tree's base, and my first thought was that it was some kind of strange offering by whoever or whatever lived here. Then I saw the black lines of corruption that traced itself from several of the bodies to the trunk of the massive tree. The bodies were poisoning it. I saw the distended belly of one of the bodies shift. Or something inside the bodies was poisoning it.

I took a step back, taking in more of the details of the cavern I had stupidly decided would be good to explore. There were more bodies at different spots along the floor, some with swollen, shifting stomachs, others looking as though they were simply taking a nap. All told I saw over a hundred bodies in the dim gloom of that unending indigo light. And among all those bodies were numerous lines cut in the stony floor. Almost as though they had been cut with a blade or a saw.

What do you offer as tribute for your need, Traveler?

The voice echoed in my mind like the high tones of a church bell. Intelligent and feminine, it carried an undercurrent of inhuman emotion that could have been a cousin of anger or amusement or both. I spun around, looking for the source. At first I saw nothing, but then at one of the black tunnels in the distance, I saw a pair of blue flames dancing in the air.

They were its eyes.

I ran into the house, shutting the front and basement door behind me as I ran down the stairs and back to the tunnel. That was enough for me. I wanted to go home and leave all this behind. I'd talk to Justin/Phil if he wanted, but after that I was packing my shit and never coming back to any version of that fucking house again.

It took what seemed like hours to make it back. I found the way easily, and even when I ran across that central burned chamber with its multitude of paths, I picked the right one without hesitation. But it still felt like it was taking forever. When I finally crossed back into Justin's cell, I was so filled with relief that it took me several moments to notice what was different.

The wall dividing the cell from the rest of the basement was back up.

I had dismantled a large central portion of the brick wall that had separated Justin's room from the rest of the house. That had now all been replaced with new bricks except for a small space two bricks wide and tall. It was just enough space for me to see Phil looking in at me.

"Hey there, honey. Been on a little trip have you? Did you have a good time?"

I ran up to the wall, realizing in passing that the cell was now lit by a pair of LED lanterns on the nightstand and chest respectively. He was setting me up in here, the bastard.

"Phil, Justin, whatever you call yourself, let me out of here."

He smiled at me pleasantly. "No can do, buttercup. And even if I did, it wouldn't do you any good. You belong to the tree now. I felt it when it passed from me to you."

I pushed against the brick angrily, but it didn't budge. "Why are you doing this?" I paused and added. "I love you."

His smile grew colder. "That's real cute. You know, you've been gone for an entire day. I only started working on the wall a couple of hours ago. Before that I did some light reading. Your precious fucking journal."

Taking a couple of steps back, he lifted my journal from a dwindled stack of bricks he had brought down for the job. "You see, the difference between your journal and mine is that I had actual problems to write about. Well, that and mine is far better written. Jesus, I had a ninth-grade education when I wrote this, and you have a masters' degree. The modern education system really is shit." He shook his head before taking a deep breath. "But no…I'm mad and hurt, and it's making me petty. Let me start over."

He sat the journal back on the bricks and approached the hole in the wall. "When I went into those tunnels again, I was so happy and excited. I thought I was about to go on some magical adventure and live a life full of freedom and wonder. Instead, you know what I found?"

My mind was still racing for some way out of this, but I thought it best to humor him for now. "What's that?"

He wasn't smiling any longer. "After traveling to over two hundred different worlds, I figured out three things. One, many worlds are filled with people much like us. After a few dozen of those, I gave up on finding a world where people aren't largely selfish pieces of shit. Two, some of those worlds are much, much worse." Phil paused, cocking his head. "Which ones did you go to? I don't know if you noticed, but I numbered pretty much every one I went to."

I stared at him dully, trying not to show how much I wanted to break through that wall and reach him. "Um, 43 and 71."

He seemed to ponder for a moment and then his eyes went wide. "71? Oh shit, really? You have an awesome sense of direction. Wow. Yeah, I don't advise a return trip there."

I shuddered at the memory. "Yeah, I don't plan to. Look, I don't want to go anywhere any more. Please just let me out and I'll do whatever you want. Stay, go, I don't care. Just don't leave me in here."

He was already shaking his head, and he actually looked sad now. "No. I'm sorry, but no. Because the third thing I figured out was that once you touch the root and enter the tunnel, you're bound to the Ghost Tree. At first I thought it was a gift. I aged incredibly slowly, I never got hungry or thirsty or tired in the tunnels, and I had all these places I could go."

Phil shoved my journal off the brick pile onto the floor and sat down. "But after a few months of that, I got tired of it. I found a world that seemed to be less terrible than most, and I settled down. I built a life there. Fell in love." He put his hands in his lap and I could see they were balled into fists. "And then one day I woke up in the tunnels. In what I call the heart room."

"I found my way back to my new world, my new life. But the tree wouldn't open the way. Eventually I figured out that I had to go back and stay with it in the heart room. I couldn't explore any world during that time. What seemed like an eternity passed, and periodically I would go back to the tunnel I needed and still see the wall up. Until finally it wasn't."

"I was so happy. I ran through into the basement, up the stairs, and I set out to find my girlfriend or any of the friends I had made. That's when I realized ten years had passed." He leaned forward, looking at me somberly. "What it amounts to is this. You can go and explore, but after about two to three years, the tree pulls you back. And after that, you have to stay with it for five times whatever time you had on the outside. I don't know if it's lonely, or it needs us for something, or if it's just mean, but that's the rules."

I started to say I was sorry, and he just raised his hand with a glare. "Save it. I'm trying to explain as a kindness. So you don't start all this totally in the dark like I was. Don't push it." He waited a second and then went on. "After I figured out how much time had passed, I gave up on staying in that world. I went to exploring again, although without the hope of a permanent life somewhere, it didn't mean as much. I figured out what I'm telling you over the years, staying for different amounts of time in different places, and after everything I saw, I realized something."

"I wasn't special. None of us are. I've seen multiple older versions of myself. They were all unremarkable. I've met people across scores of worlds, and there aren't more than a handful that stand out. But while that was depressing in some ways, it also gave me hope that I didn't have to be the one to bear this burden forever. I could find a replacement."

"As I think you may have figured out by now, I did away with my parents and brother too. It was during a dark time early on, before I had found my new world and love, but after I had become despondent in my travels. I came back and killed them in their sleep, dragging their bodies into the tunnels for a reason that made sense at the time but is lost on me now. Years later, I came back and bought the house from the bank who was left holding it. Oddly enough, people hadn't been lining up to buy the old murder house with the creepy vibes, so I got it cheap. This was in the 1950s, and I've been sitting on it since, periodically coming out to try and find a good replacement."

"But it hasn't been easy. I figured out over time that you can't just knock someone out and put them in the tunnel. You can't force them to agree to enter it either. No, they have to voluntarily touch the root and enter the tunnel for them to be bound in your place."

He laughed bitterly. "Of course, I didn't know that for sure until now. It was all guesswork. About fifteen years ago I decided it was no use and I was better off trying to kill the fucking tree even if I died with it. So I came out, got a drum of gasoline, and tried to burn down the heart room."

"Yeah I saw." He looked up at my words and grinned, giving a nod. "It didn't look like it worked too well."

His expression darkened and he stood back up. "No…no it didn't. I think I hurt it, but I don't know if it can die. So I gave up on that and went back to trying to find someone I could get to take my place, if it was even possible. That's when you came along. Well, not you. But another version of you."

My eyes widened. "What're you talking about?"

He quirked an eyebrow. "What do you think? Alternate worlds, alternate yous. Keep up. I met another version of you and got into a relationship with them. I got them to the house, but they weren't as curious and hardworking as you are. They didn't take the bait from my subtle hints or even me 'discovering' the hidden room I had made there. By the time I was getting them interested, I was pulled back into the fucking heart."

"You should have given them a mysterious note." I knew I should keep quiet since I just made him angrier, but I couldn't help it. But this time Phil was looking confused.

"Note? I didn't ever leave you a no…Oh wait. What did it say?"

"Come live in the ashes of my heart. You're saying you didn't write that? It was in your, or at least your old Justin, handwriting."

Phil shrugged. "Honestly, no note from me. I guess the Tree did that. Its attempt at being mysterious and ironic, maybe? I don't know. I wondered how you got on it so quick. I guess the Tree was tired of me too, which is understandable."

He looked away, his expression strange. "Anyway, when I could leave the tunnels again I came back here and found you. Sought you out, if I'm being honest. And you know, I actually loved you. I've been really conflicted this entire time about if I could even go through with this. Well," he glanced down at my journal on the ground, "at least before reading that."

He turned around and grabbed up a new brick, scraping mortar into the space it was going to go. I started screaming for him to stop, but he didn't pause. After a couple of minutes, there was only one brick left out of place.

"I put those lanterns in there for you, and there's a backpack on the bed with food and water. I'd suggest you travel around, just be careful and mind your time limits. Don't get too attached to any place because you can't stay forever. And I left you a new journal on the chest. Maybe you'll write about this part too. If you leave it behind when you're done, I'll keep it safe. Maybe let other people read what you wrote even. It won't matter." He paused, his eyes troubled. "I guess I'll be a villain in your story."

He started putting mortar around the edges of the final opening. "I went to 211 different worlds. And you know what? There were cells like this one in 93 of them, along with 93 corpse versions of me. Living in that room, I had always wanted to believe that my family had just made a mistake. That they were good people that just picked the wrong way when the path forked. But no, that was just who they were, through and through." He put the last brick into position and started pushing it in. "I guess everyone is someone's villain."

You saw something you shouldn't have.

Part One

So I'm posting this on here understanding that most people will think this is some unfinished story, a piece of fiction written like it really happened. I understand and accept that. I'm familiar with this reddit, and while I haven't read a ton of stuff on here, I've enjoyed what I read, and I think I "get it".

But I also don't know who to ask about this, especially without seeming crazy or turning to some weird forum that will get me unreliable answers from pranksters or crazy people. So if someone has ever heard of something like this before, or you have some thought or suggestion, please post it. Or if you think I'm making it all up, I get that too and no hard feelings.

I work as in-house legal counsel at a medium-sized, pretty profitable real estate company based in the southeast. I've been an attorney for nearly ten years, and the closest I've come to a courtroom is when I go to a courthouse to do land title searches. I've been married for eight years and we have a four-year old little boy. I say all this so you have some idea that I have a good but pretty ordinary life. I don't have strange hobbies or friends, and I don't typically go outside of the normal boundaries of my day to day existence to meet odd people or experience dangerous things.

But last Tuesday, I woke up to a strange text message. My alarm was set for 7am, but my phone buzzed about 6:40, and it stirred me out of sleep enough that I checked it. It said, "You saw something you shouldn't have". Being half-asleep, I kind of stared at it for a minute, trying to figure out what I had seen before the overall weirdness of the message dawned on me.

First of all, the sender was blank. No name, no number, no symbols, no indication that there were blank spaces like someone had hit a spacebar repeatedly and it had taken the input as characters. I couldn't even highlight anything in the sender space. Second, the font of the message was different. Not like it was a different font than normal, but there were several letters that shifted noticeably higher or lower than the letters around them in a given word. Third, I haven't seen anything. Aside from going to work, a parent-teacher conference, and out to pick up a pizza, I can't think of anywhere I've even gone in the week prior to that message, and I sure haven't seen anything weird or criminal or whatever.

I show it to my wife, and she just laughs it off. Says it's probably some marketing thing or maybe a wrong number. That seems like a reasonable possibility, so I push it aside. Two nights later, I start having bad dreams.

When I was little I used to have night terrors. I'd wake my brother up screaming my head off, and it got so bad that even though my parents couldn't really afford it, they took me to a sleep clinic for a few days when I was eight. I don't remember what help they really gave me, but I know it stopped or I grew out of it, and aside from the occasional normal nightmare I've never had any problems since.

But this dream, while it was unpleasant to some degree, didn't feel like a nightmare or even a dream. It felt very real and strangely mundane. I was at a dimly lit library, going through old books, and while I can't say what I was looking for, I know I felt a growing sensation of frustration and unease that it wasn't there.

When I woke up, instead of feeling relieved I felt panicked, and in my sleep-addled stupor I tried to force myself back to sleep, but of course that never works. After a few minutes, my phone buzzed. It was another message in the one-sided conversation from the mystery sender.

"You saw something you shouldn't have and you need to stop before your life". The message stopped there, but there was a photo attached. It was a dark picture of a man squatting down in an aisle, peering intently at a row of faded books on a low and dusty shelf. The heavy, metal bookshelves and the long aisle made it clear it was a library, and while the picture was at a bad angle and poorly shot, I could tell it was me. Not me from any library I'd actually ever been in, but me from my dream.

I felt sick as the idea bloomed and took root in me, and I considered waking my wife to show her, but something in me resisted the impulse. Maybe it was fear that she would look at me with worry, or worse, sadness and fear, in her eyes. I don't know. But I haven't told her yet. I haven't told her about the last of it either.

The dreams have continued. Me at some strange place I consider home in the dream, me at a restaurant, me walking through some unknown town on a stormy afternoon with patches of hail coming down intermittently, thudding against an umbrella with a heavy, wrought metal handle. All these things seem real, and I wake in a strange panic. No more messages for the last few days though, and while I've grown to dread and hate my phone when it buzzes, my hope was that whatever strangeness had been happening was fading and would eventually take the dreams with it. This morning I found a coin on my nightstand.

I call it a coin because it is a small flat disc in the shape of a coin and with a heft as though it was made of metal. But its surface is not metal. It seems to be some kind of mottled gray leather or scales, almost like shark skin. But it is solid and sturdy, and it has some kind of embossing, but it is hard to make out due to the thing's color and texture. And it's probably my imagination, but it feels like it's warm.

The message buzzed through a few minutes after I found the coin. "You saw something you shouldn't have and you need to stop before your life is consumed".

I think I need help, I just don't know what kind. Has anyone experienced anything like this before? I don't know what is going on and I don't think the message is fucking finished yet. Please respond if you know anything. Brief update: I appreciate the responses both public and private. Some helpful information and suggestions. I've considered trying to text back, but I didn't at first out of concern it was a phishing scam, and later because I was honestly scared and wanted to ignore it hoping it would go away. Worried it might provoke a reaction. But it is good advice and I will try it. My wife is taking our son to her parents tomorrow, so I'll wait and try it when I'm alone just in case. I do know I'm not imagining the texts though. Both my wife and a guy I'm friends with at work read them too. Haven't shown anyone the coin yet. Idk. Anyway, thank you again and I'll post an update in the next few days.

Part Two

My son is gone. I don't know how else to say it or how else to start this, and I don't know what the point of any of this is at this point, but I also feel like this is the only place I can actually talk and not sound crazy, even if it's just because everyone here thinks it's just a story I'm telling.

When I say he is gone, my beautiful, smart, funny boy Luke, that is what I mean. Not kidnapped, not run off, not missing. As far as I can tell, he has been obliterated from this world entirely.

After my first post the other day, I took to heart some of the advice I received and decided I would try responding to the text messages. I was going to wait until Thursday because I knew my wife and son would be leaving to spend a few days with her parents. Not because of all this, you understand, just a visit that's been planned for the past few months. The trip is five hours and to another state, so it doesn't happen often, but I saw no reason for them not to go this time, especially when no strangeness had seemed to touch them yet and I was about to do something that might provoke some unknown response.

So yesterday morning I woke up at 6:30, thinking I'd get up early and have breakfast with them before I went to work, as they would have already left before I got home that night and I wouldn't see them again until Sunday. When I stepped out of our bedroom, I saw Luke's door was closed. This was strange, because we never close that door so we can hear him and keep a better eye on him. But I figured he'd just shut it and was either playing or still asleep. I knocked and then opened the door, but it wasn't his room.

It was the same room, but with no sign of Luke in it. Where his bed had been there was an elliptical machine with clothes hanging off it. Instead of a collection of army men and tanks on the floor, there were boxes of books and an old t.v. The room was not full, but there was no sign of recent movement of objects to or from the room. I even thought and looked at the walls for thumbtack holes where Luke's posters had been hung, but the walls were unmarked and covered with old, faded paint.

You need to understand that two weeks ago I would have left the room immediately, assuming I had made a mistake or was going crazy, and would have sought the right room or some kind of help. But now, I am already fearful I'm going insane or that something large and terrible is coming for me. I take more care to look and consider, to see if reality is consistent with what I'm perceiving. So it was only after I went through the room thoroughly and found no sign of my boy that I checked the others. And it was only after I had searched everywhere upstairs that I began looking for my wife.

It seems odd to me in retrospect that I didn't think she would be gone too. Maybe I had some dim, animal sense of her presence in the house, or maybe I was just too overwhelmed to process any more at the moment. In any case, there she was, eating a bowl of cereal at the bar that divides our kitchen and living room. She gave me a sleepy smile at first, but it quickly faded as she saw my expression and heard what I was saying.

"Where's Luke?"

"Who? Luke?"

I tried to keep my voice even, but I could hear my fear and rage creeping in. "Luke. Our son... Where is he. What happened to his room. Why are you looking confused?"

I swear she looked genuinely concerned as she stood up and came towards me. "Honey. You need to calm down. I think you had another weird dream. One where we had a child, I guess? We don't have any children, at least not yet."

I was already shaking my head as she spoke. "No. No. You're lying, or under someone's control. We have a fucking child. His name is Luke. He's going to be five in June. He's..." I started crying some at that point, and when she reached out to hold me, I didn't pull away. We kept talking for the next couple of hours, during which she showed me photo albums, social media, emails that all either contained no trace of Luke or actual references to us not having kids yet. I agreed to go to a psychologist immediately, and my wife began making calls, but the quickest I could be seen on a nonemergency basis was this coming Monday, and I got her to agree that making this an emergency was jumping the gun, especially with what it could do to my career or bar license.

She said she needed to go into town in the afternoon and I told her to go, that I was okay. That it was probably just stress and bad dreams. In truth, I needed her to go so I had time for what I needed to do. It may be that I'm crazy, but I'd like to be sure before I commit to that path. If I get medicated, or worse, committed, it may be too late.

So she leaves, me waving and assuring her I'll stay right there, and ten minutes later I'm in my car. I'd like to say that I lied to her to protect her, and that is true. But it isn't the whole truth. I also didn't trust her entirely, and I wanted to verify Luke's existence without her.

So I head to his school. I talk first to his teacher and then the administration. I do it in that order intentionally because I know I'll likely never get to the teacher if I've already been asking strange questions at the office. I try to ask my questions calmly and with some subtlety, but that's hard to pull off when you are asking about a child that has either been erased or never existed. Both the teacher and the office said Luke was never at that school. They also acted like they didn't know me, when I have memories of going to open house, two conferences, and the Christmas program.

I sat out in my car afterward for a few minutes, crying and trying to reconcile what I knew and felt with the world I'd woken up in. I was close to giving up and going home before I was missed when something occurred to me. I knew that teacher.

Aside from related to Luke, I'd never been to that school or met that teacher. Yet I knew her name, her face, where her room was, and what it looked like. Whatever was happening, it really was happening, or I was so far gone that I was lying to myself and creating facts as needed to sustain the delusion. In either case, I made the decision to pursue it further.

I text my wife, apologizing for leaving, telling her not to worry and that I'll be back the following day. I have a long trip ahead of me. Luke was born in the same county my wife is from, the same place I thought they would be heading to today to visit his grandparents. I'd already rejected trying to confirm his existence with my wife's parents for several reasons, but I did want to check the birth records at the county probate court. It was one of the few official ways of verifying a young child's existence, and my hope was if there was some kind of....manipulation going on, maybe it wouldn't go that wide or deep. And yes, I know I sound paranoid and insane at this point, and will moreso later on.

After sending my wife a long text, I finally send a text to the unknown number. "What happened to my son?" I probably typed and erased ten different messages before settling on that one. Not too vague or specific, not overly emotional or confrontational. I waited for ten minutes for a response, but none came. Setting the phone down, I headed out.

There was no way I would make it to the probate court before it closed for the day, so I drove slowly, using the time to think. At one point I stopped and got something to eat at a fast food place, going inside just to be out of the car for a little while. After forcing myself to eat a few bites of a burger I didn't want, I was still inside when I had an idea. I had brought that strange coin with me. I didn't really remember picking it up, but I was in a frenzied rush when I left the house. I went back up to the condiment bar in the restaurant and got five packs of sugar, emptying them on the table and spreading them in a thick but even circle a little bigger than the coin. My idea was that I could try pressing the coin into the sugar to see if I could tell anything from the imprint it left behind.

I did it on both sides, and on one side there were strange shapes and what might be words along one edge, but they were faint and nothing I recognized. On the other side it seemed like there was a picture of something. Possibly a whale? I tried to take pictures with my phone, but the flash washed it out and no flash was too dark. I gave up and went on the road again.

By 10:30 I was close to the area and was going to look for a place to park for the night, having found the idea of getting a room with my card somewhat terrifying, as though someone would find me and capture me in my sleep. I had already gotten money out of the ATM before heading out that afternoon, and it needed to last me for a while for food and gas. But speaking of gas, I needed some. I'd been so preoccupied that I let it get down to the fuel light, and the only gas station within the next thirty miles was lit up but closed.

The sign on the door said "Back by midnite", and while I had no guarantee it was true, my stupidity had left me with few other options. So I sat and waited. The attendant did come back a few minutes before midnight as promised, but something else happened before she got there.

I had gotten out of the car a second time to stretch my legs and wake myself up some, pacing the lit parking lot of the gas station and peering out into the surrounding dark. In the distance I could see the dim shadowy shapes of a couple of houses, partially lit by three amber street lights that seemed to have been haphazardly placed to poorly light that spot in the road. Everything was so still and quiet. It felt like I was the only thing living in some dead or frozen world. Then I saw movement in the distance.

It was at the edge of the pool of light thrown down by the farthest street light, dipping in and out of the dark. I couldn't see much, and my first thought was that it was a large plastic bag of some sort being blown by the wind. Except it didn't move right, and there was no wind. I would just catch glimpses of it, light and dark, shiny and rippling, several feet above the ground and bobbing like an obscene balloon tugged by an invisible child. I ran back to my car and locked myself inside, and was ready to leave gas or no gas, but when I looked again it was gone. When the girl came and unlocked the door, I thrust forty dollars at her and pumped the gas as quickly as possible, getting back out on the road too fast but maintaining control of the wheel.

I didn't stop until I reached the courthouse, and I parked nearby for the night. My plan had been to sleep in the car, but there was no sleep to be had at this point. I kept watching for that shape and writing this that you are reading. If I am able, I will post this today, which is Friday. This has become a journal of sorts for me, and I still hold out hope it may lead to help, but at least it will be a record if nothing else.

Update: Apparently the lady that is in charge of birth and death records is at a funeral and won't be back until after lunch, so I will post this now. I will try to post again soon with what I found and any other update. Thank you all again for listening and trying to help.

Part Three

I've had a lot happen in the past few days. I'm currently using the wifi in the lobby of a motel I stayed at last night and I've been aimlessly wandering since Saturday, never staying at the same place more than one night. But I think that's over--it's not accomplishing anything, and I'm very tired. And that's not what happened first. That's not where we left off, is it?

I looked back at what I had posted last, and it was all accurate. The last few days have made me feel surer that I am either so insane that I'm likely in a padded room right now, rocking in my own piss and shit, dreaming up all this, including writing to you, or it's real. If it is real, I think there's a very good chance that I'm in Hell, in which case would that make it real or just an imagined torment? I don't know, but I find the semantics of it pretty funny at this point.

But back to the story, right? Got to tell the fucking story. And I do. I feel compelled, and when I'm getting it out I feel more at peace than any other time, like I'm lancing a boil. Enough of my whining. On with it.

I went back into the probate court that afternoon and met with a Ms. Mercer, who was pleasant and helpful enough, though she had no real help to give. She said that the paper records were all transferred into their database back to 2002, which of course covered Luke who was born in 2013. No sign of him. Tried every search parameter, but no luck.

So then I start asking about doing a search of the physical records. Even when they put those records in a computer system, they have to keep the originals of vital records in most states. The woman was again helpful as she could be, saying that I was in luck because they had records going back to 1982 in the courthouse, though they were about to transfer everything up to 2015 to an off-site storage facility in the next few weeks to make more room. After that, paper copies from the originals would take a written request and a few days turnaround. But again, she pointed out unironically, today was my lucky day.

She led me into a cavernous room filled with deed books and land plats, which made me realize I'd never even called into work the day before or today. Pushing the thought aside, I followed her through another door to a smaller, more densely packed room full of file cabinets. She showed me how the filing system worked and offered to help further, but I told her I could work on it myself. I planned to be thorough, so I had made up a more elaborate story that I was doing genealogical research and Luke was a distant cousin. This made it easier to explain that I would need some time to look through records for not only him, but any other lost relatives. In truth, I just wanted to be alone with the records and make sure it was not misfiled if I didn't find his birth certificate right away. Ms. Mercer nodded cheerfully and meandered away, heading to a nearby breakroom where another woman was apparently eating some variety of office birthday cake.

I began searching, and it took little time to see it wasn't there. No sign it ever had been. I expanded my search to the entire drawer, then the two drawers before and after, going through each certificate individually. It was monotonous, but as I searched I began picking up on pieces of the conversation between Mercer and the cake lady.

They were talking about the funeral Mercer had been to that morning. It was for a man who had run a local barbershop for a number of years, a man who Ms. Mercer clearly thought a lot of and had even dated briefly when they were both just out of high school. There was some wistful talk of him being kind and handsome, but what caught my attention was their tone of voice as they spoke. It carried not just sadness or regret, but a thick cord of fear. At first I didn't understand, as it was incongruous with what they were saying. Then they started discussing how he died.

The man had been found out behind his barbershop one morning earlier this week, having apparently been attacked the night before. No one knew what had attacked him, but his entire head was riddled with tiny holes. Face, scalp, even under his jaw. The cake woman, whose brother was apparently the local coroner, said they were like teeth marks, but long needle teeth, and from all angles and from nothing that he had ever seen. In any case, the damage done had been extensive. His head had been crushed and punctured severely, and according to the same coroner, and this last part had not been discussed publicly, while the injuries would have killed him, he actually died fairly slowly from suffocation, possibly while still being bitten.

About that time the women looked out at me and I realized I had stopped just sneaking glances and was staring at them. I smiled and nodded, pretending to go back to my search, but after whispering to each other for a moment, they headed back up to the front. After they were gone, I pushed the story from my mind and headed back into the drawers.

After an hour I gave up on finding Luke. I wanted to cry, but I felt too hollowed out and tired to actually do it. Turning to head back up to the front and away from the courthouse, I had a thought. My wife was born in this county too, back in 1984.

I didn't know why I felt like I needed to check her too until I did. There was no birth certificate for her either. I searched the entire drawer, a new wellspring of panic rising in my chest. Trying to catch my breath, I pulled out my phone.

First, I checked my text messages. She had sent me three the day before asking me to come home, but each time I had just sent a text back saying I was okay and I would see her when I got back. But since then, nothing. I had assumed she had given up for the moment, but now I wasn't sure. I called three times to her cell number and twice to the home phone, but there was no answer at either. They just rang.

I almost ran from the place, but I got control of myself and waited long enough to ask Ms. Mercer to run a computer check for my wife before I left. Again, nothing. I already felt myself growing numb. Thanking her, I left the office.

The trip back home was uneventful, and I honestly don't remember most of it, my head in a dull fog. I felt like I was just waiting to read the report saying I had terminal cancer after the doctor had already given me the bad news. My life was gone. Anything further was just going to be confirmation.

I pulled up at the house, and felt a rueful lack of surprise that there was no sign of my wife's car. My key worked--the house was still mine apparently, but there was no sign of my family or their belongings. I checked the house thoroughly more out of some need for completeness than out of any real hope, and found nothing. Two hours later, exhausted in every sense, I passed out on the sofa.

I found myself in another one of those too-real dreams. I was walking down a dark alleyway in some unknown, rain-soaked city, my face cold as wind whipped past me, bringing with it the spicy scent of old decay. I was headed towards the bright spot in the alley, a neon sign hanging above a door that appeared to belong to some kind of bar or club.

There was a bouncer at the door, a thick-necked man with a collapsible baton held casually in his meaty left hand. Without thinking about it, I pulled a coin from my pocket, holding it in my palm for him to see. It was the strange coin I had found or its twin. In the dream, I saw and felt it pulse and shift on my palm slightly, though my dreamself did not scream or throw it away. After a moment of studying it, the bouncer nodded and let me pass through the door.

I woke up suddenly at that point, and I saw it was still dark. My phone had gone dead, but after charging it for a few minutes it told me it was actually Saturday night around 9pm. I had slept for over twenty hours. There were no missed calls or texts, and no signs of anyone having come in while I was out. I was alone.

I took a shower, hoping it might clear my head and tired of my growing old-sweat stink. I was still numb, but I could tell that I hadn't eaten in over a day and so I microwaved some soup and sipped on it as I looked out the French doors that went out to our back patio and the yard beyond. I stood there staring for a few moments before I saw the thing floating there.

It was the same thing I had seen at the gas station or something like it. There was very little moon that night, but we have a security pole light that illuminates the back yard very well. I could see the thing coming toward me slowly, still thirty yards out but slowly undulating back and forth as it lazily crossed the distance.

I've thought a lot about how to describe this thing, and I still don't know. In some ways it reminds me of some giant pale jelly fish. In other ways it looks like a semi-opaque dry cleaning bag given obscene life. If it has a head, it is the roundish mass that moves it forward, a ball of pale and largely translucent flesh that floats in the air. At the center of this mound is a writhing ball of darkness. It reminded me of pictures I've seen of a ball of snakes mating. If this thing has a center, a nucleus, a face, this cancerous core is it.

But that is not the entirety of it. Trailing back from it, partially hanging, partially floating by some unknown suspension, are more long strands of the same pale and glistening meat. Like a comet's tail, it slowly follows behind the mound, shifting on unknown currents as smaller strands occasionally dart out as though tasting the air.

I stared at it for at least ten seconds before I was able to move. I found myself wondering if it might be filled with long needle teeth. Then I ran.

It was moving extremely slowly towards the house, so I took half a minute to put on shoes, grab my wallet, phone and keys, and get my jacket from where I had dropped it when I had come home the day before. Then I was out the door, in my car, and heading away. I looked in my rearview, but never saw it follow.

That was five days ago. I've been running ever since. Motel to motel, having given up any pretense of not using cards or worrying about being tracked. Just trying to stay away from whatever that thing is, whatever it might want. I called my job once, and to my lack of surprise, they didn't know who I was. Yet my cards still work, all my online accounts, everything that does not rely on people seems to be purring along just fucking fine.

I've been largely on autopilot these past few days, but that changed last night. I saw it again, outside my motel. Only for a moment, and it didn't come closer, but I knew that it knew I was there just the same.

So I give up. I'm going home. It'll either get me or it won't. Or maybe, just maybe, I'll go ahead and kill myself if I can get up the stomach to do it. Actually, it'll probably depend on how scared I get. Because despite everything, despite feeling utterly used up and hollowed out, I'm still fucking terrified.

This will probably be my last entry. If I survive somehow, I'll post again. If I don't, well you know. Thank you for listening to all of this. I'm so alone now, and it means so much to talk about this, even in such a strange format, even if it amounts to screaming out into the dark. Thank you.

Part Four

By the time I got home Thursday evening, I had decided I wanted the thing to come. Whether I wanted it to come back to finish me or so I could attempt to kill it would change moment to moment, but the idea of fighting back had built slowly throughout the day and remained a constant. I was tired of being a victim to whatever this all was, of having things taken away from me. Thoughts of suicide faded more and more, in no small part due to the words of encouragement I've received here, and while I was still resigned to the fact that I was likely going to die, I decided I still had a little more will to try and resist left in me.

So, of course, nothing happened that night.

When I arrived home, I checked the house again thoroughly, and it was untouched since my last visit. No sign of my family or their belongings. Now beyond the initial shock of all that had happened and slightly better rested, I had more time to study the pattern left behind by their…erasure. Not only were all of their belongings gone, but there were other things gone or different too.

My son had done a handprint in clay back in October for a school project. He had given it to me, and since then it had been displayed in the kitchen, up against the backsplash on a small stand meant for a photo or baseball card or something. It and the stand were gone.

I had a long, waxed raincoat that my wife had given me two years ago. Very expensive and nice, though I rarely actually wore it. I checked our coat closet and it was gone as well.

Even things like furnishings were different. If it was something I had bought or we bought together, it was still there. But other pieces of furniture or hangings that she had bought alone or had before we were together were either absent or replaced by something unfamiliar to me, as though to fill the hole left by the other object's absence.

My bank account was another strange anomaly. As I had previously mentioned, my job apparently no longer exists, and I have no indication of some other job that has taken its place. No business card, no strange contacts in my phone, etc. So I looked on my account to see how much money was left and where it was coming from.

I have plenty of money in there, more than I usually do in fact, and when I look at the deposits, it shows a direct deposit of close to seven thousand dollars once a month for as far back as the records go online. The name attributed to the deposits is just a sequence of letters, numbers and symbols, which—if they have some meaning—don't mean anything to me and could well be random.

I consider calling the bank the next day to try to learn more about my benefactor, but just the idea of it seems exhausting. I'm ready to be done with all of this. So I set aside my phone, pick up the softball bat I had recovered earlier in the same closet that was now missing my fancy, rarely-worn raincoat, and go to the back yard.

For the next hour I roam around outside and in, calling out to the terrible thing that is haunting me, demanding that it confront me. I can feel some ever-shifting mixture of fear, anger, and despair coating my tongue and my words. By the end I'm more begging and pleading than anything else.

But nothing.

Fine, it'll come in its own time. I go back in, eat something, and then go to sleep. I can't bear to sleep in our bed, or even stay in our bedroom for any length of time. It's too sharp a reminder of my wife's absence or nonexistence. So I set up downstairs on the sofa again, and before long, I'm deep asleep.

I have long, strange dreams that night, and while they bore the same texture of realness as the other dreams since the texts had begun, I don't remember any details of them. What I remember instead is the sudden and sharp pain in my right hand that woke me.

I tried to sit up in the shock of the pain, but my hand was immobile down near the floor, so the result was a protesting flair of pain in my shoulder as I spun/fell off the sofa and onto the carpet. I caught myself on all fours, my gaze at a good level to see what was eating my right hand.

It was another of those…things. I still don't know what to call them. But this one was much smaller. The small, glistening bulk of its body was spread out across my hand like a glove or mitten up to just past my wrist. At the time I was in such pain and terror that very little cohesive thought was occurring, so bear with me, as much of my description is based upon reconstructing these events upon reflection. The dark, ball of snakes mass I had seen on the larger one was here too, but spread out over my hand, like an inner layer to the horror that was trying to consume me. Looking at it now, I guess that is where all the teeth come from.

There were so many teeth. Needles boring down into my flesh, plucking at my tendons and scraping at my bones. As bad as that was, the overwhelming sense of pressure was somehow worse, as though the creature was competing with itself as to what method would destroy my hand first. When I looked at it for the first time, I swear it paused and considered me, though it had no eyes or face I could see. Then it went back to work, and I began to scream.

I couldn't move my hand because it had wrapped parts of itself securely to one of the legs of the sofa, and my first few attempts at pulling free just caused fresh pain with no progress. I looked around for a weapon, but I saw none within reach. I did notice where I had left the strange, leathery coin on the coffee table however. The coin had burst open from the inside while I slept, apparently having been this demon's womb the entire time. But that information wouldn't help me now. I needed to kill it.

My hand was beginning to go numb, and I knew I had little time left to save it, if it could be saved at all. Straining with the effort, I partially stood and began moving towards the kitchen, because while the thing couldn't be dislodged from the sofa, the sofa wasn't attached to anything. As I began pulling it and the sofa along slowly, it bit down and crushed my hand more, and I felt sure it would just burst, leaving me with a bloody, ragged stump. But I kept pulling, my screams having died out in my concentration and effort. I made it across the living room. Then into the edge of the kitchen. I thought about a knife, but I was afraid I would just hurt my hand or it would somehow just dislodge and crawl up the knife to my left hand spider-quick before I could drop it. I began pulling out drawers, and I found an old trigger lighter that I sometimes used on the grill outside.

Saying a frantic prayer, I pulled the trigger. Nothing. Again, and a small flame appeared at the end of the lighter. I held the trigger and stuck the flame to the creature's flesh. Dark gray smoke began trailing up from the site of the flame, and there was a terrible smell that made me gag, but that was all. No reaction from the creature at all. The pain was fading away now, but that somehow made me more afraid, not less. I cast my eyes around for some new weapon, but saw nothing other than a small cow salt shaker that must have been one of the replacement objects, because I had never seen it before. I suddenly thought of garden slugs, and having no other ready options, I picked up the shaker and turned it over.

Mercifully, salt poured out, and this time the reaction was immediate. The milky flesh turned black where the salt landed, seeming to stick to and burn the creature as it began trying to release my hand. I put my right foot down on it and my palm to hold it in place as I shook out more, rubbing my hand along the floor to catch salt crystals that missed their mark initially. The creature gave a violent shudder and then went still aside from the continued withering of its flesh. I slid my hand free from its carcass and continued to shake salt with the other until it had desiccated into a small black wad of flesh that began to crack and crumble into flakes before my eyes.

I sat staring at the remnants of the monster for what seemed like several minutes, making sure it did not somehow reconstitute itself, before turning to look at the hand I was holding cradled in my lap. There was no blood, or leaking fluid of any kind. Instead, my hand looked slightly swollen, but otherwise normal aside from the hundreds of small holes that now adorned nearly every millimeter of my flesh. Even the skin on the sides of my fingers had holes, as well as multiple holes through each fingernail. In places where I could clearly see veins, there were holes there as well, but still no sign of blood.

And no pain. No feeling at all actually. My hand just flopped limply on its wrist without even a tingle or some phantom sensation.

Trying to decide the best course of action, I looked at my phone and realized it was 2 a.m. on Saturday morning. I had been asleep for close to 30 hours.

I considered going to the emergency room for a moment, but I hesitated. I knew in the state I was in I would likely seem strange at best and totally insane at worst, and for the moment I seemed okay physically unless it had injected me with some poison, which a hospital likely couldn't help with anyway. Ultimately I decided to just go to the doctor the next day unless things got worse. While I slept no more that night, my hand stayed the same and nothing else happened.

This morning I went to the doctor. Since it was a Saturday, I wound up having to go to an emergency wound clinic across town instead of my normal doctor (if I have a normal doctor anymore), but apparently my insurance card still works and within half an hour I was back in a room getting examined. The doctor on call was a pleasant young woman who seemed very knowledgeable, but was also very curious about how the injury occurred. Rather than try to make up some elaborate lie that would probably seem implausible, I just told her that I didn't know. That I woke up outside my house and my hand was just like that.

This led her to check to see if I had some head injury or blood pressure spike that had caused me to pass out, but ultimately she couldn't say much beyond that it appeared that I had severe nerve damage, what she called "neurotmesis", based on my clinical signs and the wounds I had. She took x-rays, and she saw a small fracture in my ring finger that she splinted, but said that anything more in depth would need to be done at the hospital. I told her I didn't think I needed the hospital, but I would follow up with my doctor soon. She protested, suggesting that such a strange and severe injury should be checked more thoroughly than she could accomplish at the clinic and right away. I thanked her and left.

I drove home, trying to avoid looking at my right hand, both because it looked disgusting and because it was a constant reminder of the night before. When I got inside, I wrapped it in a bandage, not because it needed it, but just to avoid looking at the pockmarked skin. My goal had been to stay awake most of the day, monitoring my hand and watching out for another attack. In spite of myself, by noon I had fallen into a deep, dreamless sleep.

When I woke, my nose was assaulted by a terrible, rotten stench. I immediately looked at my bandaged hand, which was soggy and laden with some brownish, green bile. Stifling a retch, I ran to the kitchen sink and pulled off the wrappings. Running my hand under the water there, I saw that there was no sign of anything oozing from my hand. It was as though the holes had been turned on like some filthy faucet and then turned back off again. I washed my hand several times, and then dried it carefully, feeling new panicked sadness at the wrongness of it dangling at the end of my arm like so much dead meat. I felt tears coming to my eyes, and I moved back to the living room, noticing the pen and paper on the ground for the first time.

It was an old legal notepad that seemed vaguely familiar but I couldn't recall from when or where. Sitting nearby was a ballpoint pen of the type we kept around the house to make notes or write checks. Both had light, drying smudges of the same ichor that had been seeping through my bandages, and the pad had writing on it.

I recognize my handwriting, and I'm right handed. Based on that and the smudges, I feel sure I wrote these words with my dead hand while I slept. I don't know what it means, but what the notepad said was this:

The Magpie Song

There's a flock of magpies round me, round me,

They soar as high as you see, you see,

They took my eyes, but fairly paid,

For I rest in their eyes as even trade,

Spanning the land and the sea, the sea,

There's a flock of blackbirds in flight, in flight,

They move to and fro every night, every night,

They took my ears, beaks sharp and wry,

But it favors me with each sobbing cry,

Found in the spaces away from the light, the light,

There's a flock of crows crying loud, crying loud,

They cast shadows great as a cloud, a shroud,

They took my tongue, and so my voice,

By then I was strong--they had no choice,

It's with their pink darts I taste the tears, the tears.

There's a sky full of rooks and it's me, it's me,

See the remains in the field I used to be, used to be,

But now I move free, still young and hungry,

Still reaching out into the void.

I see you.

Shining there.

Your spirit.

Unaware.

As I finished reading it, my phone buzzed. It was a text message. It said "You saw something you shouldn't have. But now you will see and tell much, much more."

I will plan for this to be my final entry, at least for now. If I post further, it will be due to some major change or update, or if I have some new writing I need to share. God help me, but I don't know if "telling" such things is a good thing or not. I need time to think. Thank you again for all your support, I hope this post finds you well.

Part Five

I've started dreaming again. Since my hand was attacked, I sleep more and more. At first I would sleep for abnormally long periods, but it would be offset by long periods of wakefulness. Over time that is changing, and I am losing more and more time. The only potentially positive side effect of this is that I'm dreaming again, and I feel these dreams are a key to something.

I don't remember much of them, just spending time in a world that is similar to ours, but very different at the same time. As I walk there, I see cities, people, the features of a modern world. But I see dark and strange things too. I remember the alley bar from my earlier dream. I think my dream self visits there often. It's an odd and lively place, with trappings of this mysterious other place all around. Symbols on the doors, strange mutterings from a group hunched at a corner table, and music that sounds like something that would be playing at a cat diner in hell.

But in the end, a bar is a bar. And here, I can tell people know me. Most seem to respect or fear me, even though I'm wholly ignorant as to why. But it feels real, and compared to my waking life recently, it feels good. I set up at the bar, order a drink from the short, grinning bartender who approaches, and decide to make the most of this profoundly lucid dream.

That's when the good-natured buzz of the crowd died. Sensing as much as hearing it, I turn to see an older man entering the bar. He was unremarkable at first, well-dressed but not flashy, nodding to people as he entered, but saying very little as he threaded his way to a booth in the corner.

Yet I felt the room tense as he moved through it. I tried to discreetly study him for the reason why, but it wasn't until he was moving out of my field of vision that I saw it. Out of the corner of my eye I could see something much like the thing that had attacked my hand floating behind him, its tendrils wrapping tightly around his limbs and head.

I had to fight to keep from crying out, slowly turning back to my drink and trying to breathe. The thing was much larger than the creature that attacked me or even the one I had seen in my back yard. And rather than being largely translucent and flowing, it was a dark, smoky gray with sharper edges at irregular intervals along the flesh of its bulbous core. Thinking about it now, I think those might have been more teeth from its dark center, grown so long they pierced its own skin.

I sat paralyzed for several moments, analyzing the glimpse I had and trying to decide what to do next, and that's when I woke up.

For the first time in days I wanted to go back to sleep, to try and see more. Right or wrong, I've grown to feel that dream place is as or more real than this life, and that some part of myself is fighting to show it to me rather than having me decay in some dreamless slumber. But sleep was gone for the moment. I checked my phone and saw it had been nearly 26 hours since I was last awake.

The strangest thing about my increasingly odd life is that there are no real rough edges. As I've mentioned before, I have money deposited in my account from some unknown source. Everyone I knew has either been erased or doesn't know me anymore. I still eat and drink, but even if I sleep a whole day I never see signs of soiling myself or being overly hungry or dehydrated when I wake up. I feel like everything has been pruned away so I can primarily sleep and sometimes write these strange things with my corrupted hand. I worry there will come a time when I don't wake up at all.

So I go out. I go to the store, trying to avoid the strange looks my gloved hand receives. It would be easier if not for the mild distaste I see when people encounter me, like they smell something rotten. Even before they see my hand, even when I know I'm clean. I dress largely the same, and I'm not poorly groomed. Yet I feel like some dirty vagrant who is unwelcome as I push a shopping cart down the aisle. I don't even think they know they're doing it. It's like some deep, animal part of them knows I'm wrong now.

I go to the park sometimes, and that's better, especially when it's empty. I have figured out that I can stave off sleep awhile by staying in a public place. I think the dead hand doesn't want me passing out in public. But if I stay too long, my normally limp hand will begin to throb painfully and with increasing urgency until I go home and go back to sleep.

I feel like a prisoner, but I haven't given up. I'm trying to find any connection between what has happened to me and the writings my hand produces. So far what I've managed to learn is that there is a Tattersall Security--some low-profile outfit that does mainly government contracts, so that might be a connection with a story called "FM Rider". And based on some forum discussions I found, there has been a strange increase in the amount of "door graffiti" in certain parts of the southern and central U.S., and out of the few photo examples I found online, several looked like what was described in another story called "It's not a window. It's a door."

Finally, I haven't found another writing yet, or at least not a narrative. But two days ago I did find something I had done—the hand had done—while I was asleep. It was a drawing of a cave, or that's what it seemed to be at least. Below it was just one word: Mystery.

I don't know what any of this means yet, or if I ever will. But I will keep trying, and I wanted to update you on things during the brief window of wakefulness I have. If I can, I will write again, and I hope this finds you well.

The Honeymoon

Part One

The day that I married Marjorie, I felt like the luckiest guy in the world. She was smart and beautiful, and ever since I had met her six months earlier, not a day had gone by that I didn't wonder what she was doing with a guy like me. It wasn't that I'm a loser—I think I'm a good guy and look well-enough, and the only real ding in my eligibility as a good boyfriend or husband was that I lost my job recently due to layoffs. But even that was turning around, as I'm supposed to be starting the process of getting a U.S. Customs job at the Savannah docks at the end of the month. If it all worked out, it would mean better pay and benefits, plus great retirement.

It was just that Marjorie seemed close to perfect. She didn't have any family aside from an older brother she was close with, and she was the type to have tons of casual friends but few close ones. Everyone loved her, and I could tell when we went out all the guys (and a few of the girls) were jealous that I was the one with her. When she proposed to me three weeks ago, I was taken by surprise, but I'm not overly traditional. It never occurred to me to say no or put off us getting married.

Some of my friends asked me about it of course, wanting to make sure I wasn't moving too fast. That I knew her well enough to know that she was the right one and this was the right time. But I just laughed at that, joking more than once that not only was I sure, but I needed to hurry up and marry her before she realized what she was getting herself into.

Initially, we hadn't planned on taking a honeymoon for awhile so I could start this new job and we could both save up money, but the day of the wedding, Marjorie's brother Pete surprised us with an invitation to take an impromptu trip west with him for a few days. He was a very successful long-haul trucker and had just bought a brand-new semi that he claimed could comfortably hold six people, much less three, and he was heading out to California in a few days.

I had misgivings at first. It sounded like a long and potentially uncomfortable trip, particularly for a honeymoon. But Pete explained that he had a "hot site" lined up out there and he would love for us to go.

"Hot site" was the lingo he used for places that were supposed to be legitimate locations of documented paranormal activity. Ghost hunter type stuff, though it wasn't limited to ghosts. He had told us tons of stories the few times we had hung out, ranging from looking for bigfoot up in Canada to exploring a deserted high school for a ghost in the Midwest. He was passionate about the stuff, and while I didn't believe in ghosts and goblins myself, I could tell that Marjorie did. And Pete was a fun guy in my limited experience, full of interesting tales and funny jokes. I had always felt comfortable around him. Accepted. And that meant a lot.

Still…the idea was to drive to California over four days, spend a week out there having fun, and then four days back. That was a long time to be traveling with a new bride and a brother-in-law I didn't know that well. Plus, there was the financial side of it. We didn't magically have a lot of money just because he was offering a trip.

But Pete had answers for that too. His company, which he was partners in, would cover the room and the travel expenses, including a rental car for the week when we got to California. Same went for food. When I started to object to him paying for everything, he shook his head and patted my shoulder. He said it was his wedding gift to us, and it was not a big deal. He'd write off the expenses on his taxes and appreciate the company.

And naturally, he said with a wry grin, he knew that we would want our privacy. We'd have our own room on the road every night and he knew a great hotel for us to stay at once we arrived in California. The owner was a friend of his and had already said he'd comp us two rooms for the week we were there.

It all sounded great. If I'm honest, it all sounded too good to be true. I suddenly had images from half a dozen movies I'd seen where people end up being arrested as drug mules or dissected in warehouses run by sadists or organ thieves. I was probably being overly dramatic and letting my pride get in the way of a great opportunity, but I just felt uneasy about the whole thing.

But then I saw Marjorie out of the corner of my eye. I could feel her gaze on me, and as I turned to look at her more fully, I saw the hope and worry in her face. She wanted to go--wanted a honeymoon with me and time with a brother she didn't see as often as she'd like. I knew she'd accept it if I said I didn't want to do it, but how could I deny her something so simple and harmless? A few days with the people she loved most, having fun and relaxing. I knew, if I was lucky, I would be stretched thin by the new job for the next few months. This might be the last chance we had to get away and do something cool for some time.

So, I said yes. She had let out a squeal and hugged my neck, and I let my misgivings and pride slip away as I held onto her tightly. We left the following Tuesday with two suitcases, a laptop, and enough folding money to cover souvenirs and emergencies.

The first day was uneventful but fun. Pete's truck cab was truly amazing. Between its flip down seats and bed, mini fridge and television, it felt more like a small hotel room than the interior of a transfer truck. Looking out through its massive front windows as Pete drove down the interstate headed west, it was surreal seeing everything from so much higher than I was used to when driving. It was neat, but I couldn't help but think that driving the truck must be terrifying given how easy it would be to hit something and not even realize it until it was too late.

But it didn't seem to bother Pete. He chatted with us some and let Marjorie control the radio, and by late afternoon we were pulling into a small but nice chain hotel off the interstate for the night. Pete checked us in and gave us our key cards, telling us he was going to go get some sleep, but he'd see us in the morning for breakfast. We were excited to finally have some time to ourselves, so we didn't leave our own room except to pay the pizza delivery guy later in the evening.

The next morning we went to meet my new brother-in-law at the restaurant across the road, and once inside we saw he was already set up at a booth near the back, two accordion folders sharing his side of the table. Marjorie rolled her eyes and groaned when she saw the stacks of papers Pete was going through, burying her face in my shoulder.

"Oh no. It's started. My ghost hunting nerd of a brother is on the case."

Pete looked up and gave us a smile. "Yeah, yeah. Make fun. This is good intel, and I thought I could bring you both up to speed before we start making miles today."

Marjorie gave a light snort as she raised her eyebrow. "Good intel, huh? I didn't realize this was a military op. Are we going to have code names when we visit the 'hot site'?" She did air quotes on the last bit, and it was clear from her tone and expression that she was making fun of him.

This was all very odd. Marjorie idolized her brother, and short of him taking a shit on the table, I doubted she'd find fault in pretty much anything he did. And they would joke around from time to time, but not like this. She seemed mad about something, or at the very least mean-spirited in her joking. Pete just gave her a smirk and went back to looking at the papers he had, but I decided to go ahead and try to head off any further comments.

"I think it's a pretty cool hobby, Marjorie, and if we're going all this way, it's good he's done his research." Pete grinned at me and nodded. Emboldened, I went on. "And Pete has always told us good stories about this kind of stuff before, so let's see what he has to say."

Marjorie shot me a dark look and flopped down in the booth. "I guess. Let's get some food ordered first though, I'm starving."

Ten minutes later, our order was placed and Pete had gotten his presentation organized, which really just amounted to him pulling out a few pictures to show us during his account of Wizard's Folly. Carefully stowing away the rest of the papers and securing the covers on the accordion files, Pete began his tale.

****

Wizard's Folly was an amusement park that opened up in 1947. Initially it was a haunted house more than anything, as the original attraction consisted solely of the large, abandoned mansion at the center of forty acres nestled in the outskirts of the small north California town of Firenze. The town itself had been established back in 1894 by Frank Pazzi who had immigrated to New York from Florence, Italy a decade earlier before making his way west. Pazzi was extremely wealthy, and though no one knew how he had gained his fortune, he found little complaint when he poured nearly three million dollars into the town itself and another half a million into building his own nearby estate.

Firenze was small and somewhat cloistered in the expanse of wilderness Pazzi had purchased, and for a time it seemed to be the perfect community. Everyone had work, a nice house, and plenty to eat, and if Pazzi was a bit eccentric, who really cared? It was expected that such a man, with foreign ways and rarified tastes, would seem somewhat strange to the working folk who had come to the area. Once his house was finished, he only allowed a handful of people into his home as servants, and they largely lived on his grounds in one of three guest houses he'd had constructed. The only person who still lived in town was his head housekeeper, who went by the name Susanna Templeton. People said that after just a few weeks of going into that house, Templeton had changed dramatically, becoming withdrawn and quick to anger. For a time, vague gossip such as this was all the acknowledgement you would find from the townsfolk that something might be wrong. It wasn't until around 1912 that the town started talking about the missing people.

Fifty miles from Firenze there was a small clinic called Greenheart Home that catered to all kinds of cases that were too sensitive for normal hospitals and institutions. More to the point, it was a place where wealthy families would stick family members that they had decided were too much a burden or embarrassment to keep at home or send elsewhere.

The insane, the addicted, the pregnant woman out of wedlock or the deviant man, these were just a few of the menagerie that could be found housed inside its walls. From the outside, the clinic maintained a facade of genteel civility and gentle care. But the staff cared little about the comfort of their patients, and they knew the checks would keep coming so long as their charges remained quiet. Over the years it became a black pit of cruelty and abuse where people were thrown to be forgotten. Small wonder then, that it took some time before anyone noticed that every year a number of its "clients" went missing.

During the early years, when someone in Firenze saw the white truck from Greenheart Home trundling through town toward the Pazzi estate, they would just shrug and raise a questioning eyebrow. Over time this evolved into a knowing look and a furtive whisper if you were bold. But those that spread gossip and rumors about what Pazzi was doing up there were careful to do so discreetly. It was too good a town, too good a life, to risk angering the head of their little forest kingdom.

In late 1911, there was a massive fire at Greenheart Home. Thirty-seven people died, and those that survived were sent back home or to other institutions in other parts of the country. For a time afterward, everything was quiet and nothing changed in the town of Firenze. But then people from the town started disappearing.

In the 1910 U.S. Census, Firenze was reported to have 958 citizens. By the 1920 Census, that number was down to less than 500. Now most of that wasn't missing people of course. Those with better sense or more resources left the town before it got really bad, and that accounted for several hundred people over the course of several years. But in the ten years after Greenheart Home caught fire, there were an estimated 65 or more people that just disappeared.

Now listen closely to this next part, because it's important. The records are spotty from back then, particularly in an isolated town like Firenze, but for the most part the journals and newspaper articles agree with the handful of eyewitness accounts that were collected by ambitious authors and reporters scavenging the area after it was all over.

When I say these people disappeared, I mean just that. Not that they were abducted from their homes by Pazzi's henchmen in the middle of the night. Not that they were snatched off the street by mysterious figures. These were wives in the middle of a conversation with their husband and he's suddenly not there. Children playing in a swing one moment, and gone without a trace the next. There were over a dozen accounts of different people literally disappearing in front of people's eyes, to say nothing of the scores of other people that went missing when no one was around.

After a few months of this, the leaders of the town had gone to Pazzi, hats in hand, trying to probe him for information, help, or some clear sign that he was involved. Pazzi listened to their concern with all the attention of a disinterested king before clucking his tongue with concern and patting them on the head. He promised to offer rewards for any and all of the missing, and the next week there were several flybills up around town proclaiming $1000 for the return of any of those that had gotten lost.

Because that's how the townsfolk that stayed in Firenze started to refer to them. "Oh, Bill Gunderson? Yeah, he got lost last spring. His wife Polly is still running the store though, and isn't she doing a good job?" There was an unspoken consensus in the town that while concern and action would be given lip service, no one was really going to rock the boat. The flybills would be torn down until the next season of disappearances, when they would go up again for a few days. In between, people were growing tenser and more frightened, but they largely kept it to themselves.

Then Annabelle Perkins got lost. Her husband, Rudolph Perkins, had moved them to Firenze two years earlier, and while by all accounts they were well-liked and respected, it was known that Rudolph and Annabelle were both more vocal in their concerns about the periodic rash of disappearances that seemed to plague their town. Their friends and neighbors tried to mollify them, of course, and for a time that seemed to help. But when Annabelle went missing while in the middle of taking a bath one night in December of 1921, Rudolph was beyond persuasion.

He gave voice to what so many in the town knew. Frank Pazzi was the one behind the disappearances somehow. And whatever he was doing to those people, they were never seen again. It took only a couple of hours to talking to his friends to gather up a large crowd that had grown tired of living in fear and dread. Like a scene out of an old monster movie, they stormed the estate and began searching for Pazzi to demand answers.

Unfortunately, he was nowhere to be found. What they did find...well, there's not a lot that's clear from that night. I know that fifteen people went to the house, and several of them died inside, but it's unclear how or why that happened. They tried to question his house staff, but they were all gone as well, and when they went to the head housekeeper's home, Susanna Templeton was dead, having hung herself from a clothesline in the back yard.

One of the survivors of that night wrote a brief account of what they found in the house. Much of it was garbled and hard to make sense of, but one thing was clear. At some point they went into the lower levels of that house and found hidden chambers no one knew even existed. Pazzi had recruited some of his builders from somewhere else, and it must have been those men that had dug out the subterranean rooms and installed all of the cages and apparatus.

To call it a torture chamber or a dungeon is inaccurate. More accurately, it was a black shrine to some form of occult worship. There were strange symbols etched into every surface, and one of the spaces included a large pit filled with the refuse from nearly two decades of human sacrifice. It was here that the account gets especially hard to follow, as it seems to be talking about the mound of bones and flesh moving or rising up against them while also talking about Rudolph finding his beloved Annabelle even as he joined the other men in a terrible scream...it's very weird, raw stuff. The guy who wrote it died only a few weeks later, so there was never a chance for anyone to find out what he really meant. In any case, that was the deathblow for Firenze, and by 1923 it was a ghost town.

It might have just faded away forever, slowly getting consumed by the forest at its edge, if it hadn't all been bought by a man named Wilson Tattersall. The owner of a large security firm in the east that was slowly taking business away from the Pinkerton Agency, Tattersall knew the value of grabbing up land in the West with his newfound fortune. By 1932, Pazzi had gone from having been declared missing to being declared dead. With no will or heirs, the estate and the city itself reverted to the state of California, who was more than happy to sell it cheaply to the man from Virginia who was already buying up large swaths of land around the state.

It lay fallow for several more years before Tattersall began to develop it. In 1945, he announced plans to turn it into an amusement park of sorts. Keep in mind that this was ten years before Disneyland opened, so the idea of an amusement park in the mid-forties was typically confined to state fairs or a few bigger places like Coney Island or White City. The parks had rides, even rollercoasters, but between the Depression and World War Two, a lot of them had shut down. The idea of building a brand new one, particularly in the middle of nowhere, and especially at the scene of so much horror, seemed insane to me when I first read about it.

But then I realized that no one really knew what had happened in Firenze. Aside from a few articles at the time and the journals that were found by authors and researchers in the years since, it was just never widely known or talked about. And Tattersall, for all his money and ambition, started small when he rebuilt the town. He renovated the house and estate to play up the preexisting gothic architecture, remodeling here and there to suit its new purpose as a haunted house by adding secret hallways and staff areas as well as many nasty surprises for guests. The lower levels were supposed to be off-limits, however. Whether that meant that he sealed them off or had preserved them in their original state, no one knew.

When the park opened in 1947, it was called Wizard's Folly. This played into the new legends that Tattersall had been strategically inserting into the rumor mills of towns in the surrounding counties. Instead of dozens of dead and missing, there were only a couple of girls and a little boy that were victims of the cruel Francesco Pazzi, a vile man who considered himself a wizard and alchemist of sorts. He had allegedly taken the victims' blood as part of some insane ritual to make a Philosopher's Stone, which he hoped to use to convert various substances into precious metals. Instead, the ritual went awry and he wound up burning to death in the bowels of his strange home. It is said that he and his "guests" still haunt those very halls…

Or so the ads said. A bunch of bullshit, but it spread like wildfire. Most people were tight on money back then, but they were also hungry for some time away from the realities of daily life. At a penny per person, carloads of people were making the trek and standing in line to get in from the first week it was open. By the time word had spread about how terrifying the house was, how you really did need to try it for yourself, the wait to get in was over four hours.

In the following six months, the park not only grew in popularity but in size as well. This was, for all intents and purposes, an adult theme park, but the estate could only hold so many visitors at a time if it was going to be an effective haunted house. So they added a go-kart track and a tilt-a-whirl, followed by a hot dog stand that served beer. Next was a handful of booths where guys could try to win cheap toys for their dates along with a "curiosities" show that was essentially a freak show on the front end and a peep show on the back. By October of '47, they had started building a real, honest-to-God wooden rollercoaster too.

It was toward the end of that month, just a few days before Halloween, when it all fell apart. They called it a "toxic infection caused by mold", and it was traced back to dozens of people that had visited Wizard's Folly. But based on some things I've found, that was just a cover story. Over three hundred people scattered across six states reported seeing and hearing things, vomiting, and feeling an oppressive sense of being watched. This was covered up because of the two things that they all had in common. The first was that they had all visited Wizard's Folly at some point in the six months it had been open. The second was that all of them started experiencing symptoms at exactly the same time: 9:23 p.m. pacific time on October 27, 1947.

Whatever happened that night in October at Wizard's Folly, it was covered up. And the park was closed permanently the next day. Since that time, it's been abandoned and forgotten--the Tattersall company, now called Tattersall Global--still owns the place, but it's just a relic. They have a couple of guards patrolling it, and it's become a bit of a holy grail in some corners of the internet paranormal community because no one has ever managed to get in more than a few yards before they are caught and turned away.

Then two months ago a guy started posting on a forum I frequent. Claimed that he and a buddy of his worked as guards for Tattersall at the old Wizard's Folly park. People immediately called bullshit, but the next day he posted several pictures online of him at the park, and it looked legit. He said that for $5,000.00, him and his buddy would "take off" a couple of hours at an appointed time, leaving the gate open for the buyer and whoever he wanted to bring. The only rules were that they didn't break or take anything and they were out again before the two hours was up.

I wound up in a brief bidding war with a lady from Seattle, but I managed to get it for $8,000.00. Marge, don't look like that. I've got the money to spend, and this is a once in a lifetime chance. But anyway…that wraps up my presentation for now. There's more to show you, but we'll get to that later.

****

A look passed between Pete and Marjorie, but I couldn't read its significance. I was kind of blown away by everything I had just heard and that it had all come from Pete. When I told him so, he smirked at me as he forked in a mouthful of cold eggs.

"Oh, because I drive a truck you think I can't be smart? Can't read?"

I felt my face flushing crimson. "No, no. That's not what I meant at all. It's just…all that information. It's impressive is all. It must have taken you a long time to pull all that together."

He laughed and Marjorie joined in now, her earlier anger seemingly forgotten. "I'm just fucking with you, Phil. But yeah, it took a long time, even with the internet. This shit is obscure, and some of the people you run across in these circles don't like to turn aloose of the little nuggets they've found along the way. It was fun though, and I think it'll be worth it. This one is really something. I can feel it.

I gave them both a relieved smile and nodded. I didn't want to hurt his feelings and I didn't want to be stuck on an awkward trip for two weeks either, so seeing them both joking and in good spirits again eased my worries. I realized I had never looked at the pictures he had pulled out at the start of his story, so I picked them up now. Two of them were old and faded black and white photos of Wizard's Folly back in its heyday, steady streams of people headed this way and that through what looked like a cross between a carnival and a strange garden party. The last one was obviously far more recent, and it showed a chubby, balding man in a security uniform smiling uncomfortably in front of the looming face of a gothic mansion, its dark stone a stormy gray in the overexposed picture. I felt an unexpected shudder looking at that last picture, and I set them all down quickly.

Pete looked at me silently for several moments and then glanced out the window. "It's getting late. We need to get a move on. Miles to go before we sleep."

Part Two

We were off the interstate for the most part now, Pete taking us back routes that he said would be both quicker and more scenic. And he was right. We wound our way further west across the Mississippi and into Missouri, and by eight o'clock we were pulling into our stayover for the night, an older but nice motel on the outskirts of Kansas City.

I was inexplicably tired that night, and after we grabbed a quick burger at the restaurant attached to the motel, I quickly fell asleep watching t.v. with Marjorie in our room. When I awoke, I had a moment of disorientation in the darkness of the unfamiliar room, and after fumbling my phone onto the floor, I finally woke up enough to grab it and see it was just past midnight. I reached back to Marjorie's side of the bed, but it was empty.

My first thought was that she was in the bathroom, but when I looked, nothing. I tried texting her, but a moment later I heard a buzz from where her phone had been left on the far nightstand. The beginnings of real worry and fear woke me up the rest of the way and I pulled back on my pants, absently grabbing a key card off the table on my way out the door.

The air was cold so late at night, and I hadn't taken time to grab my jacket, but I didn't care. Looking around in the gravel parking lot, I saw no signs of other people, which was understandable given the hour. We were in room 103 and I knew Pete was in 108, so I headed that way to see if he knew where she was.

Something made me hesitate as I reached the door. It was only for a couple of seconds, but long enough that I heard a woman's giggle from inside Pete's room. My first thought was that Pete had hooked up with some local after we had went to our room, and I debated whether I should disturb them before I looked around a bit more. Then I heard the giggle again, and I recognized it this time. It was Marjorie.

I knocked hard on the door, an unpleasant mix of fear, uncertainty, and anger surging into my chest. I waited, counting to ten internally before knocking loudly a second time. There had been no further sounds from the room, and another ten count was nearly done before the door cracked open and I saw Marjorie's face poking out of the dimly lit murk within.

"Hey, what's up, honey? Something wrong?" Her expression was one of surprise and mild concern, but I wasn't sure if I trusted it. It was hard to tell in the blue-tinged light of the parking lot security lamps, but she looked…flushed. Flushed in a way I was familiar with, but that shouldn't be happening with another man.

But no. Pete was her brother, for fuck's sake. And not that people didn't ever lie or do fucked up things, but I had known him for months and I didn't think they were lying about being brother and sister. And I didn't think they were…I didn't think they were doing anything unnatural. I pushed the thought away and forced out a hollow laugh.

"I was just looking for you. I woke up and you were gone, and when I saw you left your phone behind, I got worried."

She smiled. "Nah, I'm fine. I just wasn't ready to go to bed yet and I didn't want to wake you up, so I came down to hang out with Pete for awhile. I'll be back down in just a few minutes. Love you, hun." I was weighing whether I should push the issue and make my way into the room, but she had already shut the door back before I could respond. Hating myself, I pressed my ear against the door and listened for further sounds or voices. I did hear something that might have been muffled whispers followed by a stifled snort of laughter, but it might have been my imagination as well. It might all have been my imagination, after all.

I went back down to 103 and sat on the bed thinking for several minutes before undressing and getting back into bed. As I was dozing off, I heard the door open. Marjorie slipped quietly into bed and gave me a hug before quickly falling asleep.

****

The morning light made the night before seem like some kind of strange dream. I went through a mental inventory of all the interactions I had ever seen between Marjorie and her brother, looking for any sign of anything inappropriate, but there was nothing. They would joke around and hug each other occasionally, but it was just normal brother-sister stuff not much different than I had done with my own brother before he died. And as for her being in his room…Well, she wanted some quality time with a brother she didn't get to see very often. Nothing wrong with her laughing and having a good time, and anything weird was just me projecting my own insecurities or making something out of nothing.

Satisfied, I tried to act normal through breakfast and the morning drive, and by the afternoon it wasn't an act. Part of this was because they weren't acting weird themselves. My fear was that they would suddenly be awkward with each other or me, or Marjorie would suddenly make a point of only paying me attention, all of which would only reignite my twisted fears. But there was none of that. Just normal talk and hanging out as the roads unspooled before us.

By late that afternoon we had made it to a small town called Brimley. It was the last planned stop before we pushed on into the heart of Utah. As we pulled into the large truck stop there, I saw it had a store that looked like a massive log cabin. After the last few days of dirty chain gas stations, something a little better cared for and homey was a welcome surprise. Pete was fueling the truck and Marjorie had ran off immediately for the bathroom, so I decided to go explore the store for a bit and stretch my legs.

The air was definitely turning cooler with each day as fall set in. We were traveling at a fast enough rate that it was actually hard to judge how much of the difference was due to the change of seasons versus the change of locale, but the feel of the crisp air as I walked to the store reminded me of autumns growing up in Virginia. The thought made me smile and glance around at the town surrounding the truck stop.

It was odd. Though it was almost five in the afternoon on a Thursday, there was next to no one else around. A couple of other customers getting gas at the pumps looked back at me disinterestedly, but the only other real sign of life was an old man frantically mowing his grass with a lawn mower several houses down a side street. A small black and white dog stood yapping happily at the man from the street, though whether it was cheering him on or heckling him, it was hard to say.

The signs of normal life, of the energetic dog, of the world outside of the truck and Marjorie and Pete—these things should have cheered me more than they did. Yet I still felt a thin thread of unease running up my spine as I entered what a sign next to the door proclaimed was “Hattie’s One-Stop Emporium”.

****

The store seemed to be an odd mix of items you would expect to find in a truck stop, those you’d find in a grocery store, and those you’d find in some kind of souvenir gift shop. At first, I gravitated towards the souvenirs, thinking it might be funny to get a random Midwest t-shirt or shot glass, or a hat that proclaimed the greatness of Brimley. Then I realized that the souvenirs were all wrong.

They weren't from around the area for the most part, yet they were oddly specific. Have you ever been in a store that has I love N.Y. stickers or California shirts, even though the store is thousands of miles from either? That I would have understood. But this was stuff like "I visited Tallulah Gorge. The first step was a doozy!" Or "Providence, Rhode Island. Home of Marco's Original Pepperoni Grinder!" Weirdly specific stuff that dealt with obscure places that would have no significance to most people passing through this little town.

The next thing was that there wasn't more than one or two of any given item. I'm not saying the store had only a few souvenirs for sale. I mean that out of literally thousands of clothes, hats, knick-knacks, cups, signs, and other miscellaneous bric-a-brac, there were a few twins or triplets, but that was it. Which made the next thing a bit easier to notice.

I think all the souvenirs were used.

I don't mean they were dirty. Aside from a thin layer of dust here and there, they were perfectly clean. But a lot of them looked worn, especially the clothes. It was almost like they had everyone that came through donate a souvenir and then the store turned around and sold it like it was new. The thought struck me as funny until I thought about the horror movie I had seen where waylaid victims' belongings were stockpiled by the killers. As I decided I needed to move to the snack area and out of this weirdness, I ran headfirst into Marjorie.

"Ow! Man, you're in a hurry," she laughed, poking a finger in my chest. "You still looking around or you ready to go?"

"Sorry, baby." I saw an extremely tall figure moving around on the far side of the food section. I couldn't see their face or body, but the top of his head was a platinum blonde, and the way the head moved, it looked as though they were moving down the aisle with a discordant and ungainly gait. Shivering slightly, I looked down at

Marjorie and shook my head. "No, no. I'm good to go. Let's get out of here."

****

I had asked Pete about Brimley when we were back on the road, and he had told me this was his first time stopping there. He said he'd had to alter his route after the truck stop he used a few towns over had burned down, but the prices were actually better at Hattie's, so maybe that was a good thing. He asked why I wanted to know about Brimley and I shrugged, saying it just seemed like a weird little town.

He laughed and nodded. "No doubt. A lot of these isolated little places are. Worlds unto themselves, I guess you could say." He slapped me on the arm. "But no worries, brother. We'll be in California soon enough, and after I drop off this load, it's on to the Folly."

The rest of that day and the next were uneventful, with no more quirky stores in weird towns or strange ideas from me about my wife and brother-in-law. I started having fun again, and by the time we had settled in at the Alpine Estates hotel an hour south from Firenze, I was actually looking forward to our trip the following day to Wizard's Folly.

Part Three

I was expecting Wizard's Folly to be a dilapidated ruin. Tall grass and encroaching woods peppered with vine-covered skeletons that had once been buildings and stands. I half expected that we wouldn't be able to get in at all, or if we did, we would poke around for half an hour before leaving dejected because the reality of the park fell so far into the shadow of what Pete's story had built up in our minds.

But nothing could have been further from the truth. As incredible as his story had been, the appearance and condition of the amusement park was even more awe inspiring. We entered easily through the front gate at precisely ten in the morning, all three of us looking around for signs of security in case the plan had somehow gone awry on the guards' end. Within moments any thought of being caught had fled however, as we were all gasping at what we were seeing.

Everything was in nearly perfect condition. The grass was cut, the buildings looked recently painted, and there was none of the expected signs of disuse or ill-repair. We had taken a rural road up to the edge of Firenze, but our route turned us left towards Wizard's Folly instead of right towards the ghost town. Because of that, I had only a slight idea of how the town compared to this place, but the glimpse I'd had of an old gas station at the edge of town had made sense. It looked long-abandoned, with rusty, old-fashioned pumps out front and morning sunlight glowing dimly through the caved-in roof of what looked like a small attached garage.

By contrast, if I had been told this park was open just an hour earlier, I would have believed it. We walked further up the main road, passing by a hot dog stand and a small building that appeared to contain public bathrooms. Up ahead, there were more buildings and the looming shadow of a massive wooden rollercoaster off to the right.

"What the fuck..." Pete's expression matched my own feelings. "What is this? Are they reopening this place?"

Marjorie looked over at her brother. "Are you sure it's okay for us to be here? This place does not look abandoned. And there's a lot more here than what you described."

She was right. We had already passed a gift shop, a small sit-down restaurant, and five different stands housing what looked like carnival games. All of them pristine and with lights blazing. Pete stopped and turned back to us.

"I mean...we're trespassing either way, right? But so long as we don't hurt anything, it shouldn't be too much hassle even if we were caught, which we shouldn't be. But...none of this makes sense. Why would the lights be on in these places? Why would everything be so...well, not new exactly, but intact?"

I knew what he meant. None of it had the feel of things that had been recently built, but rather just maintained very well. I pointed to one of the carnival game stands where you tried to pop balloons with darts. "Look at that shit! The balloons!" My description wasn't overly articulate, but it didn't have to be. Once you looked at the stand, it was obvious what was wrong. There were probably fifty balloons on a large corkboard at the back of the stand, and all of them were fully inflated.

Pete shook his head. "What...those balloons had to have been put there yesterday at the latest." He looked around, his expression growing paranoid. "I don't know what this is, but I think they're either reopening it or something is way different than what I was told. Either way, if ya'll want to go, I'm fine with it." He was looking at Marjorie, but I was the one that spoke up.

"No, let's keep going."

****

We rounded a curve and saw that the park opened up before us, with multiple paths leading off toward rides and shrouded thoroughfares that wound deeper into the property. This was also our first good look at the mansion, albeit from a distance. It was strange and imposing even far away, with dark stone and black shingles swooping this way and that like the contours of a giant gargoyle just waiting for us to get closer. A large hedge maze acted as a barrier between us and the house, and when I went to enter it, Marjorie tugged on my arm.

"No, Phillip. Let's not and say we did. I do not want to get stuck in that thing, okay?" When I nodded, she went on, gesturing towards a path off to our right. "Let's try this way. We can see more of the park and find a way around to the house if we're lucky."

Pete chimed in. "Yeah, Phil. I think she's right. We're on a clock here, so we're better off taking in as much as we can rather than taking time for the maze."

"Sure, yeah. Makes sense." I started walking with them down a brick path that led closer to the massive rollercoaster, a familiar sense of strangeness coming back to me. Why were they deferring to me so much now? Acting as though they need to persuade me or as though I was in charge? I had just been going along with whatever, which was fine, but why now did they ask my opinion? Was this some of the weirdness I was worried about? I was snapped out of my reverie by the fear and wonder in Marjorie's voice.

"My God. I smell popcorn. I smell popcorn and cotton candy."

I realized I smelled it too. Fear crawled up my back as I looked around, but I saw nowhere it could be coming from. My eyes met Pete's and he shrugged. "I don't know, Phil. I smell it too, but no clue how or why."

My roving gaze fell on the rollercoaster again. We were probably fifty yards from the entry for the ride, which a large and brightly lit sign proclaimed as "The Hunter's Blind". It seemed a strange name for any ride, much less a rollercoaster, but the thought left me as I realized something.

"Pete, didn't you say they only partially built the rollercoaster?"

He nodded. "Yeah. And you saw it in the picture too, remember? The park shut down when they were only about halfway done."

I pointed ahead of us. "Do you see any part that's unfinished on that thing? I've been looking at it, looking for a break in the track or some sign that something isn't in place yet, but I can't find it. It looks like the rest of the place—ready for business."

Pete swallowed. "You're right." He rubbed his cheek and glanced at his watch. "Okay, we've got a little over an hour left. Shit, I didn't realize that much time had passed. Anyway, what do you guys want to do? This place is weird and creepy as fuck, but obviously they have to be renovating it, right? There's no other reasonable explanation, and this is from the guy that believes in all kinds of fucked up shit."

Marjorie laughed nervously. "Yeah, I bet that's it. Has to be." She turned to me. "Phil baby, are you good with us going now? They may have more security if they're getting ready to do something with this place, and I really don't want to go to jail on our honeymoon."

I grinned at her, but it was forced. I really wanted to keep going, felt driven to explore further into the park and reach the house. But I also didn't want to disappoint her or Pete, and I could tell they were both anxious to leave.

Her brother chimed in, "It's your call, Phil. We'll do what you decide. But if you're ready to head out, we are too." Again that strange deference, that odd tension and expectation that I had never noticed before. Something about it made me want to stay in the park even more, but when I glanced back at Marjorie I pushed it down.

"Nah, it's cool. We've seen plenty, and we probably shouldn't risk it."

The relief from both of them was palpable, but I tried to ignore it. I was teetering on just telling them to go wait in the car for me, but then Marjorie took my hand and I let myself be led back to the front gate and beyond it. Within a few minutes we were back on the road in the rental car Pete had procured earlier in the morning. I found myself looking back at the park with an odd wistfulness until its dark silhouette had slipped from view.

That night I had terrible dreams that I didn't remember upon waking except for an acid taste on my tongue and the uncomfortable sensation of something gripping my thudding heart. Marjorie stirred restlessly beside me, but when I lay back down in the cool dampness of the sweaty sheets, she slipped back into a deeper sleep. I stayed awake, my mind adrift in a shadow sea of unfamiliar thoughts and feelings as I stared up at the ceiling I couldn't really see. As gray dawn began crawling through our balcony window, I gave up on getting back to sleep. The rooms really were very nice, and the hotel itself was massive and far more expensive than anywhere I had ever stayed before, but I felt trapped in there. Trying to be quiet, I got dressed and slipped out of the room.

I headed downstairs with the idea that I would just walk around a bit. The area we were in was lushly forested, and between the hotel's golf course and the series of walking paths through the woods on the resort grounds, I had plenty of options for an early morning constitutional. I've never been much for exercise, but I needed to clear my head, to be away from the two of them for awhile. So for the next couple of hours, I walked.

As I went, the thing I kept coming back to was that I felt we'd made a mistake not going on to the house. Or at least I had made a mistake. It seemed like one of those ephemeral moments in life where picking right or left will have major ramifications somehow. You can't say why it's so important, but you can feel the weight of…what, fate?...bearing down on the decision you're making. If you make the right one, you feel a sense of harmony and well-being. If you make the wrong one, you feel utterly discordant and lost.

I felt lost. I couldn't explain it, but I somehow knew I had chosen wrong, and the further I walked, the more I mulled it over, the more certain I became that I had to go back there. Then suddenly Marjorie was running up to me, telling me that we had to get back to the room and pack. That there had been some kind of major accident back at Pete's trucking company and he needed to start heading back now.

She was tugging on my arm, but I resisted with a frown. "Why do we have to go back now? Can't he just leave us and go back?"

Marjorie scowled at me. "No, idiot. We have no way of getting back then, and no money to spend on a flight or even a bus." She put her fingertips to the bridge of her nose and took a deep breath. "Fuck, I'm sorry. I didn't mean it like that. Pete's just freaked out and so am I. Apparently there was some kind of chemical spill and three of his people are at the hospital. ICU bad. He's worried about them, worried about getting sued and losing his insurance…he's worried." She reached out and touched my arm. "But that was still shitty of me to say it like that. But can we just go? He's in no shape to drive the next several days back by himself, and he doesn't want to risk leaving the semi here."

I nodded, ignoring the voice inside screaming for me to stop. "Sure, honey. I get it. Let's go get our stuff."

****

When we met Pete in the lobby twenty minutes later, he looked haggard and red-eyed. He apologized for cutting the trip so short and helped us quickly load our things before we were on the road and headed back the way we had came. I felt a growing sense of restless unease as we traveled east, but I kept quiet. Whatever weirdness I was going through, Pete had enough on his plate as it was. I felt bad for him—I knew he had worked hard building that business up, and it was easy to see how stressed out he was from fear he might lose it all.

The thing was…as we traveled throughout the morning and early afternoon, his worries seemed to slip away. Not that I expected him to stay in a state of high agitation and fear for hours on end, but I'd have expected some noticeable level of distress to hang around for at least the rest of the day, if not until he was at his company and had a better handle on what was happening. Instead, him and Marjorie were back to joking around, singing along with the radio, and generally acting like they were still on vacation. For the hundredth time, I found myself questioning my perceptions of things, wondering if I was just being an asshole.

When we had settled in at the same motor lodge we'd stayed at just two nights earlier, I suggested we all get dinner together, my treat. I could tell they were both resistant, but I pushed on with cheery determination until they gave in. I wanted to watch them out of the truck and see how they acted. See if Pete acted carefree or concerned. See if any quick, secret glances passed between them.

The meal was uneventful until the end. They were both acting abnormally normal, but that is such a subjective thing that I quickly began doubting myself again. It was only as I was leaving the waitress a tip that I glanced up at Pete's face. Marjorie must have seen it a moment before I did, because she was already up and moving, pulling Pete from the booth the same moment my eyes met his and my tongue went numb.

His face was sliding off. Or at least drooping. It looked as though he was wearing a latex mask that had gotten too hot and started to melt, the eyes and nostrils and mouth drooping low and revealing something red and wet underneath. I let out a startled grunt and put my palms against the edge of the table. I shoved the table towards him, but he was already out of the seat with Marjorie's help, so the far edge just bumped against the back of the booth he was sitting in. I went to stop Marjorie, to make her understand that something was terribly wrong, that he was a monster or dying or something, but she was already leading him away. She turned back briefly to give me distressed look.

"He's sick, Phil. I've seen this before. Go back to our room and I'll be there soon."

Before I could protest, she had turned the corner with him, heading towards the back of the restaurant and presumably the bathroom. I considered following them, but when I saw the few other customers in the place staring at me over the commotion, I reconsidered. I wasn't going back to the room, but I would wait right here instead.

I know what I saw. His fucking face was falling off. And now I want some goddamn answers.

Part Four

"Bell's Palsy."

"What? You're saying what I saw was Bell's Palsy?" I knew what it was—I'd had a dentist who had it once. But it made one side of his face droop, not look like it was falling off.

Marjorie nodded. "Yeah. Stress can trigger it, and his version of it is pretty severe and scary, but it happened once when we were teenagers. Last time it cleared up overnight, so we'll see. He's resting in his room now."

I gripped my hands together so tightly that the knuckles were white. "Look, there's been a lot of weirdness the entire trip, and I…"

Marjorie came and sat next to me, reaching over to put her hands on top of mine. "I know it. I've been focused on him too much, and I'm sorry. I just know we have the rest of our lives together and I don't get to spend much time with him. And now…he's just so upset about all this right now."

I pulled my hands away and leaned back. "You could have fooled me."

She frowned at me, her eyes growing harder. "What's that supposed to mean?"

"It means that he's been acting jolly as can be all afternoon, and then all of a sudden it's like I'm sitting across from a horror movie that you're telling me is Bell's Palsy and is caused by his extreme stress? I'm not trying to be a dick, but none of that makes sense."

She stood up, tears welling up in her eyes. "Well, it's the truth. I need you on my side on this. Do you think this is how I wanted our honeymoon to be? Stuck in a semi and going to some crappy old park? Not having any time to ourselves? But I was trying to make him and you both happy. I saw it as a way to spend time with him and to give you a trip we otherwise couldn't afford. I'm sorry that it..."

I stood up and hugged her. "It's okay. We're all just stressed and tired. If you say it's Bell's Palsy, that's what it is. Let's get some rest and see how he's doing in the morning."

****

The next morning, Pete looked normal aside from the sunglasses he was wearing. He said that his eyes were still weird looking but seemed to be improving. I thought about asking more questions, but decided to just leave it alone. All I wanted was to be done with this trip as soon as possible, and if I still felt a yearning to return to Wizard's Folly, there was nothing to be done about it now.

That evening we stopped again at Hattie's One-Stop Emporium in Brimley, and again I felt the same sense of disquiet being in the small town. I went in with the intention to just use the bathroom and then head right back to the truck, but when I made it into the stall, I stopped cold at what I found there. There was a notepad and two pictures sitting on the back of the toilet. I would have just left them alone, but I recognized them. They were from Pete's file on Wizard's Folly.

But how could that be? As far as I knew, Pete had never even gone inside the store last time we were here, and I knew he hadn't beat me in here this time. And why would he leave parts of his prized file in a gas station bathroom anyway?

Forgetting my need to pee, I grabbed up the pad and pictures before leaving the stall. I almost went out to ask Pete about it, but something made me reconsider. I was tired of getting all my information through them. Not that I didn't trust them, but it wouldn't hurt to talk to the store owners and see if they knew anything about how that stuff came to be in their bathroom or how long it had been there.

The cashier's desk was a heavily carved oak monstrosity that curved into a long "L" with two cash registers on opposite ends. Behind the counter were two elderly women that might have been twins, their long white hair tied back in matching bushy ponytails. Putting on a smile, I approached and held up the notepad and pictures.

"Hey ya'll. Me and family are just passing through, and I just found something in your bathroom that I think belongs to my brother-in-law." I pointed out in the direction of the truck fuel pumps. "He's the guy out there fueling up. Anyway, I was just in the bathroom stall and I found some papers and pictures that belong to him, but I don't know how or when he could have left them. So I know it sounds weird, but I was just wondering if you had seen someone carry them in or if you knew how long they might have been in there without being noticed?"

The two women glanced at each other with small smiles, and the one on the left was about to answer when their eyes lifted above me and the words died in their throat. I turned around to stare into the drooping breasts of the tallest person I've ever seen. The woman was of normal proportions, and her face, though a bit narrow, was actually that of an attractive woman in her early fifties. But she had to be over seven feet tall, and when she looked down at me and smiled with her long, shining grin, I couldn't help but take a step back, bumping into the counter.

"You said you had a wife, did you?" Her voice was deep but still feminine, and it possessed a tonal quality that sounded like it came from the bottom of an old stone well. The woman made a pouty expression for a moment. "That's always such a shame to hear. Always a shame when such a handsome young man is already taken." The women behind me murmured their agreement, but I was unable and unwilling to look away from this giant in front of me. I was transfixed—on the one hand, I was fearful of her for some reason beyond her surprising size, and on the other, I found her voice and words calming like a soothing balm. Not sure of what to do, I mirrored the smile that had returned to her face and nodded.

"Yes, I'm taken I'm afraid." By this point, any questions about what I had found in the bathroom had gone by the wayside. I just wanted to get out of there. But then suddenly I was swept up in a tight hug, my face being buried in her cleavage as I breathed in some combination of flowery perfume and baby powder and…something else. There was something else beneath those smells. Something earthy and raw and caustic that felt like a corkscrew going up into my nostrils. I pulled back with a gasp and found my face being gently held by her large hands as she looked at me closely with dark, wide eyes.

"You are the one, aren't you? You are, I can see it. I can feel it."

I tugged my head backward but it didn't budge in her grip. "Ma'am, I have no fucking idea what you're talking about. But please let me go. I don't like any of this."

Her face grew sad and she gave a slow nod. "Of course you don't. How could you? Lost and incomplete for so long, our Vesper, our Venus, our evening—" I unhinged my knees and let my body weight rip my head free from her grasp, scooting around her and sprinting towards the door. She screamed behind me, but it was not an angry yell. It was more of a mournful wail.

"Make them take you back, Vesper! Make them do their duty! For us all!"

If she said more, I didn't hear it. I ran off the front porch of the store and headed to where the truck had been parked, but it was gone. New panic spread across my chest as I looked around the parking lot and adjoining streets. No sign of the truck or either of them. Throwing the notepad and photos to the ground, I dug into my pocket for my cellphone. Neither of them answered after two tries each.

It was all too much. I finally went and sat down at a concrete picnic table sitting in the small triangle of grass as the edge of the gas station's parking lot. I needed a few minutes of quiet, a few minutes of peace to gather my thoughts and then…

"Heya Mister."

I looked around to see a pair of boys, one about eleven, the other maybe thirteen, staring at me. I wasn't in the mood to talk, but I was grateful for their relative normalcy so I tried to be friendly. "Hey guys. How're ya'll doing?"

The younger boy giggled. "You talk funny, Mister."

I nodded and smiled. "I'm from the South, so I probably have a weird accent to you, huh?" They both nodded back and sat down across the picnic table from me. Inwardly groaning, I turned to glance at the road again. "Hey, did y'all happen to see a big black semi around here? Just in the last few minutes?"

The younger boy went to speak but the older one poked him in the ribs before talking himself. "I did, Mister. It drove off just a little bit ago." When I asked which direction, the boys both shrugged. "I'm not sure, Mister. But they were going pretty fast."

I pulled out my phone again and sent Marjorie a text: WHERE ARE YOU? Though I hated it, I was already starting to make plans in the back of my mind for how I'd get back home on my own. But surely it wouldn't come to that, right?

I looked past the boys and down the street where, just a few days ago, I had seen the small dog harassing the man in his yard. There was no sign of life down that way now. As evening continued to set in, the shadows were pooling out their stations at the bottom of trees and cars, trashcans and garages, and the air was growing thicker with the blue haze of deepening twilight. It was a lonely road, and sitting at this decaying picnic table with these odd little boys, I had never felt more alone.

Then, at the far end of the street, I saw Pete's truck go by.

It may have been that they were heading back in my direction, but I didn't wait to find out. I leapt up and started down the road at a full run without a farewell or backwards glance. I knew logically I couldn't just chase down the truck, but my hope was that they were somehow looking for me, or that at the least, the big truck would have to slow down in the more narrow straits of a neighborhood. Yet when I reached the far end of the road, breath puffing out and hands on my knees, there was no sign of them. I stood back up slowly, my brain buzzing and off-balance. They had abandoned me. I saw no other answer.

I turned around with the idea of going back to the store on the off-chance they returned—*fat chance* I thought to myself—and to sit at the table while I called a taxi to carry me to the nearest bus stop. But I came up short when I saw that the two boys were standing right behind me. They weren't out of breath, and honestly I had neither seen nor heard any sign of them following me. But there they were. I felt a small thrill of fear and tried to just give them a nod and move past quickly. Instead of going on their way, they fell in beside me, their footfalls loud on either side of me as we made our way back toward the lights of the Emporium.

"Hey Mister. You sure can run fast." It was the younger one from my left, and I just smiled and gave him a nod, quickening my pace.

"It's probably because of his nice shoes. Where'd you get such nice shoes, Mister?" This was the older on my right, and I had no idea what they were talking about. I was wearing a pair of cheap sneakers I'd had for three years, not something fancy or expensive. I decided to just ignore them and keep walking toward the lit parking lot.

"Mister doesn't want us to know, I guess. That doesn't seem right." Younger one again, his voice coming closer to my elbow now.

"Well, maybe he just wants us to have these shoes so we don't have to go looking for some. What about it, Mister? Want to give us those nice shoes?" This was the older one again, and the thread of menace underlying his words was unmistakable. I found myself afraid and angry and ashamed of both emotions. I was being bullied by a pair of children. Children that were in their own way, trying to rob me apparently. What was going on with this place? With me?

I stopped and stepped backwards, simultaneously shoving both of them forward and further away from me. “All right, you little shits. I’m tired of this. All of this. Especially you. So get the fuck out of here before I stomp your fucking ass.” I didn’t recognize the words coming out of my mouth, but they felt good. A look of uncertain fear passed between the two boys, and I felt myself preparing to attack the older boy when I saw Pete’s truck pulling into the parking lot again. Feeling a surge of relief, I pushed past the boys and ran to it.

Marjorie opened the door and gave me a shaky smile. “Hey, Phil, come on in.”

I climbed in and slammed the door behind me. As Pete began to pull away, he dropped a greasy paper sack into my lap. Looking down, I saw it was from a chain fast food restaurant. I shoved it off my lap onto the floor. “What the fuck is that supposed to be?”

Marjorie’s smile thinned as her face went red. “We went and got us all some food to save time. I sent you a text. Did it not go through?”

Glaring at her, I gave a short and bitter laugh. “No, it didn’t go through. And that’s bullshit. I’ve been calling and texting. And ya’ll were gone for nearly thirty minutes. I’m tired of all this weird fucking shit. This town, the park, ya’ll…” I pointed towards Pete, who was driving silently with his jaw clenched. “This motherfucker is still wearing sunglasses when it’s practically nighttime. Is it so I don’t see his face falling off, because I know it’s not goddamn Bell’s Pa…”

“Fuck!” Pete was coming to a fast stop, the air brakes on the truck letting out a squealing hiss as he did so. At first I thought he was going to fight back, and I relished the thought. But he wasn’t looking at me. Neither of them were. They were looking outside. Pete let out a tired sigh. “The fuckers have blocked this way too. Even with him in here.”

I didn't understand everything he was talking about, but the "fuckers" blocking was self-evident. Spread across the road was a line of twenty or so people, young and old, small and big, all looking at the truck and waiting. Most of them had weapons of the homemade variety, though there was the occasional gun as well. And all of them bore the same look of grim determination that stated very clearly that we would not pass that way.

Marjorie slammed her fist into the back of Pete's seat. "Just run them over then. Fuck all of this. They can't stop this thing."

As if in response to a challenge, there was a loud crack followed by a louder bang and a plume of smoke from under the hood. Pete cursed again as the truck's engine warbled unevenly to silence. "Someone just shot the engine out. We're fucked."

I was looking back and forth between the two of them. "What's going on? Who are these people?"

Marjorie sneered at me, an angry contempt filling her gaze. "They're your fan club, idiot. They're here to get your autograph."

"And our asses," Pete added in glumly as he opened the door to step out.

What they were saying made no sense, but I decided to follow suit and leave the truck too. As I stepped out, I saw the twin women from the store. In the shadows of a nearby sycamore tree, I saw the looming form of the woman that had hugged me and called me…

"Vesper!" The crowd cried. "Evening Star!" The mob didn't sound angry at all, but were instead rapturously happy. "He who will save us! He who will return us to our rightful home!" It was clear that they were talking to me, and I suppressed the urge to run as they surged forward to surround me, stroking my arms and hugging my neck. Once I was in their midst, I was oddly calm, and it was only with mild and detached interest that I heard Pete and Marjorie yelling as they were pulled away from the truck and out of view.

The twin women from Hattie's stepped forward. "What name do you go by?", they asked in unison.

"Phillip. Phil. I go by Phil."

The women beamed identical smiles at me. "Well, Phil, you are very important. You have a very important destiny. Those people," they cast a glance in the general direction that Pete and Marjorie had been taken, "were meant to help you find your path, but instead they tried to keep you from it." The women's faces grew hard at this, but relaxed as they looked back to me. "But you are stronger than that. You may even be ready this time."

"Ready for what?" I blurted out. "I keep having weird shit happen and no one will tell me what's going on. And this is all starting to really freak me out." I gestured around at the crowd, the damaged truck, the town…fuck, my entire life of late, and as I did so, I found that the tall woman had stepped forward as well. The crowd parted for her and she reached down to take my hand.

"I understand, Phil. We can come on too strong. It's only because we are so proud of you. We love you so much and are excited to see you."

Frowning, I shook my head. "But why? I don't know any of you people. I don't even know if I really know the people that brought me here."

The tall woman glowered as she gave a nod. "They have done you a great disservice. They knew you were the one and yet I bet they tried to dissuade you from entering the house, didn't they?

My heart started thudding faster in my chest. "What house?" When I saw the knowing smile on her face, I stopped and nodded. "Yes. They didn't force me not to, but they worked to dissuade me without telling me no."

The woman nodded again, and I noticed several more nods and murmurs in the crowd around us. "Yes, they couldn't refuse you directly, not in that place, but they could trick you into leaving. If you had just gone inside, all of this would be over. You would understand and know who you truly are." She looked sad momentarily before brightening. "But there is still time. Do you still want to go inside the house at Wizard's Folly?"

I surprised myself by nodding again. “If it can make things better, or at least where I can understand what’s going on, yes I do.”

The woman gave me another awkward hug, though it was quicker this time and I didn’t have to free myself from her grasp when it was over. “That’s wonderful! We will start heading for it right away. By tomorrow evening we should be there.”

Part Five

We travelled in a large shuttle bus of the kind I had always associated with class reunions and senior citizen field trips to see musicals. The seats were comfortable and there was food and a bathroom, but it was still hard to ride for so long after having been on the road so many days. We stopped every few hours to stretch our legs, and I saw that Pete and Marjorie were in a second identical bus traveling behind us. They looked okay physically, but neither of them would speak to me or meet my eyes when I tried to call out to them. Whether it was out of fear or resignation, they both bore the air of condemned prisoners, and after they ignored me the first couple of times, I gave up trying.

I was mildly surprised that I wasn’t scared or worried about myself or them, but as time went on and the road unspooled before us, I felt the last remnants of my old self-doubt and fear falling away. It reminded me of watching a butterfly or moth shaking off the detritus of the cocoon before taking flight. I didn’t know if a moth remembered life before the cocoon, but if it did, I imagined it grew dimmer with each passing night.

The people on the bus with me were friendly enough, but they left me alone other than to occasionally ask if I needed anything. I only drank and ate a little, and when I slept, it was only for a half hour or so at a time. Still, I didn’t feel sleepy or especially tired. Just tired of riding and waiting, waiting and riding. I was ready to reach Wizard’s Folly and the gargoyle that lay at its heart.

By dusk the following night we were there. I had held off asking any more questions during the trip, and I found myself regretting it now. I had no real idea what I was walking into. For all I knew, these people were part of some dangerous cult and were going to torture and kill all of us. It seemed I wasn't past all fear or all doubts after all.

But they paled next to my drive to see for myself. My desire to enter the house and get rid of this terrible longing that had taken over my heart in the last few days. So I left the bus with the rest of them. We had been driven right up to the front door of the house by some route we hadn't seen during our prior visit, and when the expectant crowd parted the way for me, I stepped forward and opened the door.

Inside was dark and cool, but not pitch black. There were electric lamps and candles at various spots, perforating the shadows enough to give a rough geography of the hall I was entering and its adjoining rooms. I felt no need to explore or wander once I was inside. The house was clean and well-furnished, as well as impressively decorated in a strange gothic style, but none of that was why I had come.

I came to meet my father.

The thought had occurred to me as I traveled past the sweeping staircase going up into the upper floors and around the corner to a smaller hallway that led to a small black door at its terminus. I opened the door and began my journey down the winding stone steps into the basement and sub-basement beyond. All of this was done without hesitation, because as with so many things now, I just knew the truth of them as they came to me.

I reached the primary ritual room, the centerpiece of which was the large pit that had once contained so much death and decay. It was empty now, but I could still feel the energy radiating from it. This pit had been my womb, and I felt some connection to it. I looked around the room, my eyes adjusting to the darkness. Sitting in the corner was a small, hunched man, or something that resembled a man. I wasn't afraid, but I still approached cautiously, as I could feel great power coming from him as well.

"Father?" I didn't know why I said the word except that it was right and true.

The figure stirred from some kind of slumber, grey rheumy eyes studying me for a moment before gleaming with recognition. "Vesper? Is that you?"

I nodded slowly, almost gingerly, as I sat down near him. "I think so. My name is Phil, but I think it's also Vesper."

The man smiled, the crisscross of age lines making the expression seem more like a wound across old leather. "Phil is just your name this time. The name of your outward self. Before you were Dora. You were Stephen. And perhaps more I never knew." His eyes narrowed. "I thought I dreamed of you coming here before. Did you come here before?"

"Yes…me and my wife, Marjorie. Her brother, Pete. They brought me, but we didn't come inside the house. I never came down here. I didn't remember enough." I felt a slight shame at admitting the last, but the old man patted my shoulder.

"No shame in that. They are old and crafty. I suspect they knew just what to say to confuse you, get you back away from here without me waking up."

I jerked back at that. "Old and crafty? Marjorie? I don't understand."

The man sighed. "I know, and I hate it had to be this way for so long. Let me explain."

****

Hell is a real place. As real as this one…or more real I suppose. It is one of the chief Realms that encircle this world and an infinite number like them. There was a time that Hell was ruled by Lucifer and his fallen. It was a terrible place, but it was orderly and it served many purposes. A key cog in the machinery of Creation, if you will.

But then Lucifer was destroyed and Hell began to change. The fallen angels and other infernal demons that were left no longer controlled things, and they found themselves hunted to the edge of extinction, for the new ruler of Hell, the Hunter, was all but immune to their infernal magics and diabolical snares. With no way of fighting back, they ran.

The weaker ones hid in the shadows of the new Hell, eking out a meager existence while waiting for their turn to come as the Hunter's prey. The stronger ones fled to other realms and worlds like this one. Over the years, some formed communities like the one you visited in Brimley. And while many appreciated the respite, and some even came to enjoy their lives on Earth, most were ill-suited for it. They felt a yearning to return to Hell not that different than what pulled you to the very place you sit right now.

So they began to work and scheme. They enlisted the aid of numerous human agents and practitioners of the black arts, and over several centuries they devised a plan. The start of that plan was put into motion when a man named Francesco Pazzi came to America and founded the town Firenze. He was skilled in black magic and had been entrusted with this plan, this last hope of Hell's orphans.

And he succeeded. Year after year, ritual after ritual, sacrifice after sacrifice, he layered the blood and the pain and the power needed to craft a very special spell. It required not only human sacrifice, but demonic sacrifice as well, and over two dozen fallen angels were rendered in the process, as well as a tiny relic from the Hunter itself. A single strand of hair that had fallen from its head during its brief battle with Lucifer.

In many ways, this was the most important part. If something was going to be able to face the strange magic of the Hunter, it needed to possess a bit of that magic itself, as well as the magic of infernals and humans both. These three magics were never meant to be together, never meant to co-exist, so it was only through great skill and will and power that this was done. Only by all of this effort and sacrifice were you born.

The night you were born, men from the town stormed this house. Most were killed and others were taken. They have served various uses in the years since then, but one pair, one special couple, has lasted longer than the rest. Rudolph and Annabelle Perkins. Star-crossed lovers, you might say. Or rather, as *you* might say, your wife Marjorie and her "brother" Pete.

I know even now that comes as a shock to you. You still retain your life as Phil, and some of those old feelings are still there. But I have been sending them out to find you for decades, and I know them better than they know themselves.

When I came to America as Frank Pazzi, I had hoped my rituals would be complete by 1920. That I would gain vast power in this world and, when I eventually was forced into Hell, I would be lauded as a hero and given a place of privilege in the new infernal court. Then that fucking whore Annabelle and her stuck-up husband came to town. I had hoped that taking her would send him packing, but instead he riled the townsfolk up when you were fresh to life--and I was weak from your creation.

In the chaos of that night, you somehow slipped away. I had taken them as prizes, but I had to disappear for a time while I searched for you. By the time I found you a few years later, you were living as a young girl named Dora Wilcher outside of Omaha, Nebraska. From what I could learn, you had just shown up in town as a young woman and started living life like everything was normal. No memory of what you really were or that you hadn't existed five years earlier.

My first instinct had been to try to force you to remember, try to make you come with me. Then I realized how foolish and arrogant I was being. I was dealing with something new, something I didn't understand. That no one understood. So I decided to trust you and let you find your own way, develop the human side of your nature and grow in strength until you were ready.

For years I watched you while cultivating more money and power as Wilson Tattersall. I rebought my own house, my own property, and I waited. I had a feeling we would need this place of power again, and I was right. When Dora was in her forties, she started getting sick. I kept close tabs on you at all times back then, and I knew that the doctors you had seen had no idea what was wrong. Desperate, I sent two of my servants out to push you in this direction, hoping I could help you without disturbing your development.

Those servants were Marjorie and Pete. Except they didn't call themselves that, or Annabelle and Rudolph. Back then they were Tess and Johnny, a married couple that buttered up to you and your husband for months before springing a surprise trip on you. A surprise trip to an exclusive new amusement park that had just opened up in California.

I had waited for months for your arrival, making use of the guests we had in my own small ways, but all with the end goal of seeing you walk through those gates. Because without you, all of it was for naught. I had started to lose hope—I felt that my bindings on "Tess and Johnny" were strong enough that they couldn't betray me, but I also felt sure by that point that you needed to come of your own free will for any of this to truly work.

Then, on the evening of October 27, 1947, I saw you standing in line for the house. I have never been a romantic or even a sexual man, but you were a vision that night. I had only seen you in pictures and from a distance a handful of times over the years, but nothing could have prepared me for the excitement I felt seeing you so close to fulfilling your destiny. When you entered the house, you did remember more of yourself and your nature, but something was still wrong. You lashed out, killing several people and making others sick or insane. All of which I was happy with at the time, as you seemed to grow stronger as others fell around you. I even felt pride for my hand in it, for I had tainted many visitors in the preceding months, letting this place and you feed off them indirectly during your rampage. I thought you were finally being made whole. But then, just as quickly you were gone, vanishing into thin air.

I didn't despair as long this time, but set others to the task of finding you again. The problem is that to most people you would just look like a normal person. People I have claimed—my touch gives them unnatural life, but it also gives them a certain sensitivity. They can find you where others cannot. Over the years, without regular influxes of power, my ability to create new servants of that sort has waned.

Annabelle and Rudolph found you as Stephen Keller in the 1970s and eventually led you back here. That time, you only wanted to talk to me, largely about my life and whether my goals were noble or worthy, and then you disappeared again. I didn't find you again until now.

That damned couple—they have to do my bidding, but they enjoy their life outside far too much and have devised ways over the years to avoid finding you, to thwart the spirit of my commands if not the letter of them. When they ran across you, they had no choice but to come or the magic that preserves them would start to fail. But if they brought you and manipulated you into leaving before you could remember, their hope was they could claim ignorance and buy themselves another few decades of "searching". Alas, the magic is smarter than they are, as are my demonic companions.

I set up Brimley as a waystation years ago. A place they would have to travel through if they were bringing you to me. An independent check, if you will, to help keep them honest or stop them if they decided they didn't want the ride to end. It served its purpose in the end, and they'll be dealt with for their treachery, if you can call their disloyalty to me treason in the first place. I did abduct and magically subjugate them, but they had a lot of good years as a result, so I can't help but feel somewhat unappreciated.

But I digress. My age is catching up with me I'm afraid. Wait until you're 170 years old and see how you do.

The real question is are you ready? Do you feel whole yet? I'm not trying to pressure you, and I trust you to know when this cycle of...whatever it is...is complete, but I'm running out of time. And Hell, while vast, grows closer to being wholly under the Hunter's control every day. I've even heard stories of the Hunter appearing in this world, albeit very briefly, a few months ago and slaughtering quite a few notable occultists. No one on my level, of course, but still...it gives one pause.

I named you Vesper after the old meaning of the word. Evening star. The morning star has died and his Hell has been lost, but I believe you can champion a new era. With you to lead us, I think Hell can be retaken and made whole again. So what do...

****

He gurgled slightly as I punched into his ribcage with both hands, separating his torso like a rotten head of lettuce and letting the wet halves splatter-drip onto the old stone floor. This rotting monster, this decrepit sadist, thought that I would help him? That I would help *any of them*?

I remembered everything now. I recalled the bloody and horrible origins of my birth. I could see my husband when I was Dora. My parents when I was Stephen. Marjorie the day I married her. And yes, I had been lied to and tricked. Manipulated and moved around like a pawn. Or I suppose more like a nuclear warhead being ferried from place to place.

But I didn't feel anger or sadness. I felt joy and love for all the lives I had lived and the world I had lived them in. Unlike when Dora lost control and hurt people out of confusion and fear, I was past that now. The only negative emotion I was really feeling at this point was disgust. Disgust at this little mummy that wanted me to be a good dog. Disgust at the horde of foul things masquerading as humans outside.

I walked back upstairs, and even before I reached the doors, I could feel their anticipation, their corruption, flowing through the cracks like waves of heat. I think my father was right. It was time that I helped these demons find a way home.

I opened the doors wide and smiled at the expectant crowd. They weren't stupid, and it only took moments of seeing me now for their expressions to change, for their flesh and bones to start shifting in unnatural ways in anticipation of what was coming. That was all right. It wouldn't matter in the end.

Closing the doors behind me, I walked out into the crowd, watching with slight amusement as they shuffled back at my approach. The fear and hate in the air were palpable, and I breathed it in deeply. Scanning the crowd, I looked for any sign of Marjorie and Pete but saw none. No matter. I'd find them later. For now, it was time to show these things just what all their murder and horror had brought them. I leaned forward slightly, my voice barely above a whisper, but still resonant in the silence of the cool evening air.

"Who's first?"